Grass Shoots

Jane Bwye

An African Saga

The standalone sequel to *Breath of Africa*

Copyright © 2017 by Jane Bwye
Photography: kubikactive
Cover Design: soqoqo
Editor: Sue Barnard
All rights reserved.

No part of this book may be used or reproduced in any manner whatsoever without written permission of the author or Crooked Cat except for brief quotations used for promotion or in reviews. This is a work of fiction. Names, characters, and incidents are used fictitiously.

First Green Line Edition, Crooked Cat Books. 2017

Discover us online:
www.crookedcatbooks.com

Join us on facebook:
www.facebook.com/crookedcatbooks

Tweet a photo of yourself holding
this book to **@crookedcatbooks**
and something nice will happen.

This book is dedicated to my sons
and daughters, Jo, Colin and Kathy,
Heather, Anthea, and Dennis;
and to their families.

Acknowledgments

I am again indebted to my erstwhile colleague, John Sibi Okumu, for his advice and encouragement, as well as valuable editorial input. If I have failed to portray the African perspective with due authenticity, it is despite his efforts, and I accept full blame for any mistakes.

Thank you to Shani Struthers and Nik Morton, my Beta readers, for taking the time to offer advice. You gave me the confidence to go forward, and submit my book to Stephanie Patterson, the mother Cat of Crooked Cat Books, who embraced my efforts with customary warmth. It is special, belonging to this supportive community of authors. And Sue Barnard, my editor, made the final process an absolute pleasure.

Because the book addresses the question of charitable giving, I had an excuse to return to Kenya in 2015 to do research. My first objective was a mineral sands mine in Kwale County on the Kenya coast. My son, Colin, conceived and nursed Base Titanium from the start. He led me on a personal tour of the project. It was their investment in local villages and farms which caused me to reflect on how big business can become involved in sustainable community projects to the benefit of all parties, without the stigma of patronisation.

I flew to Uganda for a week, and am indebted to Geoff and Geraldine Booker, founders of the Sussex charity, Quicken Trust, which supports the Kabubbu Village Project. I stayed at the village Tourist Resort with Geoff and Geraldine, who facilitated my research. I have unashamedly drawn on my observations and conversations with the people involved in this amazing project, and thank them all for giving freely of their time, and for injecting me with their enthusiasm and joy.

My final, and most precious, stay was for ten days alone in my daughter, Anthea's, weekend hideaway at Maanzoni, south of Nairobi. There, I communed with nature, while planning this book.

On my return to the UK to start writing, I discovered St. Peter's Lifeline, which supports a village called Kajuki in the shadow of Mt. Kenya. Thank you to David Baldwin, the founder of the charity, who inspired me to support it with the proceeds from my first book, *Breath of Africa*. He introduced me to the concept of the Grameen system for microfinancing businesses. I could not resist including this idea for the imaginary village of Amayoni in the Kenya Highlands.

Jane Bwye

Praise for Breath of Africa

"Reminds me of Doris Lessing's 'The Grass is Singing', in the depth of feeling by Jane Bwye of the dark continent."
~ R. Nicholson-Morton, author / editor

"...a gripping historical novel."
~ Juliet Barnes, author of 'The Ghosts of Happy Valley'

"Bwye handles deftly not only the historical and political aspects of this story, but also the social changes that come with the passing decades."
~ Alison Gomm. Lady Margaret Hall, Oxford Brown Book 2014.

"The book could only have been written by someone who was there at the time, so deep is its accuracy in assessing the events and feelings of the age."
~ Christine Nicholls, biographer of Elspeth Huxley.

About the Author

Jane Bwye lived in Kenya for over half a century, where she was an intermittent freelance journalist, business owner and teacher. She has written a cookbook, *Museum Mixtures*, in aid of the National Museums of Kenya, and a History in commemoration of the 50th anniversary of her church in Eastbourne.

Her first novel, *Breath of Africa*, published in 2013, was nominated for the Guardian First Book Award. It draws on her experiences growing up in the country she still calls her home.
A novella, *I Lift Up My Eyes*, (2015) is set in Sussex.

Grass Shoots, the standalone sequel to Breath of Africa, completes a family saga through to modern day Kenya.

A world traveller, Jane has bought a bird book in every country she visited. Now living in the UK, she is a business mentor, and indulges her love for choral singing, horses, and tennis.

Follow Jane here:

Website: http://janebwye.com
Facebook: http://www.facebook.com/JLBwye/
Breath of Africa Facebook group:
https://www.facebook.com/groups/110264945726473/

Grass Shoots

As rain falls, grass shoots of hope spring from the scorched earth and spread in pricks of green over the wasted land. Desert flowers lift their delicate petals to cover the dunes in a mosaic of colour, then quickly fade as dusk descends.

The cycle of life is ever apparent in Africa, vibrant yet vulnerable to the sweep of destiny. But there is always hope.

There is a glossary at the end of the book.

PART I

Kenya 1998–2003

President Daniel Arap Moi has won a fifth term of office, and the US Embassy is bombed by those linked with Al Quaeda. Richard Leakey is made a Government Minister, and then deposed for 'abuse of power'. President Moi forms a Coalition with Raila Odinga, and Uhuru Kenyatta is appointed his successor. But in 2002, Mwai Kibaki wins landslide elections, and re-introduces free primary school education.

Chapter 1

"Blast those wretched parking boys – they're more a menace than a help!"

Paul Clayton swung the steering wheel to turn off the tarmac onto an undulating waste land. He waited for a car to back out. In front of him a scruffy boy who should have been at school was gesticulating with dramatic exaggeration as he waved out the departing vehicle.

"I don't need that ragamuffin to show me into a space I can see for myself."

"At least there's some sort of order here since they came," said Emily, hanging onto the strap as the car dipped into a crater full of water. The *toto* gestured right and left while the car inched forwards, then he held up his hand to impose an immediate halt. He looked to the left side of the car, and beckoned Paul on a few inches before stopping him with a sharp tap on the bonnet.

"I bet he's landed you in a puddle."

Emily opened her door. "No, he hasn't. Look – there's a stepping stone just where I need it!"

She tested it gingerly, encouraged by the *toto*, and caught his proffered hand as she jumped onto dry ground.

"I look after your car, *bwana*." The boy held his palm open.

"I'll pay you when I get back," Paul growled, "provided it's in one piece."

"You want it washed?"

Paul shook his head. "*Hapana*."

Emily thanked the *toto*, pressing a coin into his hand.

"*Asante sana*." Thank you.

"You didn't need to do that," grumbled Paul. "Now he'll

guide us into that same puddle every time we come here."

"What's the harm? At least he's offering something instead of just begging."

"And if I'd refused his help and parked along the street instead, he'd have punished me. Look." Paul indicated a gleaming Mercedes, flush-parked alongside the nearby pavement. "I bet he's let that tyre down."

Emily saw the right front wheel-rim resting on the tarmac.

They stepped out of the stark sunlight into the Five Bells curry house. Her eyes adjusted to the darkness and she was grateful for the fan in the foyer. It cooled her skin and dried the perspiration on her dress.

While they waited for a table, she spoke to the proprietor, pointing through the window. "Mr Gomez, is the owner of that Merc dining here?"

Gomez glanced out and grimaced. "He is; I'll have to tell him."

Minutes later a well-dressed man with a protruding belly burst towards the exit.

"Where's my driver?" he shouted from the pavement. "I told him to stay with the car – those wretched parking boys... I'll deal with them if it's the last thing I do!"

"He's one of the *wabenzi* – a government minister," whispered Gomez. "They've been using the street parking to avoid the *totos*. I hope this won't mean I'll lose his custom, even though he doesn't always pay his bill."

"You'll have to lay on an *askari* to guard against the *totos*!" Paul laughed as they were shown to a corner table. He took the menu from the table and turned to Emily.

"What'll you have today? I'm going for my usual *murg makhanwala*. You can't beat it."

"Prawn curry for me, please," said Emily, placing a damask napkin on her lap and holding out her hands to the waiter for a hot towel.

She examined the tastefully-furnished restaurant. Walls painted crimson with dashes of soft brown enhanced the opulent ambience. Gleaming brass ornaments adorned wall-mounted shelves, and latticed partitions threaded with indoor creepers created intimate nooks. Buoyant conversation hummed around them.

"This is a good place to be," she said, thanking Paul for his generous habit of treating her to lunch every Wednesday. "It has more ambience than the Thorn Tree."

She remembered her first day in Nairobi, over a year ago, as if it were yesterday. She had walked more slowly than everyone else, watching the dawn break over a wash of pale cloud spreading from the grassy plains of the game park. The cloud snaked in sinuous wisps over the airport runway and infiltrated the stagnant waters of Nairobi dam, suffocated by a sea of water hyacinth.

She looked back the way she'd come. A tight mass of tin-roofs filled the dusty hillside, where open drains exuded their odoriferous poison. Downhill from the slums and across a ribbon of potholed tarmac, once a proud dual carriageway, thousands of people paced haphazard paths towards the industrial area of the city. Feet pounded the dust, legs moving like automatons, faces expressionless, set steadfastly on the purpose of getting to work on time.

The gleaming white teeth of those nearest to her were clenched in concentration as they negotiated the puddles, careful not to contaminate their shoes. She would have to wipe away the grime on hers once she reached the city streets. Leaping over a clump of grass, she collided with two men in white shirts and collars stiffly cutting into their flabby necks.

"*Pole*." She apologised.

She touched her head, its crinkly hair combed into short plaits against her scalp, conscious that the dark shade of her face stood out against the whitened skin of other girls. Teetering on high heels and almost turning an ankle, she steadied herself against an obliging arm.

"Thank you."

The path flattened out towards the buildings, which lined the main highway. A beggar, wearing a threadbare overcoat which drooped over his thin frame, sat cross-legged on a soiled piece of sacking. He looked old, but his eyes were lively, darting here and there as he tweaked at a dirty piece of cloth lying before him.

The lines of commuters detoured around him; one or two paused to drop a coin onto the cloth. He drew the corners together, rattling the coins in the hope of attracting more attention.

Emily held up the stream of people as she clutched at her shoe, adjusting the strap. Her yellow blouse parted to reveal firm breasts thrusting gently against its fabric. She paused above him and fumbled in her bag for a fifty-cent piece. He held his hands prayerfully together and bowed his head in thanks as the silver coin dropped onto the cloth. He swiftly hid it under a fold. She sensed his beady eyes devouring the movements of her body beneath her tight black skirt.

The two men in spotless white shirts behind her stopped at his picket to exchange words.

Emily hurried on, losing herself in the seething mass of people tramping the city pavements, and paused in Cabral Street off Moi Avenue. She peered at the tarnished gold plaque outside a formidable carved door, comparing the name with that remembered from the piece of paper in her bag. Yes, this was the place.

Opposite, a window advertised Ocean Spice, open for lunch and dinner only. She could see cars passing along the roads at both ends of the short one-way street. The two men stood at the corner, watching her.

She turned towards the door. Drawing a tissue from her bag, she wiped at her soiled shoes, eyeing the approaching men through the crick of her elbow, then she stood sharply upright and knocked at the door.

She knocked again. As the men drew near, she grabbed the handle and twisted it. Thankfully, it opened. The door swung heavily shut behind her, and she rested against it, letting out a sigh of relief in the dim hallway. Somehow, she knew they wouldn't follow her in here.

A wide staircase rose to her right. On the landing above

gleamed another gold-coloured plaque. She gathered courage and started up the boards, worn into grainy unpolished steps which creaked as she climbed.

Swing doors opened into the reception area of Davis & Finchley, Solicitors, and a round face crowned with a halo of red hair peered at her over the counter.

"Can I help you?"

Pulling down her skirt and tweaking at her blouse, Emily approached the desk. A notice pinned to its side said *Secretary Wanted*. She had come to the right place.

"I'm looking for a job."

"As a secretary?"

Emily nodded.

"We do have a vacancy. I'll have to ask Mr Winston, the senior partner. Do you have a CV?"

"Excuse me, I have only just qualified. It would be my first job."

The receptionist smiled. "That's fine – so long as you can touch-type. Where did you train?"

"At a secretarial college in Mombasa."

The smile grew wider. "Ah, Caroline Clayton's?"

"Yes. I took the Diploma Course."

"She's good; we've had girls from her before. If you'd like to leave your name and phone number, I'll get in touch when Mr Winston can see you."

Emily hesitated, thinking of the Kibera slums and the tin shack she'd stayed in the night before with the cousin of Martha, a friend at college. There was no electricity there, or a telephone connection.

"Excuse me, but I don't have a contact number."

The face disappeared, and all Emily could see above the desk was a massed bouffant of frizzed hair. Surely it must be dyed? She peered over the counter. The lady was consulting a diary, then she scraped back her chair and stood up.

"Please take a seat while I speak to Mr Winston."

The diminutive receptionist passed through the inner door, and Emily perched on the nearest of two armchairs facing a low table. She pulled her skirt down over her knees and waited, staring unseeing at the portrait of President Daniel Arap Moi on the opposite wall.

Several minutes later the receptionist returned, beaming at her. Emily noticed the dark brown eyebrows. Yes – the bright red hair had to be dyed.

"You can come back and see Mr Winston tomorrow at ten o'clock," she said. "We've been trying to find somebody for weeks, and you're the only one with acceptable training. I'm sure you'll be successful. Can you start straight away? There's a huge backlog of work. My name is Molly, by the way."

Emily nodded gratefully. Caroline had told her that secretaries were in demand in Nairobi.

She had the whole day to herself, and Caroline had given her money to spend. The bustle of Nairobi was vastly different from the leisurely humidity of the Kenyan coast, where she'd been brought up at an AIDS orphanage. People pitied her when she told them about her background, but Emily appreciated her luck in having a benefactor like Caroline. Her mother had died when she was born, and (like so many girls of her age) she'd never known her father. He'd disappeared in the course of Kenya's turbulent post-independence history.

Emily juggled the coins in her purse, remembering the fifty-cent piece she'd given the beggar on her way into the city this morning. She must be careful how she spent her money in future, but she did need clothes; perhaps a more comfortable skirt than the one she'd borrowed from Martha, and a pair of sensible sandals of neutral colour would be a good idea if she had to walk to work every day.

She had an hour or two to kill before her lunch date.

Emily teetered down the stairs and pulled open the door, peering timidly along the street. The two men had gone.

She walked back to Moi Avenue and up Kenyatta Avenue to the New Stanley Hotel, stopping at Woolworths on the way. She emerged, swinging a plastic bag containing the clothes which were too tight for her. Her elegant calf-length skirt, complementing the flow of a new floral cotton blouse, made her feel more comfortable. It was nearly lunch time. She found an empty stool at the counter of the Thorn Tree café, and looked upwards at the elongated trunk of the yellow thorn which strained towards the roof of the multi-storied hotel.

A man rose from a nearby table to pay his bill. He looked disconcertingly like the beggar she had seen on her way to town. But it couldn't be him, surely – not this smart gentleman in the tweed jacket?

Emily glanced at the watch Caroline had given her for her twentieth birthday. Paul was nearly an hour late, and she was hungry. She caught the eye of a waiter, and then had second thoughts. There were cheaper places to eat than the New Stanley.

Climbing down from the stool, she picked up the Woolworths bag and headed back towards Moi Avenue, where she'd noticed a street-side café. She glanced behind. Perhaps those two men had not been trailing her after all? Caroline had warned her about male predators in Nairobi, but Emily was determined to leave Mombasa in order to earn real money in Kenya's capital city. It was time she left the safe nest offered by her *mzungu* guardian and stood on her own two feet in the African world. Besides, Paul worked in Nairobi. She knew she could always seek refuge with him if she had to.

She threaded her way along the crowded pavement, wondering what had happened to Paul. It was unlike him to let her down. Perhaps he'd found a girlfriend? She smiled to herself as she thought of the serious-minded man, whom she'd always looked on as a big brother.

On his holiday visits to Mombasa, he used to take her for walks along the sea front, peering through binoculars at the birds. He would exclaim at the most ordinary bird flitting above the steamy city, while she saw only dull buildings towering over hot pavements crowded with people chattering and shouting at one another as they hawked fruit and vegetables from shanty market stalls.

Nairobi was more vibrant, alive and glittering. People were purposeful and sophisticated; there were so many opportunities here, and maybe she would be able to fulfil her purpose in life. She'd always wanted to make a difference, to pass on something of what she'd received from Caroline. But first, she had to earn a living.

Emily entered a street-side café and ordered a hamburger, then took a seat near the window to watch the world go by. She needed to buy more clothes, and find a better place to live than the Kibera slums.

Later in the afternoon, as she stepped onto the path winding up the hill towards the slums, she saw the beggar eyeing the stream of people returning after their day's work. She let a copper coin drop onto his dirty piece of cloth and noticed that one limb was foreshortened, its tatty trouser leg lying flat along the ground beyond his knee.

Paul had eaten his curry by the time Emily came out of her reverie. She cleaned her plate, savouring the spicy sauces, then dabbed at her mouth with the napkin and thanked him for the meal.

"You don't need to keep on taking me out like this, Paul – I forgave you ages ago, you know."

"But I want to take you out, Emily. Haven't you realised that?"

She smiled across at him, glancing into his grey eyes peering at her through spectacles. His mouse-coloured hair formed an unruly halo of curls around his elongated face. Was that the beginning of a moustache she could see on his upper lip? It would suit him, she thought.

He was fifteen years her senior, and she felt lucky to have someone like him as an anchor, someone solid and reliable who cared about her. He didn't look a bit like Caroline. Perhaps he took after his father, who'd died before Paul was a year old. Caroline was also guardian of Paul's friend, Sam. Three children, Emily thought, one family; Paul – a white boy, Sam – a half-caste, and years later herself – an African. That was how the nation of Kenya should be: a mixture of races and colours, all part of one family. Caroline never did see colour.

"A penny for your thoughts?"

"What? Oh, sorry."

"You were far away, and it's time to go back to work."

Paul signalled a waiter to bring the bill.

"I was thinking about Caroline taking in Sam. I've never met him. Why did she do that?"

"Sam is the son of Mum's school friend Teresa, who died," said Paul. "He's a palaeontologist, working at a dig in Italy as part of his PhD, and when he returns to Kenya you'll meet him. But to go back to your question, Mum has this ideal about all the people of Kenya living as one happy family. An impossible dream."

Emily led the way out onto the street, crossing the road towards the car.

"I don't agree with you, Paul! Look how the Africans, Asians and Europeans have learned to live together in an independent Kenya."

"Ah – but what about the tribes in the country? Surely you haven't forgotten how the Kikuyu are always fighting the Luo, and how the Luhya and Kamba are jealous of both?"

The parking boy appeared at Paul's shoulder for his promised payment. As she stepped over the puddle onto the stone and entered the car, Emily noticed a man on crutches standing nearby. The boy ran up to him and handed over the money.

Paul backed the car out and swung onto the street, heading towards the centre of town.

"We've moved beyond petty tribal infighting," she assured him. "I'm a Luhya, sharing a flat with a Kikuyu girl, and we're the best of friends."

"You wait until the politicians stir things up at the next elections – they'll have you all at each other's throats!" He stopped the car outside her office. "I can't see you next Wednesday, as I must go upcountry to do an audit. I'll give you a call."

He raised an arm and Emily watched him drive off, smiling to herself as she pictured him bending over his desk worrying over figures. Accountancy suited him, somehow. She looked forward to meeting Sam, and as she completed her pile of dictation for the afternoon, she thanked God that she no longer had to commute to the Kibera slums every day.

Chapter 2

The beggar looks around furtively as three *totos* approach him. The steady stream of commuters has dried up. He shifts position, easing out the leg which ends abruptly at the knee, and hobbles heavily onto home-made crutches. Cocking his head sideways, he beckons the boys towards a shanty made of tin in a nearby alleyway. The door bears faint marks of a *Stop* sign, and he smiles to himself as he creaks it open. The authorities have erected a new sign on the highway and haven't drilled it with holes as a deterrent to thieves. He'll send one of the boys to take it down. The metal is thicker than that of the kerosene tins which make up the walls of his shack, and it'll serve as a roof against the forthcoming rains.

"Where's Ken?"

"We couldn't find him, Ouma. Perhaps he's sick."

These boys are unreliable, but what can he do? Whatever he says, they always return to the habit of sniffing glue or hovering near the exhausts of cars for a quick fix. Then they drop out of sight. When will they learn that it is better to work for him than spend their days in a stupor?

Ouma sniffs, pinches his nose and a stream of liquid squirts onto the ground. He hawks and spits, then hobbles into the hut, leaving the boys to toe the dust outside. Unearthing a key from a hole beside the door and grabbing a torch to light his way, he goes to a cupboard in the far corner and turns the lock. Two shiny crutches stand alongside a tweed jacket, and two pairs of trousers lie neatly folded over a hanger. A prosthetic leg is propped against the back of the cupboard. The stiff coupling hurts him, but he needs it today.

He strides purposefully out of the alley, immaculately-creased grey trousers concealing the prosthesis attached to his lower leg. His shiny black shoes avoid a bloated plastic bag which tumbles towards him. Despite the blazing sun, the tweed jacket hangs from his shoulders. He has business to do in the city.

The boys have disappeared. They'll regret it if he sees them hovering round the strings of cars crawling along the highway in the rush hour.

A *matatu* – taxi – crammed full of commuters pulls up beside him, but there is always room for one more. He squeezes in, jostling against the mass of bodies, which allow him a modicum of space, and they balance against each other as the vehicle rides the potholes. It stops at City Square, and Ouma walks along Moi Avenue before turning towards the New Stanley Hotel.

He is early for his appointment. Sitting at a table for two in the middle of the open air café, he snaps his fingers at a passing waiter.

"A cup of black coffee!" It's too early for beer, and he needs to keep his wits about him.

A mother and two small children sip sodas at a nearby table. A young woman with a Woolworths bag perches on a stool at the counter, the flow of a floral cotton blouse draped over the soft curves of her breasts. There is something about her which stirs his memory.

Shouts and a brief commotion herald the arrival of a minibus. It pulls into the loading area, and a uniformed driver opens the boot to fill it with luggage. A group of pink-faced tourists emerges from the foyer, cameras and binoculars dangling round their necks.

Ouma drops four teaspoons of sugar into his cup and leans forward to pull out a chair for the man approaching his table.

Alex Gomez is a dapper gentleman, small and self-effacing, but he has a quick brain and an eager eye for making money. Ouma met this restaurateur a few months back when he asked permission to have a pitch outside the

Five Bells.

"I've noticed several of your customers parking their cars on the waste land near your restaurant," he says, after exchanging pleasantries and offering his guest a coffee. "I could tidy it up a bit. We can mark out parking bays, which will mean more cars and customers for you. We could even repair the potholes." Ouma notices Alex's eyes glimmer.

"The land belongs to the council, you know."

"No matter, Alex; the Nairobi City Council have so much to think about, they're not going to bother with it for years. Besides, if we make it look better, they'll be grateful."

"And what's in it for you, I wonder?"

Ouma smiles. "Don't you worry, Alex, I won't interfere with your business. I have ideas of my own."

As he rises to pay the bill, the woman in the floral blouse glances at him. He turns away to signal a passing *matatu*. It is time to go back and remove the uncomfortable prosthesis.

There she is again. This time her heels are thicker and her shoes are red. The skirt is green, longer and not so tight-fitting.

She extracts a coin from the same handbag, and Ouma inclines his head, putting his hands prayerfully together as she drops it onto the sack before him. He opens his eyes. The coin is copper, and he clenches his teeth as he watches her receding figure. That girl is learning fast, and her face reminds him of the past.

The shirts of the two men trailing her are less white than they were in the morning. Sweat-stained patches under the arms have left their marks.

They pause beside Ouma and report – nothing much, really – but he tells them to remain discreet and watch.

Maina fidgets, eyeing the lithe, sinuous figure disappearing into the crowd towards the Kibera slums.

"And let's have none of your private plans, Maina," warns Ouma. "I know all about your connections with the pimp who controls the city centre. You're not to touch that girl. I pay more than he does – just you remember that!"

The other man hangs back. "Don't worry, Ouma. I'll keep an eye on him."

"Thank you, Musumba. I'll hold you responsible."

Musumba strides after his friend. Ouma picks up the sack, pockets the coins, and hobbles towards the alley where the boys are waiting.

Ouma laments the fact that few people care for the street boys of Nairobi. The Undugu Society is a brotherhood which gives them basic education in the slums, but it is overwhelmed by the numbers which vary from day to day. The boys return to living in the alleyways of Nairobi, in culverts, under cars; glue-sniffing, petrol-sniffing, hallucinating. It's a losing battle, but Ouma is slowly gaining the trust of his little band of four, and he aims to improve their prospects. A step at a time, he tells himself, is better than nothing.

The boys settle, each into his self-demarcated area of the alleyway. Pieces of dirty cloth are bundled into makeshift mattresses as dusk swiftly turns to night. A wash of light from a billboard at the far end creates shadows where rats and cockroaches lurk. But they barely notice these creatures of the night.

Ken has not returned. The boy is a natural leader, older than the others. He ran away from the relatives who took him in as an orphan and sent him to the Undugu school, but he doesn't always attend. He is a bright boy, but he needs to find more money, he says, by whatever means possible. Ouma fears for him. The city police show no mercy to the street boys they catch, beating them and forcing them to confess to crimes they may not have done. And the remand homes are dens of iniquity and violence.

They share out bruised mangoes found in a hotel dustbin, and slurp at dregs of milk squeezed from abandoned Tetrapaks. Joseph has found a sliced loaf of bread and he divides it into four. They eat well tonight.

Ouma produces a thermos of tea and pours the steaming liquid into a cup, which is passed between them.

He reminds them of the benefits of working for him as he

looms over their still forms, huddled beneath the spreading pages of yesterday's newspapers.

Later, he hears a scuffle and opens an eye. Ken is back.

Before dawn, the boy has disappeared again. Ouma peers into the gloom of his ramshackle hut. He scrambles under his mattress, comprised of several layers of used gunny sacks, tipping them over in folds as he rummages for his torch. The light is weak. He must buy more batteries today.

He opens his cupboard to extract his pin-striped trousers, then sits on a low wooden stool to draw them on, tucking back the right leg below the knee and securing it with a shoelace. Then he takes a blue long-sleeved shirt from a shelf and pulls it over his head. He draws a leather purse from the pocket of his tweed coat and counts the money. It is time to visit the bank.

Locking the cupboard and dropping the key into its hiding place, he picks a felt hat from a nail on the wall and leaves the shack. Swinging easily along the alleyway on his crutches he emerges onto the pavement to hail an approaching *matatu*.

"It's the old *mzee* again – give him room on the front seat!" shouts the tout, holding his palm open for the fare.

Ouma jostles for position among the crowded passengers. The vehicle swings into the road, several bodies clinging to the open back door while the tout hangs out of a side window, shouting for fares.

The traffic stalls as they approach the city centre. The lights on the highway are not working, and cars creep over the roundabouts, giving reluctant way to horn-tooting drivers bullying their way through the blockage. Street boys in tattered clothing thread between the waiting cars. They knock at hastily-closing windows to show their wares – postcards, pens, glossy magazines and even small toys; stolen, probably. They don't come near the *matatu*.

Ouma stiffens. One of the boys working the outside lane is familiar. He recognises Ken's red T-shirt and tips his hat down over his face. The boy is offering a magazine to a harassed housewife who hasn't wound her car window up in time. Two children bounce on the back seat. The woman turns to chastise them, and Ken scampers away, clutching a purse to his chest.

Ouma curses under his breath. Is Ken doing a bit of freelancing? Or – worse – is he working for somebody else?

Several cars are parked in the waste land opposite the Five Bells when Ouma arrives. Joshua is helping a lady into a dark blue saloon car. She takes his arm and steps onto a stone in the middle of a puddle. A short man with a moustache holds the door open for her.

Ouma retreats beyond their sight as Joshua waits for payment, then comes to him with the money.

"How much has he given you, Joshua?"

"Five shillings."

Ouma nods approvingly. "He's a good man."

"You know him, Boss?"

"I used to, in the old days."

His eyes mist over as he remembers the attempted coup in 1982. Before he was shot in the leg, he'd tried to catch up with Paul and Sam, carefree teenagers who had hitched a ride back to Nairobi when their car broke down.

He'd spent many hours face-down in the blazing sun with others on the verge of the airport road, not daring to move lest the trigger-happy rebels let off another round. He could not help moaning as daggers of pain shot up his leg, but didn't dare raise his head. Others were groaning and sobbing around him. He let the tears trickle down his face. Then silence.

A car engine started up, a motor bike roared, muted voices murmured and the sun lost its heat. He stayed still.

A toe nudged his side. "This one looks dead."

He opened his eyes. Had he passed out? He tried to turn his head. Gentle hands felt for a pulse at his neck.

"No, he's not. Stretcher!"

He heard the click of beads, and a female voice giving orders as he was lifted up.

"Careful now – look at his leg!"

He awoke in a hospital bed. Excruciating pain came from his right leg, yet when he reached down to touch it, nothing was there. He felt around the bedclothes and his heart lurched. Slowly, carefully, wincing with pain, he eased himself into a sitting position. The outline of one leg showed beneath the covers; a cage raised the blankets where the other should have been. How had that happened? He let himself fall back onto the pillows, crying out in anguish. A nun hurried in and patted him on the shoulder.

"I'm Sister Brigid," she said. "I'm afraid we've had to amputate your leg. What you're feeling are phantom pains." She straightened the bedclothes and settled the pillows comfortably under his head. "You must think about getting better; you've been very ill. We'll get your name later. For now, you must rest."

He felt a sharp prick in his thigh and fell into a deep sleep.

Ouma looks around him with a start. Where is Ken? Several new cars have arrived, and Joshua is still working alone.

He wipes at the sweat creeping down his cheek. It does no good to dwell on the past. He must forget the dark years of depression which dogged his mind. He's come through it now.

But later that night, lying on the makeshift bed in his shack and listening to the heavy breathing of the parking boys sleeping on the pavement outside, he lets his mind wander.

His memory had slowly returned, and with it came nightmares of pain and depression. He decided to change his name – again. He was known as Charles Ondiek as a youth, until the need to avoid a Mau Mau curse made him change to Charles Omari. Now he would call himself Ouma. In the uncertain political climate, it was safer to remain incognito, and as a journalist he knew too much for his own comfort. He would start a new life. With a leg missing, he could hardly carry on as before.

He told Sister Brigid that all he could remember was his name – Ouma – and he knew someone called Jackson at the Nairobi Museum.

His brother came to see him, closing the door politely on the nun who showed him into the room. He sat on the bed and Ouma saw recognition and relief in his eyes.

"We've been so worried about you, Charles. Caroline has asked everywhere and Sam is beside himself with anxiety."

"Sam – he's all right? The boys got back to Nairobi safely?"

Jackson nodded. "Not without last-minute drama, I can tell you!"

"And the coup?"

"It failed. *Rais* Moi has tightened up security, and heads are rolling."

Ouma leaned back against his pillows. "Thank goodness!"

"You seem to have suffered more than most."

Ouma grimaced and his face crumpled. "My leg has gone; my temperature keeps rising, and the nuns say I may have to spend months here."

"I'll tell the family. They'll want to see you."

"No – please!" Ouma begged him. "Don't let them see me like this. I couldn't bear it. No-one must know I'm here. You must promise me! It's too dangerous." Ouma didn't tell Jackson that he remembered hearing the rebels talking and had recognised one of them.

There was a gentle knock on the door and Sister Brigid tapped her watch. "We mustn't tire him – perhaps you can come to the office, sir? Ouma seems to have lost his memory."

"I'll pay his bill," Jackson said quickly. "But please don't let him have any other visitors."

"That won't be difficult – he is too ill for visitors, as you can see."

Ouma was frightened to leave the hospital. The nuns

settled him into the annexe and called in a psychiatrist who prescribed medication, then more pills to counter the side-effects. He lost weight. Frightening dreams troubled him at nights, and his days were spent in a stupor of sedation.

They reduced the dosage and he enjoyed moments of clarity. He studied his surroundings, resolving not to let anybody know that he was getting better. He felt the nuns were watching him closely; he was watching them, too.

He decided it was time to cope on his own, and needed to break his dependency on the drugs. He pretended he'd taken the pills, and flushed them down the toilet. Each successful day without medication was a major victory, and he gained confidence. Every day after breakfast he used the crutches the nuns had given him to hobble to the gates and sit on a bench in the shade beside the entrance. He asked Jackson for money, saying he needed it to buy newspapers and extra food. One day, when the nuns had become used to his daily ritual, he caught a *matatu* into town. He knew he had three clear hours before Sister Brigid checked on him at lunchtime, and by then he would be beyond their reach.

As the *matatu* approached the city centre, a feeling of elation crept over him. He was free! At every stop, new passengers crowded him further into the back corner of the vehicle. The intimate presence of a large *bibi* pressing her breasts against him aroused forgotten feelings. The incessant chatter and the shouts of the tout made him feel he belonged to the world, and he savoured the familiar odours of his fellow men.

He was alive!

He stepped out at the Machakos stage and let the crowd hurry past while he fiddled with his crutches, nearly falling over when a *toto* brushed against him.

"Mind the *mzee!*" shouted a smartly-dressed woman, yanking the boy's arm as she strode towards another *matatu.*

Ouma followed her through the organised chaos of rushing people and minibuses parked at haphazard angles all over the place. Touts called out destinations above the cacophony, and after several wrong tries, he found a vehicle bound for the city centre. Emerging at the market, his courage high, he chose a table in a café and stood his crutches against the wall, then looked round for service.

Nobody noticed him. He gazed out of the window and watched the people walk by. Sun streamed onto the pavement and through the window. His eyes drooped.

A sharp nudge on the shoulder caused him to start.

"Are you going to eat, *bwana*? If not, we need your table. It's self-service, you know."

Ouma groped for his crutches and made for the counter, paying for a cup of coffee and a *mandazi*. He had not eaten a doughnut for years. But when it came to returning to his table, he could not manage the crutches and the tray at the same time. He felt so helpless.

"Let me take it for you, *mzee*."

A smart young lady with a copious *kiondo* dangling from her arm came up beside him. With a grateful smile, he let her help him back to his table. That was the second time today somebody had called him *mzee;* he was a respected elder. He studied the retreating figure, her bottom wiggling at him with mouth-watering exaggeration. Biting into the *mandazi* and savouring its sweetness, he put four teaspoons of sugar into his coffee before sipping it down. People strode with purpose along the street outside. He didn't have anywhere to go.

He thought of Jackson. Of course – he would get a taxi to the museum. He felt in his pocket, and then the other one, but he couldn't find a single coin. What had happened to the change from the *mandazi?* He was sure he'd come with two hundred shillings.

That girl who'd helped him from the counter must have dropped it into that brightly-woven bag she carried. He looked round, but she'd disappeared. Seething with frustration, he grabbed a crutch and waved it towards the counter, shouting for the manager.

The more he protested, the more the manager tried to calm him down.

"I can't help you, *mzee*. I don't know the girl you're

speaking of. She doesn't work here. I'm sorry, but you must leave. You are making too much *kalele*."

Ouma felt lightheaded as he emerged into the sunshine. The passers-by formed a space round him as he floundered onto the pavement, leaning heavily on his crutches. He would have to walk to the museum. Which way was it? He couldn't remember.

He turned left and started up the street. Car horns and shouts interrupted his progress. People made angry gestures at him through their windscreens. He gritted his teeth and carried on, until something bumped him from behind and sent him sprawling.

He lay there, chest heaving miserably. A hand helped him up and guided him towards a doorstep.

"Sit here, *mzee*, and rest. You're lucky that car didn't hurt you or break your crutches. I've put them here, leaning against the wall."

Ouma batted his helper away. His back was hurting and his eyes misted up. His head buzzed madly and he couldn't breathe. He kicked out with his good leg catching a crutch, which clattered to the ground beside him. Pausing, he wondered at the noise. He didn't need them; it was their fault the car had knocked him down. He had to find Jackson.

Ouma tried to stand up, and toppled over onto his stump. The pain shot through his hip in excruciating waves and he cried out in agony. Hands grabbed at him and pulled him while he fought them off, shouting obscenities at the top of his voice.

Ouma stops himself from dwelling on this further nightmare of pain and depression in hospital, while he nurses a broken hip.

He forces his mind forwards to more pleasant times, when in a window of near lucidity he finally discharged himself into Jackson's care, and they went to commune with the spirits of their ancestors in the secret family cave overlooking Lake Magadi on the Tanzanian border.

For a while, he'd enjoyed peace and freedom from stress in his new surroundings. He helped Jackson from time to time, clearing away the rubble as his brother painstakingly traced the ancient rock art for transfer to the Museum. He practiced walking round the confines of the cave on his crutches.

"It's a wonder how you managed to get me up here in the first place," he said.

"Don't you remember? It took us hours – you managed the last bit by sitting with your leg over the edge and moving sideways, an inch at a time."

"It won't do to try and go back in a hurry, then."

"That was why I brought you here. There's no fear of you escaping again, until you are completely well!"

His old fever sometimes returned, together with the nightmares, and once Jackson had to go to Nairobi for more medication.

Later, a thunderstorm and flash flood transformed the dry plains into a fresh expanse of green, and the waters of the lake rose to cover the soda ash.

"Our old Mau Mau enemy, Mwangi, drowned in a flood like that," said Jackson as they sat on the ledge overlooking the lake.

The news marked the beginning of Ouma's long, slow road to recovery.

He shifts position on the pile of sacks which is his bed in the tin shack against the alley wall. It's a long time since he sat near his ancestors on that ledge, with binoculars focussed on the thin line of pink flamingos which encrusted the shores of Lake Magadi. But for the moment, there are more pressing things on his mind. The boys are growing up, and their needs are escalating. He must expand his business.

Chapter 3

"I have to go to the south coast to do an audit. How about you taking some leave, and we can go down together?"

Emily looked at Paul with surprise as she wiped her hands on the hot towel offered by the waiter. Their lunch meetings at the Five Bells were not as regular as before, and her social life had blossomed into a full-blown whirl.

"I don't know that I've got time, Paul. Life is so hectic."

"It would be a chance for us to visit Mum in Mombasa," he said. "You haven't been to see her since you started working."

"Is it as long as two years?"

Paul nodded. "She's been asking after you."

Emily pulled a face. "I've not contacted Caroline for a while – you make me feel guilty."

Her life suddenly seemed superficial and meaningless. Emily remembered the ideals she had shared with Paul, which vaguely addressed better lives for orphans who had no hope for the future. She had been one of those.

She'd not saved any money either. Where had it all gone? It was easy to get caught up in the glittering whirl of city life, to forget the down-trodden found at every corner and alleyway. She hardly noticed them now.

Paul peered at her through his glasses. "Well?" he said. "I can give you a lift to Mombasa and leave you with Mum for a week while I go to work. Then perhaps we could spend the weekend at Diani Beach before travelling back to Nairobi?"

Emily raised her eyebrows and cocked her head.

"I can book you a separate room at the hotel I stay at, I hasten to add!" He laughed. "Think about it."

It would be nice to relax for a change and spend more time with Paul, who was a caring, generous person. And he was right; it was time she saw Caroline again. Her benefactor had sold the secretarial college and now lived in a house in Likoni, south of Mombasa Island.

Emily had not taken leave this year; it would only be a matter of coinciding dates with the other secretaries.

Paul picked her up in his dark blue saloon car and Emily placed the nibbles and drinks she had brought for the journey on the back seat.

"It'll take us the whole day to get there," he said. "I'll have to drop you at Mum's and then go straight off to Diani for the night, ready to start work on Monday."

The journey was a nightmare of dust, heavy lorries, tankers, and potholed tarmac. Road works near Athi River held them up for three hours. Emily was glad to stop for refreshments at Hunters' Lodge after the first hundred miles. As Paul indicated right to pull into the petrol station, a white pick-up screamed past, barely missing them. It skidded onto the opposite verge, bounced off the ragged rim of the tarmac and came to a halt against the trunk of a thorn tree.

Paul stopped in the forecourt of the petrol station, swearing loudly.

He was shaking with shock. Two men emerged from the other car, and Emily went to see if they were all right.

"Come back here, Emily!"

She looked over her shoulder. Paul was leaning over the bonnet of his car, fighting for breath. She laid a hand on his shoulder.

"Are you okay?"

"Leave them alone; they're probably high on *bhang* or some other drug. You'll make matters worse. And I'll be fine. Just go in and order a cup of strong black coffee for me, and something for yourself. You'll probably suffer from delayed shock, too."

The two men were inspecting the front of their car, pulling twigs from the bumper, and one of them turned to look at her. She held her breath as she locked eyes with him over the distance. He seemed familiar. But he turned back to his car, which reversed and sped down the road.

"That man, Paul, he reminded me of someone. Do you remember me telling you about two people who always seemed to be following me, especially when I first came to Nairobi?"

"And I said you were imagining things! Come on, let's go and get something to drink; we've a long way to go."

When they drove through Mtito Andei, fifty miles down the road, Emily glanced to her left. A white pick-up was parked in the forecourt of the petrol station. Could it be the same car? But she said nothing to Paul.

It was a tedious drive in the hot afternoon sun. Emily nibbled at the ham sandwiches she had brought, and passed one to Paul. She shifted uncomfortably, her shirt sticking to the seat, and allowed herself to nod off until they passed Voi. Only a hundred miles to go.

"Would you like me to drive?"

He smiled across at her. "There's no need, I'm used to long journeys. But you can drive when we get to Mackinnon Road if you wish. The tarmac there will be in better repair, and I'll appreciate a rest before facing the south coast road in the dark."

He pulled over as they came to the first of several long straight stretches of road. Emily moved into the driver's seat and listened to the hum of the wheels on the tarmac as the road dipped towards the coastal strip. She was free to accelerate and enjoy the rush of cooling wind in her face through the open window. There was no fear of meeting one behemoth overtaking another as they approached a brow, for the daily convoy of oil tankers travelling northbound from Mombasa port would be nearing Nairobi by now.

As they descended to the coastal plains, Emily looked to her left, catching a brief sight of the sea. The road deteriorated, and oncoming vehicles weaved sharply between the potholes in a dangerously haphazard manner.

"Like me to take over?"

Emily hesitated. "Would you mind? This stresses me out! Besides, I don't want to be responsible for damaging your car."

She stopped at a dusty kiosk which sold mangoes and limes. "We might as well buy some for Caroline – and I could do with a soft juicy mango. Let's share one."

Emily borrowed a knife from the vendor and cut into one, giving half to Paul. She sliced hers into cubes, turned it inside out, and sunk her teeth into the succulent orange flesh. The juice dribbled down her chin and she reached for a tissue from the pocket of the car. Paul smiled at her through a gleaming mess of mango, so she passed him a tissue and he wiped his fingers before taking the wheel for the final leg.

Mombasa Island was deserted on the sleepy Sunday evening, and only a few cars clanked onto the Likoni ferry with them as they headed for the south coast.

Paul parked beside a bougainvillea bush which creeped over the latticed roof of Caroline's garage. She greeted them, flashing a torch to light the way to the front door.

"The electricity's gone – again," she said, giving them both hugs. "Can you stop for a cup of tea, Paul? I know you have to get on to Diani for the night, but it won't take a moment to heat the kettle on the gas ring."

Emily hadn't seen Caroline's new home on the cliff overlooking the harbour entrance. The welcoming glow from hurricane lamps gave the veranda a peaceful aura, and a gentle breeze cooled her cheek. She sank into the softness of a cushioned sofa, gazing out over the moonlit channel. Mombasa Island was in darkness, but the winking lights of the ferry reflected in the water, and the dark hulk of a cargo ship slid past, sounding a warning honk.

She spent the next few days in peaceful idleness, settling into the slow, humid rhythm of the coast, as she caught up with Caroline's news and allowed herself to wallow in lavish care and attention.

"It should be me looking after you, Caroline."

"Nonsense. You're a working woman, and you deserve a

break. Besides, I've nothing else to do but walk the dogs and look after the garden, which is mainly rockery anyway."

Caroline looked thin. Her legs were covered with scabs, where she'd scratched herself when walking on the cliff edge, or been wounded by the dogs who loved to jump up.

"Your skin is paper-thin, Caroline. Don't those sores ever go septic?"

"Sometimes, but I try to be sensible and keep them clean. Now, I'd like you to meet some of my neighbours. Would you mind if I asked them for drinks one evening?"

"'Course not."

But Emily groaned inwardly at the prospect of suffering the obtrusive attention of old-fashioned colonials. It was forty years since Kenya became a nation, but the old settlers still lived in the past, regarding Africans as an incongruity within their segregated social life. They didn't know how to treat her, and it sometimes made her smile.

She helped prepare bitings and stood by to welcome the guests as they arrived, wondering how Caroline could flit so naturally between their two worlds. She got on with everybody in her friendly outgoing way, and people responded to her charm. The party was more enjoyable than Emily expected, and the guests showed a genuine interest in her. But when the wine and beer flowed more freely, words slurred and obscenities crept into the conversation. Emily cleared the empty glasses and withdrew into the kitchen, watching out of the window as the guests weaved unsteadily along the stony road back to their homes.

"Thank you for enduring my party," said Caroline. "It does them no harm to be reminded of a different Kenya once in a while – and it's good to have you here after all this time."

Caroline engulfed her in a bear-hug, and Emily resolved not to leave so long between visits in future.

She joined the afternoon ritual of walking the dogs on the beach. As soon as the sun lost its heat, the neighbours stepped out with their knobbed walking sticks, while their dogs cavorted amongst the seaweed, throwing up sand and racing each other in circles. Greetings were exchanged and meetings arranged for the next day as the residents stopped to rest and talk. And the waves pounded the reef with an incessant roar.

It was a long time since Emily had felt the grainy sand between her toes. Standing in the ripples and gazing out to sea she let her feet sink into little troughs of water. A ship appeared as a faint blob on the horizon from the south, taking shape as it crawled into port.

At the end of the week, she helped Caroline prepare a meal ready for Paul's return.

"I don't see him often enough. Having you down here at the same time is very special. I'm so proud of you both." Caroline chatted and flitted about the kitchen, as Emily peeled the potatoes and prepared the vegetables.

After dinner, she helped clear away the table and then joined Paul on the upstairs balcony while Caroline locked up below. They stood together against the rail, their shoulders touching, and watched a great ocean liner turn southwards after dropping the pilot outside the harbour entrance. Its lights winked as it slid slowly out of sight into the vast Indian Ocean. Feeling insignificant, Emily wondered what lay beyond her own horizon.

Caroline came up the stairs to say goodnight. "I get quite tired these days if I stay up late," she said. "But you don't have to go to bed now. Just turn off that hurricane lamp in the corner before you retire."

"We can turn it off now," said Emily, coming away from the railing. "The half-moon is light enough for us."

She gave Caroline a hug and watched her go downstairs.

Paul turned, stretching his arm out to encircle her shoulders. He pulled her gently towards him and they stood gazing at the moon-washed waters. He had never done that before. A feeling of peace and security flowed through her; he squeezed her slightly and she nestled her head against his chest. His lips brushed her hair; she closed her eyes and let new feelings of delicious intensity engulf her.

"Are you going to come back with me to Diani

tomorrow?"

She pulled away and looked up into his eyes, dark orbs in his head silhouetted against the starlit sky.

"I feel guilty about leaving Caroline…" But she couldn't help herself. "Yes, please!"

He squeezed her arm. "I'm so glad. I've arranged a little surprise for you in the morning. I'm excited too. I've found a gem of a place for watching birds."

They stayed a while, standing close, listening to the occasional hoot from a passing ship. The sky clouded over. Emily's emotions were in a whirl. Paul didn't kiss her again, nor did he try to hold her tightly. He didn't say anything, either.

They left early on Saturday morning, Paul driving along the single strip tarmac past the coconut palms of Tiwi. The edges of the road had worn away, creating a sharp drop, and Paul had to perform a careful balancing act with two wheels on and two wheels off the road whenever they met a car coming the other way. Emily held her breath. He was driving too fast, but he handled the car well.

The road widened as they came into Ukunda. Several *dukas* crowded each other on either side; fruit and vegetable vendors lined the dusty verges, and idle figures lounged in the sun.

"This is not a nice place to be, and you mustn't ever get out of the car along this part of the road," warned Paul as he continued along the highway towards the Tanzania border. "We're going to detour into the Shimba Hills. There's a dam up there, and a new business venture which I know will interest you. My clients have ideas which remind me of the Bamburi Cement Factory on the north coast. You've heard of Rene Haller's Park, I presume?"

"Of course," said Emily. "I often went there with Caroline. There are some wonderful nature trails in the excavations."

"I know – perhaps we can go there together one day – but the one I'm going to show you will be closer to your heart."

He swung off the highway onto a dirt road past a rough

wooden signpost, but they were going too fast for her to read it.

"There are valuable minerals in these hills," he said. "And my clients, an overseas company, have started mining the sand. They've got their priorities right. I'll show you."

He pulled into a track which led to a school. Dozens of uniformed children were playing in the grounds.

"It must be break time," said Emily.

Paul stopped outside an office block near the entrance. "These don't belong to the school," he said. "They're temporary headquarters for the mine, who sponsor the school and run it in partnership with the local people."

"This is new. I've heard of missionaries sponsoring schools before, but not high-powered businesses."

"It's not only schools they're helping. You'll see for yourself once I've cleared it with the office. I'll leave you with the foreman to have a good look round, while I do a bit of bird-watching at the dam."

Emily thanked him, and smiled to herself. She didn't like bird-watching. It made her neck ache, and she could never find the birds through the binoculars, however patiently Paul tried to show her.

She waved him goodbye, and followed the foreman through a large maize *shamba;* the stalks towered over her.

"This maize bears three or four cobs, and sometimes more," he said. "We're using seeds imported by the company, and we've been taught how to plant them properly spaced apart. We use special mulch to keep the soil aerated."

He bent down to take up a handful of brittle, sweet-smelling material, working it through his fingers. It looked like ordinary soil, only darker. With such a crop the people could produce more than enough for themselves, Emily thought, as he told her of plans for building a maize mill to grind, package and sell the staple food in local shops.

The next two hours sped by as he drove her round a series of experimental fields belonging to local farmers.

Bibis wearing company uniforms worked in lines,

harvesting neat rows of potatoes. The tubers were of a standard size for hotel kitchens to make chips for the tourists. The foreman told her that field trials had been held in different parts of Kwale, teaching local farmers the correct technique. In order to maintain the quality, they had to use imported seed potatoes, but the yield more than justified the expense. A new agricultural industry was being born, suited to village small-holdings, and not as a result of charity or foreign aid.

Emily's hopes were raised as she recalled her ideals of helping the poor. This was the way to do it – through meaningful sponsorship, until the people could take ownership of their livelihood. She could become involved in something like this, instead of dull secretarial work in a Nairobi office.

On the way back to Ukunda she talked non-stop, telling Paul every detail of what she'd seen.

"I said you'd be interested, didn't I?"

"I'm more than interested! Don't you see this is how the people can really improve their lives?"

"Yes – but it's only one small project by one company. Can you imagine the same thing happening all over the country? I certainly can't."

She wound down the window and let the breeze cool her cheek. "It's not just one business. You're forgetting the Haller Park."

"That's for wildlife and the environment."

"And this one is more important, because it's for the people!"

"We have many charities here, Emily, and the missionaries have been around for decades. The problem is when the projects finish, people are left without the means to continue, and everything goes back to square one." There was a tinge of frustration in his voice.

These were standard objections to charitable works, because of their 'unsustainability'. Emily hated that word.

"Don't you see this is different? The people are being taught something which is close to their hearts. They're shown how to grow their own crops in a more profitable way, on a small scale."

"And aren't electricity and water supplies, health care and schools also close to their hearts? That's what the government should do. I don't see the difference, Emily. And you've only seen one part of what this company is doing. As well as funding schools, they're also bringing in electricity, providing boreholes and health clinics. They're even going to build a road here."

This confused her, but there had to be something special about this germ of an idea.

"You're making me lose the thread of my thoughts, Paul. If what you're saying about that road is true, it's also different from charitable works. Think of the local businesses which can spring up along it."

"The Kenya Government builds highways using international aid, and they open up new areas for development," said Paul, laughing. "And this company is helping itself by bringing in the road."

"That's what I think I'm saying, Paul! Isn't investment and a business arrangement better and more likely to succeed than a mere handout?"

"Only if there's no corruption involved," mumbled Paul as he swung the car off the main road towards the seafront.

"Now you're confusing me even more," she said, giving him a playful punch on the arm.

She would have to think deeper on the subject, but it was too hot now. The sun blazed through the window onto her bare skin. She fanned her face with her hat as he pulled into a petrol station, and then turned the car onto a winding track through dense bush. The heat was suffocating.

"Are we nearly there?" she asked, as tendrils from hanging branches scratched at the paintwork. Protruding roots jolted the wheels, causing her to bump against Paul's sweaty arm on the gear lever. Her shirt felt wet with perspiration, and her jeans, frayed off at the calves, clung tightly to her legs.

Paul rounded a sharp corner. "Only a hundred yards to go," he said, giving her a lop-sided smile.

The hotel car park was an expanse of glaring concrete, which hurt her eyes.

"Watch out – the ground is hot!"

But his warning was too late. Emily had kicked off her flip-flops into the well of the car and opened the door to stand up and stretch. With a shriek of pain, she jumped into the air, to dance away the searing agony in a series of barefoot leaps towards the haven of shade in the hotel.

The cool marble floor of the foyer immediately relieved her agony. Paul carried in his bag and went to the check-in desk. She dared not offer to help empty the car.

Her room overlooked the front lawns, dotted with coconut palms revealing glimpses of deep blue sea through the swaying fronds. Emily headed for the shower, revelling in the luxury of cool water and a soft towel to sooth her skin. Refreshed, and wearing a red and yellow patterned *kitenge* (its soft folds covering her bikini), she met Paul in the downstairs bar. In quiet companionship they sipped their *dawa* cocktails through straws. The vodka, lime and honey mixture was too sweet for Emily's taste, so Paul suggested she top it with soda water.

"That's better," she said, savouring the scenery and relaxing into the slow thrum of lethargy characteristic of the Kenyan coast.

Later, she discarded her *kitenge*, kicked off her sandals and walked between the palms to the white expanse of the beach, Paul striding at her side.

"You'll need something on your feet," he told her. "The sand is hot."

She was doubtful. "My black skin is tougher than yours, even on the soles of my feet. I'm sure I'll be okay."

The fine sand above the high tide mark was indeed hot, but not as searing as the concrete of the car park. Emily dashed through it, her feet sinking deep, and waited for Paul on the firmer damp ground lapped by the sea. A floppy white hat covered half his freckled face. He linked her arm as they strode along together, but she broke away and ran for the sheer joy of it. There was no end to the beach; not even a distant point jutted out to break its wide expanse. Green foliage fringed the shore and blue waters rolled in from the reef.

That evening, they dined under the stars, rising between courses to dance to 'sixties music played by a local group. Caroline had taken her into Mombasa and helped her to buy a silver gown with a modest cleft and a deep slit on one side, which clung to her curves as she moved. Paul held her close, rocking to the rhythm, and she let herself melt in his arms, feeling along the length of him.

Was this love? She knew Paul so well, and yet now she didn't know him at all. Why didn't he kiss her? Why didn't he say something? Was he feeling the same sensations?

He led her back to the table, leaving his hand over hers as they sipped their coffee and nibbled at mints, listening to the music and watching the dancers sway in front of them. She studied his profile. His modest clipped moustache under a fine straight nose broke the elongation of his face. The receding hair over his temples gave him a distinguished look. How could this man of the world feel anything for a girl like her? Perhaps it was just passion, brought on by the sea and the sun.

She got up to go to the washroom, feeling his eyes on her as she weaved between the dancers.

Others were watching her, also. Two people stood beneath a palm near the hotel steps. She had to pass them, and her heart lurched as she recognised the man from the white pick-up on the way down from Nairobi. He leered at her, taking a step forward, and she bounded up the steps into the safety of the foyer.

How would she avoid him on her way out? Emily stayed a long time in the washroom, repairing her lipstick, refreshing the makeup round her eyes and tweaking at her evening dress. But she couldn't stay here for ever.

She approached the steps, eyes darting from left to right. The two men had gone, thank goodness. She glanced over to their table near the dance floor, but Paul wasn't there. Had he gone to his room? The band had packed up, and the waiters were clearing the tables. Emily approached the table. Perhaps Paul had left her a note.

A figure lunged out of the shadows of a bougainvillea bush, and dragged her into the darkness.

Steamy breath, laced with beer, filled her senses. Fingers grabbed at her gown, tearing at the slit, and a large muscular body pressed fiercely down, grinding against her. A hand engulfed her mouth and she couldn't breathe, but she fought frantically, kicking out and trying to scratch at the flesh under the shirt. The face – that ugly, screwed-up face swelled with lust and inward effort – hung above her. She felt his fingers groping between her thighs. She closed her eyes. It was no use; she couldn't last much longer. Where was Paul? Why didn't the waiter come to her rescue? She went limp.

And suddenly the man was still. A voice hissed fiercely, and he got to his feet.

"What do you think you're doing, Maina? Stop it this instant! If Ouma gets to hear of this…"

She heard an angry grunt followed by a scuffle, and bodies crashed into the bushes. Footsteps pounded in the sand and she listened to them thudding towards the beach.

Emily stirred, and rose to her feet. She couldn't find her shoes. But she had a name: Maina. She would never forget that name, or that smell. And she would remember the face, too. She couldn't stop shaking. Thank goodness she'd been rescued before he'd done her worse harm.

She gathered her torn gown about her as best she could and stumbled towards the stairs, grateful that the place was deserted. No light showed below Paul's door next to hers. She hesitated, but she couldn't let him see her like this.

Safely in her room, she turned on the shower and stayed there for what seemed like hours, trying to wash away the dirt and the shame. But in bed the shaking returned as she recalled with raw fear the weight of that repulsive body over hers. She prayed, thanking God she'd escaped an even worse fate. She tossed and turned, grappling with her emotions, trying to calm herself, until in the early hours of the morning a hopeless rage filled her with exhaustion.

The sound of gentle knocking penetrated layers of sleep as Emily stirred, rubbing her eyes.

"Emily?"

It was Paul. She grunted an acknowledgement through the door.

"Are you okay, Emily? This is the third time I've tried waking you. It's nearly ten o'clock."

The sun streamed through her window and tiny particles of dust danced in its beams. Emily stretched and felt for her slippers.

"I must have overslept – give me half an hour."

"I'll be downstairs; I'll tell them to keep breakfast for you."

She let her nightgown drop to her feet and stood before the mirror, examining herself, feeling for bruises on her back and thighs, grateful that her black skin didn't show the damage. She was surprised how calm she felt as she stepped into the shower and again scrubbed herself vigorously, wincing as she felt more bruises. Choosing a loose calf-length skirt and sleeveless top from her wardrobe, she prepared to go downstairs.

"I'm sorry I didn't wait up for you last night," said Paul, rising to pull out a chair for her. "But you were so long away that I thought you'd gone to your room and forgotten to say goodnight."

Emily sat gingerly on the edge of her seat. "I know – but I didn't forget..."

"It doesn't matter, my dear." He took hold of her hand and searched her face. "I should have waited longer. Are you hungry?"

She shook her head.

He leaned forwards, his face close to hers. "Are you okay, Emily?"

His lips softly brushed her forehead, then her cheek. He squeezed her hand and she glanced up into his eyes, then quickly down again.

"I should have done that last night. We should've gone for a walk along the beach and had a long talk. I should've —"

"It's not that, Paul."

But he wasn't listening to her. He stood to put his arm round her shoulders, drawing her close to him. She winced, and pulled away.

"What's the matter – have you hurt yourself?"

"No… Yes," she said, miserably. And then she told him what had happened to her last night. The words came out in a short rush, just telling him the facts. Then, she sat there in silence, fighting to control her emotions.

He held her hands, stroking them with his thumbs; he didn't try to make her look at him again. It was a long time before he broke the silence, and his voice was shaking.

"I'm so sorry. Did he…?"

"No, Paul, I was lucky; he didn't rape me."

"I'll never let that happen to you again," he whispered. "Never. I'll never let you out of my sight!"

She couldn't help smiling at the absurdity of his fervour, and then he smiled, too. But she was glad he didn't try to hug her again, and it wasn't just because she was bruised.

"I'll be okay, Paul." She shuddered violently, remembering. "I just need time – I think."

Chapter 4

Ouma surveys the scene of his enterprise. The car park looks pristine in the early morning light; the boys have filled in the puddles and used stones to mark four neat rows of spaces for cars.

He rests on a crutch and jingles the coins in his pocket. The charge is three shillings for an unlimited period. Each boy receives one shilling and they keep the tips. He doesn't begrudge them, as there are other pickings to be had, and he can see a lucrative industry growing if he handles things right.

It's time to expand into other areas of the city. He's noted one place, conveniently close to the Kenya Cinema on the station end of Moi Avenue, but he needs to take another look.

He snaps his fingers at Ken who approaches from the direction of Uhuru Highway. The hum of traffic is increasing with the rush-hour.

"You're late. The *memsahibs* will soon be arriving to do their shopping, and you need to straighten up those stones again. Where are the others?"

"They're coming, Boss." Ken glances in the direction of the jam-packed highway. "But Joshua isn't here. I don't know where he's gone."

Ouma rolls his eyes in despair. "How am I to run this business if I don't have the people to help me? You boys are so unreliable."

"Would you like me to find more boys for you? I know many—"

"And I know your friends, out for quick money to spend on bad things."

Ouma shakes with frustration. There's a limit to what he can do. He can't go running after the parking boys to claim his due every time. His crutches feed the pity of soft-hearted housewives, but he is too slow to catch drivers who want to avoid paying. It needs careful thought and takes time, and he cannot operate without help.

"Ken, I will promote you to manager of the car park and you can use your friends. But you must be here every day without fail."

"I can't be here all the time, Boss. You know I go to the Undugu school in Kibera. But I'll find you someone to help. I can come first thing in the mornings and in the evenings when there's more money to make. I have some ideas."

"I'm sure you have ideas – but I hope you will tell me before you decide to put them into practice."

Ouma is tempted to trust Ken, but the boy is too acquisitive for his own good. He hangs around the highway in the early mornings on the look-out for open car windows and unguarded belongings. Ouma is sure the other boys are in league with Ken, and he can't stop them from selling trinkets to the motorists while they wait in the traffic jams. They are probably out there this minute, harassing the drivers. He suspects that Musumba might be behind that little enterprise. The tall, gentle-spoken man, whom he recruited to be a calming influence on Maina, has a stomach which protrudes over his waistband, betraying signs of good living. Ouma hopes the wares are not stolen.

He watches Ken reset the stones in straight lines, and guide a car with elaborate gestures into a space. It is the first of the day, but the charade is played out and the *memsahib* hands Ken three shillings.

The boy waves in an increasing trickle of cars. He has an endearing way with the housewives, who instinctively trust him. He tells them their cars are safer under his care than those in the street, where ragamuffins let down the tyres of people who can afford to pay the council charges.

The park is two-thirds full, and two more boys have arrived. Ken hands Ouma a plastic bag full of coins. Ouma counts them and gives Ken his due, then watches his new manager scamper off to school in the direction of the Kibera slums.

That's another problem. Kibera, the largest and poorest slum in Africa, is a hotbed of thieves and a breeding ground for AIDS. Ethnic violence often breaks out in the close confines of the shanties, where discarded rubbish clogs the open sewers. The expanse of rusty corrugated iron roofs is an eyesore on the landscape of Nairobi, with its various hues of brown, green, orange and dirty grey. Looking down from the Langata Road below the Nairobi Game Park entrance, Ouma has seen it many times. At least from that distance you can't see the slimy filth or smell the putrefaction.

He could share a slum shanty with any one of his relatives who have drifted away from their upcountry village to the big city, but he prefers his alleyway. It is a healthier place for the boys who are better off under his eye. He doesn't want to control them, he wants to teach them that being honest and reliable is the best way. And although Ken says he goes to school every morning, Ouma has his doubts. Kibera is not a good environment for anyone, however sharp and intelligent. But nowhere else can he get education, and the boy deserves to better himself.

If only the new government would acknowledge Kibera's existence and provide basic services, instead of letting it run riot at the mercy of unscrupulous entrepreneurs. But the President is too busy grappling with the corruption handed down from the past regime. The whole country is in a mess.

Ouma sighs. It's not up to him. All he can do for the moment is look after his own welfare and that of the four boys who have drifted under his care. He snaps out of his reverie. He's heard that Kibaki is bringing in free primary schooling for all children. He must ask the nuns about schools in the area. It's time to pay them his monthly visit.

Joshua arrives looking sheepish, but Ouma says nothing.

He transfers the coins into his pocket and hands Joshua the empty plastic bag.

"Here – I have to go somewhere. I'm putting you in charge. I've counted the cars and have a list of the number plates, so I'll know how much should be in that bag when I come back. Don't let the others cheat you!"

He has another reason for keeping the registration numbers. The drivers who escape paying are made fully aware of their misdemeanour the next time they come, and they often end up as his best customers.

Hobbling on his crutches, he heads towards Kenyatta Avenue, the main road into the city centre. He stops occasionally to recover his breath and lay out a sack to sit and beg, the empty trouser of his foreshortened leg protruding into the pavement. He scatters a few silver coins before him to encourage people to give generously, and thanks God for the Asian community who never fail him. It's something to do with their religion, which promises that givers are rewarded. Ouma is always careful to catch their eye as they approach, then he grovels his thanks whenever a note wafts downwards. Every few days he goes to the bank to make a deposit, and it is time for another visit. Today is going to be busy.

Before arriving at the imposing portals of the bank, Ouma enters an alleyway and extracts his tweed coat from the depths of his sack, then stuffs the sack behind a dustbin. He increases in stature, puffs up his chest and sheds his air of dishevelled poverty. Swinging his crutches with aplomb, he negotiates the wide steps and heads for the counter.

The teller greets him by name as he pushes through his bag of notes and coins. Another five hundred shillings is added to the coffers. He tips his cap and thanks her in perfectly enunciated English.

Leaving the bank, he ignores his chattels in the alleyway. Head high, he creates a wide swathe around him as he negotiates the lunch-time crowd and strides purposefully towards Moi Avenue. There is a likely piece of unused ground at the station end. If he can gain a foothold here, his takings will more than double. He turns into a cul-de-sac, which allows limited angle parking, and inspects the terrain.

A strand of barbed wire straggles between him and half a dozen dusty shrubs on the other side. He curses his crutches. If it weren't for his leg, he could duck under the wire and examine the area thoroughly. But it looks smaller than he remembers, and there is a large city car park beyond.

A strong aroma of coffee reaches him and he goes towards a nearby eating place. Beckoning at a waitress, her bulges oozing from a tight black mini-dress, he gives his order. He realises he has been here before, and a feeling of panic wells up, threatening to choke him.

A flight of wooden steps rises to the food counter, where more tables are occupied by diners. He sees the waitress approaching with a tray bearing his coffee, and catches her eye. The years slip away as another pair of eyes superimpose themselves on his vision. Black, deadly, menacing eyes. Mwangi's.

Ouma shudders at the memory and gets up quickly, grabbing his crutches. He leaves the café, and ignoring the girl's cries he escapes along the street. He can't help it; the shaking only subsides when he has turned the corner onto Moi Avenue. He heads in the direction of the *matatu* terminal. He cannot understand himself. A primeval fear has overwhelmed him, and yet logic tells him that Mwangi met his end years ago. How can that evil influence, the cause of all his suffering, still be present? Is he to be forever haunted by the man?

He grits his teeth, glad that he is going to see Sister Brigid today. She will calm him. And it is probably time he went to church.

She greets him in the hospital gardens, placing a pair of secateurs in the pocket of her apron and wiping the earth from her hands as he hobbles up the pathway.

"Hello, Ouma! I've been pruning the roses. One cannot trust the *shamba* man to do that properly. You're just in time for elevenses."

She opens a side door and Ouma gestures her to go in first.

"Excuse me a second." Sister Brigid disappears into the

washroom and Ouma wanders into the nuns' communal area. He spent many hours here when he lived in the annexe at the bottom of the garden during his recuperation.

He goes to the window and studies the building. Long wisps of dry grass scratch against it in a light breeze. The paint is peeling off the door. He remembers his room, one of three, and a sitting area with a kettle and a cupboard where the nuns always kept a tin full of biscuits.

He turns as Sister Brigid enters the room.

"Does nobody stay there anymore?"

"No. We've been wondering what to do with it. Our patients are all short-term now, because we've opened a new respite centre outside the city."

She bustles towards the counter and places two cups of tea and a plate of biscuits on a table in front of the sofa. He leans his crutches against the wall and lets himself down into the soft springs.

Sister Brigid lifts her cup and takes a sip. "Why do you ask?"

"Just wondering." He smiles at her. A thought has crossed his mind, but he won't mention it yet. "Have you heard anything further about President Kibaki's election promise of free primary education? All this business about fighting corruption is in the news, and I fear the education bit has been set aside. I have four street boys under my care – did I tell you? A couple of them are quite bright, and would benefit from going to a good school."

"Yes." The nun's eyes light up as she nibbles at a biscuit. "There is a school in the next street down, where our nurses send their children. You probably walked past it on your way here. They've started building more classrooms, but it's not free – the children must have books and pens, and the new extension needs funding. But where are your boys living?"

Ouma shrugged.

"You're welcome to use the annexe. I'll have to ask the Mother Superior, but I'm sure she'll agree so long as they behave themselves. It's such a waste of good space."

Ouma forces himself to remain passive. "It would need repairing, and it is rather near the hospital. But thank you, Sister. It may be the answer to prayer."

Sister Brigid glances at her watch. "I have to go on duty now. I'll ask her later."

Ouma visits the tiny hospital chapel, trying to dismiss the picture of Mwangi's evil eyes which hover in his mind as he kneels in a pew. He's been free of fear since Jackson told him the Mau Mau oath-giver had died, and he resolves never to go near that café again.

On his way back to town he lingers outside the school. A labourer is feeding a churning cement mixer while two others trundle wheelbarrows under the eyes of a supervisor. The classroom wall they are building is two feet high. A dozen children in dusty uniforms are playing in the rubble, and a harassed teacher hurries towards them. The sound of voices chanting times-tables wafts towards him through a window which has no glass.

Ouma hails a passing *matatu* to take him back into the city centre and, deep in thought, wriggles into a seat between two *bibis*.

Joshua greets him outside the Five Bells and hands over a bag full of coins.

"Ken is back, Boss. He's had an idea."

Ouma grunts, not sure that he wants to hear about any more ideas from his new manager, who approaches with Musumba trailing behind. They have tried out their scheme, Ken tells him. There is a standpipe nearby, and Musumba has bought buckets and liquid soap. Three *totos* are cleaning cars in the line closest to the street, the water running in puddles along the side of the pavement. Ouma doesn't recognise any of the boys.

"We're asking two shillings for a car wash!" they shout. "It's good money."

Ouma tells Ken it is an excellent idea. He directs the boys to clear the ground and channel the water into the ditches along the highway, which need cleaning – again. The City Council should be grateful to him for doing their work.

Alex Gomez is certainly grateful. As long as his customers use Ouma's car park, they can safely while away the hours in his curry house, spending money on food and hard liquor. But the government ministers with their gleaming Mercedes Benz cars and uniformed chauffeurs, look askance at Ouma's enterprise.

Ken devises another scheme, and Ouma suspects that Maina is involved this time. The chauffeurs drop off their employers at the door of the restaurant, and are guided into the car park. Money changes hands, and as long as the patrons remain oblivious, the drivers can enjoy a certain amount of freedom. When they head for a discreet brothel a block away, Ouma understands the natural urges of men and remembers his own profligate youth. And Ken provides a warning service the instant their bosses show signs of leaving the restaurant.

It's all very well, thinks Ouma, so long as everything goes smoothly.

A man stumbles out of the Five Bells, clutching at his protruding belly. He coughs as if to clear a blockage in his throat, then staggers over the road and vomits into the ditch. He looks round, trying to focus. His car is not where he left it.

A *toto* appears at his side.

"Can I help you, *Bwana*?"

"Where's my driver?"

The boy leads him into the darkness and he splashes through a puddle, bumping into a car; he leans against the bonnet to steady himself. A torch flashes onto the number plate.

"Your car, *Bwana* – is it this one?"

"No. Where's my driver?"

The torch jerks ahead of him, pinpointing number after number in a line of vehicles. He stops.

"That's the one!"

"Wait here, *Bwana* – I will get your driver!" The *toto* scurries away.

His eyes attuned to the night, Ouma watches from the shadows. The man stands still, waiting. Ken has disappeared round the block, heading for the brothel. He comes back, followed by the driver in crumpled uniform, fumbling at his clothes. Ken comes to stand by Ouma.

"This is bad," whispers Ouma. "That man is a top minister in government. Your idea to make money will come back to bite you."

The sound of a blow and a sharp cry is followed by the clunk of a car door opening. Headlights flash and, wheels skidding, the vehicle dashes out of the car park.

"That driver is going to lose his job, isn't he?" mutters Ken, shaking his head.

"And you will lose much more, if we don't act quickly. Come!" Ouma rounds up the boys and they slink off into the night.

He is not surprised when President Kibaki issues a directive to ban all parking boys from the city. They cannot be seen near this place again.

It's time to speak to Sister Brigid, for the police will soon scour the alleyways for vagrants to arrest. Punishment will be merciless. He has heard stories of police violence, and has no desire to wait and see if they are true.

Chapter 5

"Shut your window, Emily."

"Why? The heat is stifling, and the fan in your car doesn't work properly."

"I've ordered a brand-new model with air conditioning. It's being delivered in two weeks' time. Just wait until you see it."

Emily felt the perspiration dripping down her neck as she looked over the cars towards the university playing fields. Nobody was using the running track. She didn't blame them. She rested an elbow on the window and leaned outwards, trying to catch a breeze on her cheek, but the sun was relentless and the dark blue sides of Paul's Peugeot were too hot to touch. The traffic crawled along at walking pace, and now it stopped – again.

"I hope it's not going to be the same colour as this one. It's an oven in here."

She heard a shout from Paul's side and twisted her head to look behind him. A boy was gesturing dramatically to attract her attention. He bobbed up and down, pointing to their rear wheel. Her heart sank. They had a puncture? Not here, in the middle lane, surely? Paul's face was grim as he put the gear into neutral and engaged the handbrake.

"Have you shut your window?"

"No – why?"

"Just do it!"

Emily reached for the handle as Paul opened his door to place one foot onto the tarmac. He leaned round to have a look.

"The tyre is okay. And there's no *toto;* he must have gone." He shut the door.

"Thank goodness for that!"

She felt a movement at her side, and an arm reached across her. The stench of stale body odour blasted her senses, and a face, eyes intent on the well at her feet, filled the window. He caught hold of her handbag by its long strap, flipped it over her lap and disappeared.

"Hey …!"

At that moment, the traffic started moving and Paul let out the clutch.

"He's taken my bag!"

She couldn't see the boy for moving cars.

"That'll teach you." Paul frowned at her. "We're already late; and you'll never catch that *toto* anyway."

A surge of anger swept through Emily. She tried to calm herself down, knowing that Paul was right. She was lucky she didn't keep much money in her purse.

"I've had that black handbag for so long, it's become part of me," she complained. But she'd taken a good look at the boy's face, and would never forget that smell.

After her ordeal at the coast, Paul had insisted on taking her out to lunch twice a week, and they went regularly to the theatre together. He was always there, almost suffocating her with his attention but never making advances. The awful nightmares which interrupted her sleep over a period of months had petered out. She'd not had one for ages.

Paul pulled up outside her office.

"I'm sorry about your bag, Emily, but—"

"I know; I should have kept my window up. You're always telling me to watch out for thieves. I know better now."

"I'm going to an upcountry farm on an audit next week," he said. "I'll be back on Friday to pick up my new Peugeot 607. It's a bank holiday weekend. Would you like to come back to the farm with me on Saturday morning? I'll have a few loose ends to tie up, then we can go on a little safari. I don't think you've ever been north of Nairobi?"

"I haven't," she said. Was she ready for this – and what

was Paul thinking?

"I promise I won't try anything you're not ready for."

He'd read her thoughts.

"I'll book two rooms at Barry's hotel in Nyaharuru for the Saturday night," he said. "But if you'd rather not, I can easily cancel. I'll call you on Friday."

They left for Nyaharuru after work.

"I'm so glad this car is white!" said Emily, savouring the smell of new leather as Paul opened the passenger door for her. "It will reflect the sun much better than that old dark blue one."

"You forget – it has air conditioning. I can't wait to find out how it behaves."

They headed northwards through the Kikuyu smallholdings on the outskirts of Nairobi, and Paul turned left off the highway to take the old escarpment road. The sun was low on the horizon as they stopped at a lookout.

Emily gazed at the burnished bronze of the cumulus clouds billowing against the azure sky; the great expanse of the Rift Valley spread beneath her. Paul placed his arm round her shoulders and pointed out the landmarks.

Mount Longonot rose in stark volcanic mass from the valley floor, and the dim outline of the Mau Hills were a hazy line in the distance beyond. Gradually the blue turned to purple and the lingering sun etched the clouds with a molten outline. Golden bars of light grew from breaks in the cloud, fanning out to touch the dimming valley floor. And suddenly darkness fell.

Forty miles later they topped the climb up the Aberdare Mountains and spurted through large patches of sticky mud. Paul weaved the sliding vehicle precariously along deep furrows in the road, and Emily clutched tightly at the strap above her head as he accelerated through puddles which gleamed in the headlights. His car met the challenge well, but it was splattered with mud when they arrived at Barry's Hotel, dimly lit in the heavy mist. The rushing sound of a waterfall filled her ears, and she took a woolly sweater out of her bag, pulling it tight round her.

"It's much colder at this altitude, isn't it?"

"A good meal and a drink by the fire will solve that!" he said.

They had drinks at the bar, and roast beef and Yorkshire pudding for dinner. There were no other guests. Emily wasn't used to eating so much at night. She flicked through a wildlife magazine afterwards, with her feet up beside a fire that blew smoke into the room. Paul had immersed himself in a detective story. The smoke made her drooping eyes smart, but she was grateful for its warmth.

"I'm going to bed, Paul."

"Goodnight, my dear. Don't be alarmed if you find a hot water bottle in your bed."

When she got into the bed, a strange object wobbled under her toes, but was deliciously warm. She manoeuvred it up her body, curled herself around it and fell into a deep sleep.

The following morning the country glowed under a bright sun.

After breakfast, Paul led her down a rocky path to the waterfall, swollen from the previous day's rain. Great gushes of foaming water leapt out with a thunderous roar to crash into a frothy pool. She gasped and caught his arm, slipping on the treacherous stones. Trembling, she put her hands to her ears.

"I can't bear the noise – it's so frightening!"

He put out an arm to stop her from turning back. "Wait – you're safe with me. And watch! I love looking at waterfalls; nature is so majestic and powerful."

"Nature is dangerous, too, Paul."

But she watched, and was fascinated, and started to understand a little of his excitement.

He drove her through fields awakening in the sunshine. Little farms bordered by scruffy thorn hedges or sisal plants lined the dirt road. One or two cows, the odd sheep and an occasional field of pyrethrum broke the monotony of grassland, which was dotted with mud huts in various stages of dereliction. A man on a bicycle wobbled towards them, and a boy with a stick goaded a donkey and cart along a parallel track.

"They haven't recovered from the post-Independence Settlement Schemes forty years ago," he told her. "The commercial farming of colonial days is only suited to large acreages, and these people want their own little plots of land."

"But that's natural, Paul! You must feed yourself first, surely, before thinking about selling to others?"

"But are they even feeding themselves? Look at these acres of wasted land, which in my youth were filled with wheat and barley as far as the eye could see. The people haven't got the means or the know-how to improve their lot, and how can they hope to feed a nation when the men-folk give up and drift to the towns to seek quick fortunes? You'll soon see how it should be done. The farm we're going to used to belong to the only Europeans left in this part of Kenya. They refused to hand over to the Settlement Scheme, and when they died, it was sold to a top government official. It's now managed by a white man, and is an example of what can be achieved."

"Hummmph..." Emily snorted. "I bet the owner is one of the fat cats deep in corruption, and using public money."

But she couldn't help admiring the extensive fields of crops drinking in the recent rains. The farm was neater than the scrappy *shambas* they had passed earlier. Giant tractors were parked in a yard, and as they approached the homestead, she saw dozens of *bibis* in uniform bending over orderly rows of vegetables. Long lines of piping loomed overhead.

"Those are used for spraying water in periods of drought," said Paul. "They'll be taking them down, now that the rains have broken."

He drove past an enormous shed. "This is where they sort and pack the vegetables for export. It's big business. The cartons are loaded onto freight 'planes in Nairobi every night, ready to be taken to European markets for the following morning."

"What vegetables are they?"

"Courgettes. Baby marrows, to you!"

"I never knew they looked like that in the field. Our marrow plants are large sprawling vines which creep all over the place."

"These are a different, specially-cultured variety; they're picked when young. Impressive, isn't it?" He stopped the car. "Come, let's take a look inside the shed."

He spoke to an *askari* near the door, and led her into a packaging area filled with tables piled with the small green vegetables. Groups of women sorted them, discarding the misshapen ones onto the ground.

"What happens to the rejects?"

"Most are thrown away. Some are taken home by the *watu* and sold in local shops, but the people don't like them."

"What a waste. Why don't they take them to Nairobi?"

"It isn't cost-effective to sell them locally."

They got back into the car and drove up a bricked road towards the homestead, a low stone building covered with creepers. The manager's wife offered them morning coffee and home-baked cakes, and chatted with Emily while Paul completed his work in the office.

"Would you like to drive?"

"Do you trust me, Paul? I'd hate to be the first to spoil your lovely paintwork."

"Don't worry, my dear. A pristine new car is a liability in this country. I won't rest easy until it gets its first scratch."

"I'll try to keep the scratches small, then!"

She took the wheel for the rough road to Nanyuki. The Aberdares stood starkly on her right, overlooking acres of dry grass and withered crops, for the rains had not yet reached here. In front of her rose Mount Kenya, topped with cloud and veiled by hazy heat. Mirages appeared regularly on the road. And even through sunglasses Emily was mesmerized by the shimmering waves, which turned the horizon into a sea of motion.

Perhaps it was this, or mere slowness of reaction, which caused her not to notice a billy goat until it was too late. It darted onto the road from a nearby group of huts and crashed into the passenger door with a sickening thud. Emily stopped the car and rested her head on the steering wheel, taking deep breaths. She looked up.

The goat was alive. It limped away bleating loudly. They got out to examine the paintwork, which despite the dent was not even scratched.

"And so your nice new car has had its first dent."

"Don't worry," said Paul. "It'll only need a gentle push by a panel-beater to take it out."

"I'm not worried. Remember what you said – I've done you a favour!"

They waved their apologies to the goat's owner, and Emily had to shake herself awake several times as she weaved the car along the empty road. When she pulled up at a fork in the road to ask him which way to take, she noticed Paul had nodded off.

Several miles later they entered a dusty village. Faded signs on lopsided shops indicated they were in Rumuruti. Paul woke up again.

"We shouldn't be here…"

"Well, you told me to take the left hand fork fifteen miles ago."

He smiled sheepishly. "We'll have to go back. But never mind. It's a lovely day, the office is paying for the petrol, and time is no factor."

Emily made a U-turn, and after taking the correct fork, stopped under a scraggly thorn bush beside the road for lunch. She rested awhile, then left Paul to sleep with his hat over his face while she wandered through the brittle grass in search of green shoots.

Everything was covered with dust; even the wait-a-bit thorns were suffering. Carefully avoiding the wicked barbs, she plucked at their tiny white fluffy flowers and breathed in the sickeningly sweet scent. A lorry lumbered past, but she had the wind in her favour and watched as the red dust billowed out to cover the opposite side of the road in a thick carpet.

She roused Paul, packed up their picnic and motored on through the green oasis of Nanyuki, crossing the bridge where sparkling clear water trickled between well-trodden banks.

"We're about to come to the worst tarmac road in the country," said Paul, stirring. "I think I'd better take over."

Emily stopped the car and they changed places. The sharp sides of massive potholes created havoc with his brand new tyres as they weaved over what was left of the tarmac towards Timau. Mount Kenya lay hidden beneath folds of cloud, which blackened on the lower slopes, drenching the forest. But the large estates at its foot had enjoyed no rain for over a year, and the farmers were in dire straits.

The country was beautiful. Rolling acres of fertile fields stretched out in alternating patterns of brown plough and yellow grain ready for harvest.

"They only require a little rain each year to turn a good profit," said Paul.

Mount Kenya looked down in its awesome majesty. Its forested slopes harboured buffalo and wild pig, he told her, the farmers' worst enemies. Away to the north lay the wild African desert, broken by an occasional range of hills disappearing into a heat-hazed horizon. Here, thought Emily, I am indeed a mere grain of sand.

"Farming is prosperous when the rains are good, but it's hazardous," said Paul. "They have hair-raising adventures shooting at buffalo in the middle of the night, trying to keep them off the crops."

Emily pointed at some objects hanging in a line on a fence. "What are those?"

Paul stopped the car and took up his binoculars. "They are bush-pig heads," he said. "The farmers put them there as warning to the animals that grazing the crops means certain death."

Emily shuddered with revulsion.

"Life is harsh for the farmers. Their characters are moulded by destructive drought, the parching sun, and danger from wild animals. They struggle against many odds to earn a living and the right to live as they please."

They turned back to Nanyuki and checked into the Silverbeck Hotel. Emily, relaxed after the bliss of a hot bath, was happy to repeat the formula of the previous night: a drink, followed by a supper of roast beef and Yorkshire pudding.

"I have a surprise for you," Paul told her the next morning. "After breakfast, you must be sure to wear your jeans."

He turned left off the main road towards the mountain, which stood in stark outline against the golden rise of the sun. A narrow winding track took them towards a group of dilapidated wooden buildings, as wisps of grass scraped the chassis. They passed horses grazing behind a strand of wire, and pulled up in a yard where a hen clucked at a trio of scruffy chicks. Three ponies waited, bridled heads looking over makeshift stable doors, and a woman with a halo of frizzy blonde hair waddled towards them in skin-tight jodhpurs.

"Mr Clayton? Welcome. I have chosen Swara for the lady. She used to be as swift and graceful as the antelope after which she's named. But now she loves to go slowly and look after beginner riders."

She called to a *syce*, and the man led out a small brown pony with grey hairs round its muzzle. "See, she has our most comfortable saddle."

Emily met Paul's eyes, and held her breath. How could he do this to her? She'd never been near a horse in her life, and had no desire to ride one.

"Come," he said, taking her hand. "Swara won't bite you."

Emily knew he meant well. She touched the pony's neck. Paul covered her hand with his, making her stroke the rough hairs and feel the wiry mane. She glanced down. Her hand was black with dirt and she wiped it on her jeans.

The *syce* led the pony to a mounting block and encouraged Emily to step forwards. The saddle was covered with fluffy sheepskin. She put her foot in the stirrup, and Paul eased her upwards. Lifting her leg over its back she let herself sink into the soft fleece, admitting that it was indeed comfortable. But she dreaded what was going to happen next.

The *syce* snapped on a leading rein. Emily grabbed the front of the saddle as the pony took a first step. It walked in a slow circle. She gradually became used to the unsteady gait, feeling every bone in her body move to the sway of the horse. She tried, unsuccessfully, to relax while Paul mounted a taller, grey animal, and they followed another horse out of the compound.

"You're not going to make me to ride by myself are you, Paul?"

He laughed. "Of course not! We're just going to walk round a field. Come on – smile. It's not as bad as all that!"

She tried to smile as the *syce* led her in a wide circle behind the guide. Paul rode alongside, encouraging her and making her laugh by pretending to fall off. He showed her how to hold the reins, and when she was able to balance without clinging onto the saddle, he took the leading rein from the *syce*.

"Don't worry, Emily. I'll look after you. Trust me?"

How could she not trust him, uncomfortable though she was? She gave him a little smile and nodded bravely as they followed the lead horse up a track towards the mountain. Paul's leg brushed against hers from time to time as they rode side by side when the track was wide enough. He pointed out a herd of impala behind the bushes, and a shy duiker skulking in the undergrowth. A flash of blue caught her eye and he cried out.

"That's a lilac-crested roller! Did you see it?"

She laughed, happy at his delight at spotting the bird. Her pony plodded onwards, sure-footed and unperturbed. She'd never felt so close to nature before, and the wild animals ignored them.

"They don't associate people with horses, or with cars," said Paul.

It was true, and her confidence and sense of familiarity with the wild became deeper as the ride continued.

The following morning she suffered stiffness in unusual places, but ate a good breakfast before the drive back to Nairobi. They detoured to Nyeri. The road twisted and turned, and at each bend Mount Kenya seemed to change position. The air was so clear that, even though they were thirty miles distant, its cloud-capped peak seemed directly to bar their way.

They stopped for lunch at the Outspan hotel near the entrance to the Aberdare National Park. Emily laughed when she saw that here again the menu offered roast beef and Yorkshire pudding. She took Paul's elbow and directed him to the cold buffet table.

Afterwards, in the car, she sang contentedly to herself and Paul shared her mood, adding his baritone to her soprano. Approaching home, the traffic thickened into a crawl, but neither of them minded the delay as they reminisced over their weekend.

"Remember when we talked about my friend Sam?" said Paul as he drew up outside her flat. "He's returned from abroad, and I've found out that he's stationed near Magadi. Would you like to come with me to meet him?"

Emily nodded.

"But first, I want to take you to a very special place, not far from where Sam is guarding his ancestral secrets. I've never been there, but I have a friend in the Mountain Club who is organising an expedition to Ol Donyo L'Engai, the Mountain of God. Have you heard of it? It's a volcano just over the Tanzania border, and it has started to erupt."

She had never heard of it, and she wasn't too sure about going there, but after all he'd done for her, she didn't like to dampen his enthusiasm.

Chapter 6

Ouma regards the decrepit building at the back of the hospital with misgivings. It calls up too many unwanted memories. But it's all he has to offer the boys, and he is grateful to Sister Brigid for organising it.

Ken runs on ahead through the long grass and punches open the door, breaking the cobwebs which festoon the frame. Joshua is close on his heels.

The two boys stand in the drab and dusty room, looking round them in wonder as Ouma hobbles up the pathway on his crutches. He is followed by the twins dragging plastic bags containing their worldly belongings: a bundle of rags, two dented tin mugs and toys they have made from pieces of wire. They look at the cracked cement floor, and with excited whoops start trundling the toys on wobbly wheels, going faster and faster in decreasing circles.

"Look – one, two, three rooms! And a roof over our heads!" Ken finds the bathroom and turns on the tap. "Water!" He tests the toilet, misfiring with his stream onto the floor, but he flushes it with a flourish and the twins stop in surprise at the noise. Then they too want to have a try, but can barely reach the rim and their aim is worse than Ken's.

Ouma glances into the nearest bedroom. It is the one he used when convalescing. The bed is still there, the curtains in tatters at the window. He shudders, wondering how he is going to manage in this place of bad memories.

"Ken," he calls. "You and Joshua can sleep in this room. Look – it has a bed you can share. The twins can take the next one. Put your bags there, boys. You'll have to sleep on the floor."

He opens the door to the third room. It is smaller than the

others, and quite bare. The tiny window has been boarded up, but there is a key in the door. He tries it, and it works. He dumps his bag onto the floor and pulls out an old foam mattress. His cupboard can go against the wall in the corner, when he can find someone to transport it from the alleyway.

The twins jump up and down on the broken sofa in the main room, causing clouds of dust to fill the air. Joshua sneezes.

"Can't we sleep on this?" they shout.

Helped by Ken and Joshua, they grab a corner each, and pushing and pulling, scrape the sofa along the floor, gouging runnels in the broken concrete as they manoeuvre it through the bedroom door. Ouma tries to pull it shut, but it jars against the warped frame, and the twins resume their bouncing.

Ken fills a kettle with water from the sink in a tiny kitchen alcove, but it leaks. He tries the light switch, and a weak glow emanates from a bulb hanging from the ceiling. The twins stop bouncing and point upwards, chortling with joy, and Ouma notes with relief that the switch is out of their reach.

He closes the door to his room, turns the key and pockets it before going out. Sister Brigid is pruning rose bushes against the wall and glances up as he comes, parting long wisps of grass with his crutches.

"I'll clear it properly for you," she says, brushing away a strand of hair and tucking it into her wimple.

"Don't worry, Sister. It's better as it is. We don't want to betray our presence to the police."

"I see your point. The boys approve of their new home?"

"They do. I'll let them enjoy the novelty for a while, but I want to ask you about that school."

"I've already spoken to the headmaster. He'll take the boys. You can send them at the beginning of the week."

"Bless you, Sister."

"And God bless you too. I think you will find that Mwai Kibaki's crackdown on parking boys is a blessing in disguise. But there's something I want to ask you. I've had a letter, and I have to look for somebody…"

Ouma's mind jumps forward, finding obstacles, imagining what would happen if any of the boys strayed back to their old haunts, and if the police got hold of them. How is he going to control them? It will be all right as long as he is here to see them to school every morning, but the temptation to skip lessons and work for Musumba along the highway will sometimes be too much, and they'll be recognised. He has to keep begging at his pitches in the city as it's his only source of income now. Somehow, he has to feed them and buy uniforms.

"I've had a whip-round of the hospital patients," says Sister Brigid later. "We're buying material for the boys' school shirts. I'll sew them this weekend. One of the mothers who come for ante-natal check-ups has some old shorts they can use for the time being. Her children have grown out of them."

Will there be no end to these blessings? And how is he going to repay her kindness?

Ouma accepts graciously, but his life becomes more difficult as he tries to control the boys. It is simple at first, but when the novelty of going to school wears off, they try to slip away from classrooms of sixty children, with only one teacher.

Ken does well at school. He has learned to value his education, and luckily the others follow his lead most of the time. But one day when Ouma takes a *matatu* into town, he sees Joshua weaving through cars jammed in the traffic.

The only solution is to remove the boys from Nairobi's temptations. The only place he can think of is his home village. He hasn't been there for years, but Joshua and the twins are from that area. What will happen to Ken after he takes his primary exams? Ouma remembers a high school near Lake Victoria where Ruth, his estranged wife, went.

What has made him think of her after all these years?

A rush of memories overcomes him. He abandons his pitches and stays at the annexe for days, allowing scenes of the past to fill his mind. He regards the dilapidated building strewn with the boys' possessions, the dirt, and the poverty. He doesn't belong here. It's time to move on.

The end of term is weeks away, and he can't act before next year, when Ken takes his exams. But he'll go away for a few days. He'll have to leave the boys here, but Sister Brigid will see they have enough to eat. He knows she gives them left-overs from the hospital kitchen when she thinks he's not looking. They'll relish the freedom of his absence, and he could do with a break.

"Don't you worry, Ouma. I look forward to mothering your boys while you are away," says Sister Brigid. "But I keep forgetting to ask you. I've had another letter from a lady in the UK. Did I tell you? She supports a charity through her church. They've helped provide beds in our hospital in the past. Her name is Louise, and she's been asking if I can find someone she used to know, called Charles Omari Ondiek."

That name – Louise. Ouma can't help himself, his eyes widen and he holds his breath. Louise – could it be?

Sister Brigid is watching him. "Your English is very good, and I've often wondered about your past. Could it be that you used to know people in the UK, before you lost your leg and your memory?"

Ouma flinches, but Sister Brigid is talking again.

"Have you ever met someone called Charles Omari Ondiek? Perhaps your brother Jackson can help."

Has she guessed his secret? Ouma composes his face into an expression of thoughtfulness, and shakes his head in bewildered fashion.

"My memory surprises me sometimes, Sister. It suddenly has a jolt and another piece of the jigsaw goes into place. I'll see what I can find out about this man."

He must get away from here before she asks any more questions. He'll travel home tomorrow.

Ouma screws up his nose to endure the proximity of his fellow passengers. He is crushed into the back seat of the rickety bus as it speeds round the hairpin bends of the escarpment. Through the grimy window he regards the steep mountainside towering above him, where exposed roots of trees cling precariously, holding the soil and rocks together. The bus brakes as a car coming the other way swerves to avoid a fresh fall of rocks.

The passengers lurch forwards, and Ouma's head hits the seat in front. His crutches slide along the aisle. Shrieks of fear rise as the bus teeters on the brink of the ragged tarmac. The passengers on one side can see nothing between them and a steep drop to the valley floor. The driver wrenches at the wheel to regain control, and after a nerve-racking sideways wobble on two wheels, the tyres gain purchase on the gritty verge.

Wild laughter and chattering break out as the tightly-packed passengers in a euphoria of relief help each other recover their belongings. Someone hands Ouma his crutches. Baskets are overturned, boxes have burst open; pots and pans roll under the driver's feet as he de-clutches and brakes before spinning round the bends in a race to get to the bottom of the escarpment. The faster he goes, the more passengers he gets to before his competitors, and the more money he makes.

Ouma grits his teeth. There is no need to hang on to anything, as his shoulders are tight against his neighbours.

The bus stops at Naivasha and he stumbles past the others as they queue at a kiosk for a coke. He heads through the heat and dust towards the Belle Inn to sit on the veranda, a mug of cold Tusker beer in his hand, and nibbles at a samosa. It's a pleasant break from the hectic rush, squalor and odorous presence of his fellow passengers. He watches the traffic trundling past, then snaps a finger at a passing waiter to ask for the bill.

Refreshed, he steels himself for the onward journey, squeezing back into the rear seat to rub shoulders with a toothless elder in a tattered jacket.

Another stop in Nakuru, and the driver has to check an ominous clanking coming from the exhaust. It will take time to repair, and they won't be continuing the journey until the next morning. Ouma is forced to look for a place to sleep. It is not advisable to spend the night in an alleyway in a strange town, and his savings are being eroded more than expected. But he finds cheap lodgings above a bar along a road leading towards the Lake Nakuru National Park.

The following day repairs on the *matatu* cause further delay, but he enjoys a more comfortable onward journey, as a number of passengers have caught an earlier vehicle.

The bus leaves him at the stop nearest to his home village, and as he swings along the red road on his crutches in the loose dust, he passes a cluster of shops. One or two brick buildings have appeared in his absence, but the makeshift bar where he conversed with his dying father a generation ago is still there. The men inside are strangers. He orders a Tusker beer and drinks it out of the bottle, eyeing a group of *totos* playing in the dust nearby. It is late afternoon and he feels chilly in the high altitude. It's time to re-discover his family, but a strange reluctance overcomes him. He gives himself a mental shake. There will be new people to meet. His daughters will have provided him with grandchildren, or even great-grandchildren. And Ruth – has she found another husband? Will she be there? Will he even recognise her?

The path leading towards the family enclosure has not changed. He rounds a bend, but the hedge of dried thorns is no longer there. Instead, a barrier of sisal plants surrounds an area smaller than he remembers. The ground is swept clean, and a girl with a baby at her side is squatting outside a mud-and-wattle building. A tin roof has replaced the old thatch he remembers, but other dwellings in the compound are more familiar, and in need of repair. The girl fans a fire under a pot standing on three large stones and glances up at him, rising slowly to her feet. She adjusts the baby onto her hip. Her face has a familiar shape, and the eyes slide downwards in shy deference. She brings him a stool to sit on and disappears into the hut.

Ouma tries to lower himself onto the stool, but sees a plank of wood resting on two chunks of firewood against the side of the hut. It is higher than the stool, and he tests it with his hand before propping himself downwards and resting his crutches against the wall. A hen pecks at the dry earth, clucking over three scruffy chicks. A meagre patch of broken ground to his left holds brown stalks of maize with bean plants in between, the dry pods bursting and ready for harvest. A stand of bedraggled bananas grows nearby.

A woman appears from the door of the hut. She is wearing a faded yellow frock, and regards him with inquisitive eyes buried in the wrinkles of her face, which is transformed into a smile as she recognises him. She shuffles forward and bows, taking his hands.

It is Simaloi, a relative from Jackson's side of the family. She has learned the art of sorcery, she tells him, and will be going to guard the cave of their ancestors when her mother retires. There are many questions, and his answers fill the evening hours. He is surrounded by women, who share a simple meal of mashed maize and beans accompanied by groundnut stew seasoned with curry powder. He smacks his lips and, wiping the drools from his mouth with his arm, stretches to take more.

Ouma sleeps soundly that night on the floor of a widowed uncle's hut. In the morning he walks to a shielded area of land to relieve himself, and then goes back to the girl. She tells him that Simaloi will stay sleeping for many hours. Two small boys emerge, wiping their eyes. She plucks a banana from a hand of fruit hanging nearby and gives them half each. There are no men in this home. Life here, like his own life, has deteriorated since his father died. But he learns that Ruth has sent word; her family are waiting for him in their village.

Ouma walks northwards along overgrown tracks and winding pathways, using his crutches to sweep at the undergrowth and frighten away any lurking puff adders. The irregular thump of his progress catches the attention of old friends and acquaintances, and he stops to rest and exchange news. They tell him that there are no young men in the villages anymore; they have gone to the towns to look for work and hang around beer halls.

Abandoned mothers who have returned to the shelter of their paternal homesteads regard him from the doorways of their huts, surrounded by children. Young girls, backs laden with sticks, turn sideways to allow him room to pass on the narrow paths. Boys struggle to carry plastic containers slopping with water from a trickling stream in the valley below.

On reaching a secondary road, Ouma flags a lift on a donkey cart, his leg dangling over the back as the *toto* wields a stick to urge the animal on. Arriving at Ruth's village, he makes his way along rocky uneven paths to reach her home.

She welcomes him, holding herself proudly. He notices the wrinkles on her face, and reminds himself with a jolt that she is a few years younger than he; they married nearly forty years ago. Two women linger in the background. He doesn't recognise them, but of course they must be his daughters. Ruth confirms it with a nod and they come forward to greet him, four girls of varying ages clinging to their faded cotton frocks. His grandsons are at the mission high school near Kisumu, they tell him, but they will send word.

The home is built of bricks and has three rooms. She shows him into hers, decorated with pictures of the saints. A wooden bed stands along one wall, with a table beside it and shelves underneath with neatly folded clothes. A light hangs on a wire from the ceiling. He sees a calendar on the wall and studies the picture.

"Is this where you went to school, Ruth?"

She nods. "And so did your children, and your grandchildren," she says proudly. "They have done well."

"And so have you," he says with a smile.

Over the following days, he basks under the attention of his new-found family. His daughters live nearby. Maria left her husband and came home when he took a second wife, Ruth tells him, and Naomi's husband died in a *matatu* crash. Ouma's grandchildren are intrigued by his stump. It frightens them at first, but he gently quells their fears and allows the older boys to try out his crutches.

"Next time I come," he says, "I'll see if I can bring some more – or maybe you can make some at your carpentry classes? You can practice on them, and we can have races. I bet I'll beat you every time."

"No, you won't, *kuka* – we'll practise hard! When are you coming back?"

Ouma glances at Ruth, who returns his smile. He feels comfortable here, but there's much to do in Nairobi.

Chapter 7

Emily pressed up against Paul in the crowded room as they sat listening to a talk on Ol Donyo L'Engai at the Mountain Club. They had come for last-minute news of the erupting volcano, and instructions on how to get there. It was safe to go, they were told, provided they were sensible.

She was the only African in the party. Not that it bothered her, for Molly from the office was coming with them. But the thought of climbing this "Mountain of God," especially when it was erupting, caused shivers down her spine. Paul encouraged her to write down detailed notes so they wouldn't get lost, which helped her to focus.

They drove the first hundred miles to Namanga on the Kenya/Tanzania border in the comfort of Paul's car, but Emily was dismayed at the lack of space in the hired Land Rover waiting for them at the border. Six spare gallons of petrol crowded the back of the vehicle, together with several containers of water. Four people had to squash into the back seat, and two others mingled with the luggage in the boot. Emily and Paul were the navigators, so they had the privileged seats next to the driver. This made her feel guilty. Twelve miles out of Namanga they turned right off the tarmac onto a rough track, and she had to concentrate on her notes.

They dipped into a *donga*, and at the bottom of the little valley she looked for the landmark of a giraffe's skull hanging on a thorn bush, where they had to turn left. Paul saw it at the last minute, and the driver swung the steering wheel. The car clung to the track, bouncing over ruts and bumping through *dongas* for twenty miles. They passed numerous giraffe and surprised a kudu. Emily watched the majestic chestnut-coloured animal with its pale stripes as it blended into the bush. She'd never seen one before.

Several gerenuks scampered away, their long necks reminding her of baby giraffe. The car crawled past a dry dam.

"At least that means we've come the right way," Emily said, consulting her notes. But there were six more miles to go before the next turn. As night fell she peered ahead, identifying another faint left fork, and they bumped along a track for a further twenty miles.

"Next instruction: at mile 49, pass a large pile of stones and turn sharp right."

The tiny village of Gelai loomed in the headlights.

"Oh dear, we've missed the turning," said Paul, telling the driver to go back.

Emily searched along a stony *donga* bed for a faint track in the dark, which should go off at twenty degrees, making them almost double back on their tracks. She couldn't see anything. Suddenly the driver swung the car sharp left, then reversed and drove forward.

"Here it is!"

The track turned into a cattle path, and as the vehicle bucked over boulders and dipped through ruts and ditches, Emily wondered if they were indeed going the right way. She couldn't imagine how the driver could keep his eye on the "road" and control the vehicle at the same time. And an occasional squeal came from the boot of the car, where the two unfortunate members of their party were being thrown from side to side against the jerry cans.

Emily allowed her head to nod against Paul's shoulder and she closed her eyes.

"Look – there's the Masai village!"

Emily awoke to peer into the limits of the headlights at vague grassy mounds in the bush. A water hole crept into view.

"The Mountain Club warned us not to pitch camp near the water, or we'll be run down by cattle in the morning," warned Paul.

She groaned. They drove a further mile through the scrub and it was nearly nine o'clock before they stopped. She wished she had never come.

Molly had cooked a ready-made stew for supper. "All we have to do, folks, is make some packet soup, heat the stew and fill up with bread and cheese," she shouted.

"How can you be so cheerful after such a journey?"

"I'm just immensely relieved it's all over." Molly punched Emily in the shoulder. "Look – Paul is making a camp fire."

Emily sat sleepily to one side while the others lounged round the fire, singing and cracking jokes. There were four camp beds between eight of them. She dossed down on the ground between Molly and Paul. She'd never used a sleeping bag before, nor had she slept out in the open. At Paul's prompting, she made a hole for her hips, then snuggled up against him, fitting her body into the curves of his back. Strange noises broke her sleep, the volcano rumbled at intervals, and great cracks of lightning rose into the night sky. Emily counted three herds of cattle walking past at different times, and a hyena howled.

Dawn at last. She consulted her notes. It would take three hours to get to the mountain, and they had to start climbing before ten o'clock in order to reach the top and get back in daylight. The driver picked up a faint pair of wheel tracks towards a Masai *manyatta*, comprising half a dozen roughly-thatched huts surrounded by a barrier of dry thorns, after which it petered out.

Paul looked over Emily's shoulder.

"Our directions say head straight for the mountain until the foothills show a gap. We have to head for it, cross a sand river and look for tracks up the other side, which will take us to the ridge at the start of our climb."

"Isn't that rather vague?" said Molly with a feeble laugh.

Emily remained silent as they jolted over tufts of grass, through *dongas* and past several hills. They couldn't mistake the volcano, for a huge cloud of ash billowed from it. The sky to the left of the mountain was dark with thunder clouds. She gave herself a mental shake. She and Paul were the leaders; she couldn't let everybody down, even though the awesome spectacle of God's power made her want to run away and hide.

The sand river was deep with ash, and the driver engaged four-wheel drive. Falling particles settled on the vehicle as it floundered up the bank, and ash mingled with rain smudged the windows in a matter of minutes. The car ground to a halt and the men got out to push, to no avail.

"Let's stay put for a while, and see if the rain stops," said Paul.

But twenty minutes later it was still pouring, so they donned anoraks, found their water-bottles, packed lunches and cameras, and stepped out. In a matter of seconds, they were all covered from head to toe in filthy grey ash.

They left the driver with the car and followed Paul, treading in his footsteps in a long line for what seemed like miles before they found the ridge. Two faint paths led upwards.

"The Mountain Club told us to follow the left hand path," he warned. But three people decided the right one would be shorter. "We should keep together!" he called in vain.

They slipped and slid down a gully and clambered through deep ash up a ridge, avoiding hidden crevices and boulders. As they neared the crest, Emily stopped. A tremendous roar sounded above the periodic cracks of thunder coming from the crater. Swirling clouds of steam rose from the mountainside, turning into a torrent which tumbled down the canyon to their right. The deafening sound pulsated through her as she watched. It was travelling too fast for lava, she told herself, remembering films she had seen of red molten lava creeping down volcanos in other parts of the world.

There was no sign of the three who had taken the other route.

As they climbed higher, she saw that the glistening black mixture had lost momentum and spread onto the plain below. She wondered if it would cut off the Land Rover and prevent them from leaving the mountain. She had visions of having to camp on the slopes, and tried to work out how long their food and water would last. At least Paul had left instructions at home for the Mountain Club to be warned if they hadn't arrived back by the end of the weekend.

She must take her mind off such gloomy thoughts. The other three joined them. They had had to cross three gullies, and after they'd negotiated the first, the furious liquid lava had roared down it, cutting them off.

"Now that we're all happily together again, I'll lead the way," she told Paul. "For as long as I am able, at least!"

Her boots sank six inches into the ash at each floundering step, and all the while the mixture of rain and ash was making her hat and backpack heavier. She turned her head away from the stinging wind, to prevent the gritty particles from falling into her eyes. She felt cold and wet and bedraggled, but strangely excited. Every so often a deafening crack of thunder would sound from the bowels of the volcano, the noise going right through her, and she would stop and look upwards. To her right, the roar of another torrent down the gully added to the racket.

After five hundred yards Emily stopped. Paul joined her and they waited for the others to catch up. She looked back. The Land Rover, grey in the distance, was a long way from the trickle of watery lava which glistened onto the plain below. Her visions of having to spend the night on the mountain thankfully faded away.

Feeling too cold to stop for long, she insisted that someone else take the lead. It felt wonderfully effortless to tread in the ready-made footprints, and her spirits rose. She trudged steadily upwards through the fine ash, which deepened with every step. Straggles of thorn scrub scratched at her legs, and colossal boulders covered in the miserable grey substance stood in her way. The whole world was grey and wet and cold.

Little cracks appeared to the left and right of their path, and she wondered what would happen if the ash slid down the steep side of the ridge they were climbing. Eventually, a rim came in sight. Slowly but surely, never daring to stop for longer than a few seconds in case they should not have the heart to start again, they headed for the top.

Paul stopped. Emily looked eagerly over the rim ahead to discover that they were not at the crater after all, but on a ridge which stretched out to the left and up yet another thousand feet.

"The crater rim is an hour's climb away," said Paul, hanging his head.

They sat down on the wet ash and waited for the others. Nobody felt like eating anything although it was long past lunch time. As soon as the food was brought into the open, it was covered with unappetising black, salty ash.

They discussed their next move, and Paul echoed Emily's fears that the ash might slip from beneath them. The next phase was even steeper than before. As if to prove the reality of their fears, a mini avalanche fell away from the ridge and tumbled into the canyon below. It left a bare portion of rock which quickly became grey again.

The dampness penetrated Emily's anorak, and she began to shiver. Two deafening cracks of thunder filled their world, and forked lightning flashed in tongues out of the summit. The particles of ash mixed with rain took on the calibre of stinging pebbles, and they turned tail and headed for the bottom.

Spirits rose as they slid and slipped down their previous tracks, already three-quarters obliterated. Fears of an avalanche lingered at the back of Emily's mind, but the cracks didn't widen, and when they reached the Land Rover, a silvery colour in the drying ash, the rain had stopped. They retired for two miles to get away from the heavy downpour and peeled off their hats and anoraks, laughing at each other's faces creased with black, before washing away the grime and changing their clothes. They piled back into the car and rode across the *dongas* and through the parched grassland to look for a camp site.

Near a thorn tree seven miles from the volcano, they made a roaring camp fire. All through the night Paul kept it burning, and the mountain spewed out a billowing black mushroom against the stars. Every few seconds pinpricks of light appeared from the crater, and sometimes a great flash of forked lightning illuminated the cloud. Thunder rumbled, but it didn't frighten Emily any more. She had experienced the awesome might of the Mountain of God, and was filled with wonder at the glory of nature around her.

Lying in the protection of Paul's comforting frame on the ground beside her, she found his fingers and, turning over, he squeezed her hand then held her close. With their sleeping bags between them, she let her body melt into his, allowing a delicious ecstasy to fill her senses. Then she turned her back and he settled behind her, throwing an arm over her body to keep her close.

Chapter 8

The herdsman, Ondiek, pulled at his blanket to form a hood over his head. Wrapping one foot round the ankle of the other, he leaned motionless on his spear, then stiffened. It was a clear day, and he saw a cloud of grey ash rise from the distant cone of Ol Donyo L'Engai over the Tanzania border; the Mountain of God had not yet gone to sleep. It was sacred to the local people, and its recent eruption had caused consternation. He looked north towards Magadi and waited, watching as dust billowed on the horizon. A vehicle was straining through the sand on the lakeshore. The cloud hung in the windless air, tracing its erratic progress in his direction.

It could be Paul, who had sent an email. They hadn't seen each other for a while, and this was a long way from Oxford, where they'd renewed their boyhood ties. But Ondiek was on home ground now, and he needed time.

He and Paul had made the journey from Nairobi to Magadi many times in the past, cresting the southern shoulder of the Ngong Hills and descending in a serpentine through two steep escarpments. The change in altitude marked a transition from the cool, rarified air of the highlands to the enervating humidity of the Great Rift Valley.

Leaving the Olorgesailie prehistoric site on the left, the road passed through scrubby acacia and sparse undergrowth sheltering herds of goats and cattle. Dramatic fault scarps and strange volcanic shapes marked the way, and weird brown anthills encompassed tree trunks, turning them into miniature baobabs. There was a wealth of birdlife here, and Ondiek smiled, remembering that Paul always paused on this part of the road to spot the hunter's sunbird with its distinctive scarlet chest.

The trail of dust stopped, dispersing into the clear blue sky. A softly-moulded hillock of sand stood beside the track a few hundred yards from the turn off. Paul would be taking his bearings to avoid losing his way to the camp.

Ondiek's dappled goats strayed out of sight, and he moved silently through the scrub to round them up. The car passed him, thorns scraping at its paintwork, and he followed it into camp. He was disappointed to see that it carried two people. He must be careful.

He herded his goats towards a rusted drum of water.

"Where is everybody?"

The figure standing on the bare swept camp circle was more portly than Ondiek remembered, but the guttural voice of his friend was unmistakable.

"At the dig."

Ondiek hesitated, and then threw back his hood. Paul bounded forward and the men embraced. Ondiek turned towards a black circle of ashes in the centre of the camp to coax it into a fire, but Paul hung back.

"I want you to meet someone special," he said. "I hope you don't mind me bringing Emily along. She's part of our family, after all, and I find it hard to believe you two have never met."

"Caroline's family?"

Paul nodded. "Yes, Sam. My mother took her in when she left the AIDS orphanage at Watamu. We were away on our studies at the time, and then you went off to visit digs all over the world, and I came home to start work."

Ondiek looked towards Paul's car as a young woman stepped onto the dusty earth. Dressed in tight jeans and a green and yellow sleeveless top, she came towards him. Every movement of her lithe body spoke to him as she held out a limp hand. Her hair was freshly braided in tight lines across her scalp, and she raised her head. Her full lips glittered, she removed her sunglasses, and the world stopped as he lost himself in the depths of her eyes.

She lowered her gaze, and Paul moved beside him.

Remembering his manners, Ondiek pulled up three camp chairs and offered them refreshments. The men sat down beside the charred remains of a fire, and caught up with their news.

"They told me in Nairobi that Kenya's distinguished palaeontologist had simply vanished into the bush, Sam!"

Ondiek recoiled; he hadn't been addressed by that name since returning home, and now Paul had used it twice. He recovered himself quickly, but Paul noticed.

"What's wrong?"

"I'm known as Ondiek here. I'd almost forgotten my former name."

"So you've taken your uncle's name, the man whose footsteps you followed?"

Ondiek nodded, looking around for Emily. She had retired to the car.

"Your uncle Jackson is not at the Museum either."

"He's retired, long past his due date."

Paul nodded. "I suppose I'm not surprised – but he's the sort of person who goes on forever. What's happening – and why are you dressed up like a tribesman? Surely you haven't both gone permanently native out here in the bush?"

Good old Paul – never one to pull his punches. Ondiek smiled as he caught himself thinking in white man's phrases again. It was a difficult question to answer. So many of his people had gone abroad and then come back, only to disappear again into their tribal lands. But he wasn't like that; he knew his country needed him. How to make Paul understand, without revealing too much?

"Remember when we used to come here with your mother? You found a hand-axe."

"Yes – and you told us about your ancestors' cave in those hills..." Paul gestured in the direction of the horizon.

Ondiek stiffened. "That's sacred ground." He changed the subject. "Want to see what they've been doing at the dig?"

He gestured to Emily, inviting her to join them. The heat

closed in as he mustered the goats and led them down an erratic track through the scrub to a dry riverbed. Two sweat-glistening students were sifting sand near a pile of rubble, where stone-age hand axes were scattered.

Ondiek pulled his blanket into a hood and left his goats to nibble at the bushes on the river bank. He beckoned to Paul and approached the research graduate from the United States who led the group.

"These people are here to see you, *Bwana*."

He retired to the bushes as the two men conferred. He watched Emily nudging idly at the rubble with her toe, her profile silhouetted against the sky. Then Paul raised his binoculars to study the distant escarpment, and came to squat down in the shade.

"That cave, Sam, with one corner glinting white in the sun – it's a signal, isn't it?"

Ondiek beckoned them further into the bushes, away from the dig and out of hearing.

"They only know me as the herdsman down here, Paul. And I want to keep my identity a secret for a while longer. I need to trust you both…"

The last thing Ondiek wanted was to have strangers tramping clumsily around the sacred area where his tribal secrets were hidden. And he sympathized with those who allowed themselves to melt back into traditional life after the hustle of western civilization. There was a therapeutic quality about the simple task of herding goats. If he went to Nairobi, the family would crowd around him like vultures, expecting favours, and his earnings would dissipate among the relatives. He had seen it so often. It was the custom, and it had broken better men than him.

"But you haven't contacted your sponsors, the Oxford and Cambridge Society. I've been to a few of their get-togethers. They've asked me about you."

"There is much I have to do," Ondiek said, "and we aren't ready yet."

"We? Who's we?"

"My uncle, Jackson."

Paul nodded sagely.

"So – let me guess: Jackson is up there, guarding your ancestral cave. I expect that your old cousin Simaloi has passed on, and he has taken on the mantle. And you are here in disguise, to make sure no foreigners stumble upon your secrets. Nothing has changed since we were boys. What's all the fuss about? Although I must confess I'd love to see what there is in that cave."

Ondiek sighed. He would not reveal the family secrets to Paul, but maybe his friend could help in some way.

"Simaloi is still guarding the cave, and will eventually make way for her daughter, who is also called Simaloi." He paused. "If I tell you that Jackson and I are working on a massive project in that cave, which could mean worldwide acclaim for our museum, would you be prepared to keep it to yourself until we go public?"

Paul gave him a hearty slap on the back.

"I knew it, Sam! Of course I'll help you – but as a mere accountant, there'll be limits. What is this project, and what would you like me to do?"

"Better still, I'll show it to you. But not now." Paul glanced at Emily. "There's no access, even for a Land Rover. You'll have to go on foot, and the only woman who goes there is a sorceress. I hope you are fit. It will take you the best part of a day. But I need to warn Jackson. Meanwhile, you can tell the Museum Director and the Oxford & Cambridge Society that you have spoken to me. But don't tell them where I am."

"No problem. You're right, but I won't have to do any training, as Emily and I have recently climbed Ol Donyo L'Engai."

Ondiek regarded Emily with surprise. "You went up that sacred mountain?"

She nodded. "Paul protected me. It was scary, but we survived! Is it sacred to your people?"

"It is."

He set aside his spear and opened the passenger door for Emily. He hadn't had the opportunity to talk to her much, but no doubt they would see each other again – it was another reason to keep in touch with Paul. She gave him a warm smile and put on her sunglasses as Paul started the engine.

Ondiek watched their cloud of dust disappear into the sky line, and wondered if she had also felt the magic of their meeting.

Chapter 9

"I think that's enough for now, Jackson. We have to prepare the cave ready for Paul's next visit."

Ondiek sat back on his haunches and surveyed the cave paintings, spread across a vast portion of the rock face. The task of exposing and tracing them had been painstaking but fulfilling, and he was sorry it was complete.

"The next phase is to create a replica of the site and display it in the museum. But we'll have to obtain permission first."

He knew Paul would be impressed by the scale and quality of the paintings. They didn't need to show him the sacred ground, which was deeper inside the mountain.

"I don't know anything about rock art," said Paul. "But even I can see that this is far superior to the rather jaded exhibition copied from a site in Tanzania, which has been in the museum ever since I can remember. Sam, I apologize for the scathing greeting I gave you last time. I can see you haven't dissolved entirely into the bush after all! But that reminds me…"

Paul reached in his pocket and pulled out a letter. It was from the Oxford and Cambridge Society.

Ondiek tore it open. They had invited him to become a member of the Society and serve on the Committee. It would mean taking his place in Nairobi society, with its old school tie and all that it entailed. He would play a part in screening candidates for scholarships.

He would have to become Sam again. But did he want to do it yet?

He had to think of an excuse. He showed Paul the letter.

"I can't accept their offer. My family is spreading its tentacles, and putting pressure on me to take a wife. That is a much more attractive proposition, don't you think? I was half-expecting you to bring your girlfriend with you again."

"Emily?" Paul laughed. "You told us the walk here was not for the faint-hearted, so I didn't offer her the opportunity. I'm glad I didn't, as the walk has nearly killed me. She's more of a city girl, despite our recent trek up Ol Donyo L'Engai. I see the mountain is still spewing ash. I can tell you it is a far more dramatic sight when you're up close."

Paul gestured towards the mountain silhouetted against the distant sky. Ondiek raised his eyebrows.

"I'm surprised she went with you. Even I would have hesitated to go near the Mountain of the Gods, especially during an eruption. She must have had an ulterior motive."

"Emily and I are just good friends, Sam."

"Are you sure? She's an attractive girl, and I thought you always wanted to marry Africa."

Paul looked away. "I wish…"

Ondiek did not pursue the matter, but his heart gave a little leap. He would like to see Emily again.

"Come and help us scatter the paintings with protective earth. It'll help preserve them and disguise their presence."

They hung sacking over the earth, and heaved some rocks to secure it at ground level, keeping it close against the wall. The tracings needed packing for transportation to the museum, together with photographs and measurements.

When all was done, the three men squatted around a camp fire at the mouth of the cave for a meal.

"You and I will set out before dawn tomorrow," said Jackson, nodding towards Paul. "It'll be a long day – so I'm going to sleep early."

He disappeared behind a hessian curtain deep within the cave.

"Aren't you coming with us, Sam?"

"No. Jackson has the experience, and I hope he hasn't lost credibility at the museum. And someone has to guard the cave."

"But there's nothing more to guard, Sam!"

This persistence on calling him by his old name was beginning to irritate Ondiek, but he was careful not to let it show.

"It's still our sacred place, the original art is *in situ*, and until a permanent custodian is appointed, I will stay here."

That was final.

"Oh well – I suppose I'd better get some sleep, then. I'm not looking forward to the trek back to the Land Rover carrying all that luggage. I expect Jackson will make me walk even quicker than you did. That reminds me," Paul rose to get another letter from his backpack, which he handed to Ondiek. "The Museum Director asked me to give you this."

Paul went to the rear of the cave and reached for the sacking behind which Jackson had disappeared.

Ondiek had to think quickly.

"Hey, Paul – you can't go in there! That's Jackson's place. Put your sleeping bag here on this ledge beside mine. I see you've got one of those new sleeping mats – might you bring one for me next time you come?"

"So I'll be allowed to come again, will I?"

"Of course."

Ondiek stood on the ledge outside the cave and watched Jackson and Paul weave through the bush, bearing their precious burden.

Now he could ponder over his future, and seek inspiration from this ancient place. Life would be easy if he tended his goats and foraged for food, with no care in the world but to guard the spirits of his ancestors. However, there was another mission to fulfil and his University training to justify. Superstitions of old hounded his people, and it would take time to coach them into accepting today's world.

His people held the key to what he believed was the true cradle of man. Perhaps only generations to come would be ready to expose their treasures for the sake of scientific progress. But never should they forget their ancestors, nor deny the spirituality of their shrine. It was a fine balance.

He tore open the letter Paul had given him from the Museum Director. It was a job offer in the Department of Palaeontology, a dream he had strived for all his life.

The future was now clear. He would resume the name of Sam and ensure an increasing number of African scholars passed through the portals of his University. Eventually, he would realize his goal as Head of Department. It didn't matter how long it took. One day, tribal tradition and scientific research would join forces to expose the secrets of his ancestors.

No matter if it didn't happen in his lifetime. The seeds were planted.

There were more immediate problems to address. When the season closed, he would visit his home village, but he had no intention of bowing to tribal tradition when it came to choosing a bride.

PART II

2004-2008

Wangari Maathai wins the Nobel Peace Prize.

2006 sees a severe drought followed by floods, which cut off the north of Kenya. The Anglo Leasing phantom company scandal is exposed, China is given permission to prospect for oil off the coast, and 35,000 Somali refugees arrive in Kenya.

1,500 people die after the disputed 2007 Presidential election, and President Mwai Kibaki agrees to power-share with Prime Minister Raila Odinga, thus heralding the return of multi-party politics. But there is no investigation into the election violence. Rampant corruption is exposed, and the vast overseas holdings of former President Daniel Arap Moi, supporter of President Mwai Kibaki, are revealed.

Chapter 10

The boys are away at school when Ouma returns from meeting his family, warmed by their welcome after years of absence. There are no unwashed cups beside the sink, and the floor is swept cleaner than usual. In fact, Ouma inspects it more closely and finds it's been scrubbed. Sister Brigid greets him casually.

"There you are, Ouma! Come and have a cup of tea."

He follows the little nun into the common room, beads clicking as she walks, and settles into an armchair. She puts on the kettle and he stirs four teaspoons of sugar into his cup.

"Was it good to be home again? And did you find what you were looking for?"

"It was better than expected, Sister. The school is still there, if that's what you mean. Although whether I can afford to send Ken to it is *shauri ya mungu,* up to God. Have the boys behaved themselves while I've been away?"

"Of course." Her eyes twinkle as she goes to sit beside him. "And they look very smart in their new shorts. We found some material and I've made them a pair each while you've been away. Just you wait and see! I have so much to tell you – but first I want to listen to your news."

There isn't much he wishes to say, but Sister Brigid manages to drag every detail out of him. He tells her about Ruth, and pretends he has fitted another piece of jigsaw into place in his memory.

"She was my wife," he says, then falls silent.

Sister Brigid wants to know all about Ruth, how many children she has, and especially about her two elder daughters who must have children of their own by now.

"You must remember; I was here when Ruth had her babies in this very hospital."

Sister Brigid pauses, and Ouma awakens to the impact of what she has said.

He regards her with wonder. "You knew," he said. "You knew all along…"

The nun gives a gentle nod and a faint smile, then rises to take his cup and pour him another. She sets it on the table, brings him the sugar, and picking up a pair of secateurs from the window sill, goes out to prune the roses.

Ouma is grateful for the period of privacy she has allowed him. He closes his eyes and listens to the steady tick of the clock on the wall opposite. His secret is out, but perhaps it's been no secret for a long time. He wonders when Sister Brigid first realised who he was, and whether Jackson dropped a few hints. It doesn't matter anymore. He is surprised how calm he feels. In fact, he is relieved that there's no more need for the stress of pretence.

He gives a little huff of mirth. Perhaps this could have happened earlier if he'd been brave enough. But no, there are too many complications in his life; too many uncertainties and dangers to avoid. Mwangi, his biggest threat, is dead, but has the evil power of the Mau Mau oath died with him?

Ouma gives himself a mental shake, remembering his faith.

His thoughts turn to Sam, his only living son, whose mother succumbed to Mwangi's curse. Thanks to Caroline, he and Sam found each other only a few years before that fateful day which changed his life. Ouma recalls the blessing of their first meeting at the Museum, the little book he gave Sam as a memento and the times they spent at Caroline's home getting to know each other. How could he have forsaken Sam, left him abandoned once more, the minute disaster struck? What made him do it?

He puts his head in his hands. Mwangi, of course, and that cursed oath. He'd wanted to shield Sam from its force. But what pain the boy must have gone through, not knowing what had happened to his father. Life is so complicated.

Remorse fills his soul, and the peace of moments ago is shattered. He raises his head to look through the open door at

Sister Brigid's silhouette bending over the roses beside the driveway.

The boys are coming through the gate and stop to chat to her. She straightens her back and points towards the annexe. Ken hangs behind, and then turns towards the hospital. Ouma reaches for his crutches and props himself upwards, pausing to let the stiffness out of his back, then he goes to the door and waves. Sister Brigid grabs Ken's arm and firmly points him towards the annexe. Ouma smiles. She is telling Ken to change out of his uniform first. Ouma hobbles along the path to meet Ken at the doorway of the annexe. The pristine cleanliness of the room has given way to a jumble of abandoned clothes on the floor, and splashes of water spill from enamel mugs as the boys crowd round him, mouths full of bread, crumbs falling to the floor.

"Ouma – you're back! What have you brought for us?"

Sister Brigid is at the door, her face trying to mould itself into a frown.

"Now, now, boys – what's all this rumpus? Twins, pick up your clothes and fold them away in your room. Ouma has brought a special treat for supper tonight. I'll bring it to you later."

She winks at him and disappears towards the hospital. He raises his eyebrows; he's brought no treat, but Sister Brigid is a wonderful woman.

The boys crowd round him. "It's good you're back," they say. "That nun is so *kali.*"

"Fierce? I know, but she's right," says Ouma. "Go and tidy away your things."

He rests his crutches against a chair and fumbles in his pocket, then sits down.

"What have you got in your hand?"

He allows them to force open one hand and then the other. Their faces fall and the twins turn away in disgust. Ken and Joshua stay to riffle through the contents of his hands.

"They are just beans," says Joshua.

"And here is some maize," observes Ken, examining the other hand. "What have you brought these for?"

"I've got more in my pocket. They're special seeds all the way from my home village. I've brought them for you to grow and eat."

He watches their faces, smiling at the puzzlement and the gradual dawning of enlightenment. Ken is not too sure. Ouma can see that the boy's mind is working hard. Growing plants means physical work, and dedication.

"But we haven't anywhere to plant them!"

"I'll show you how to plant them in cotton wool in jars on the window sill and we can watch them sprout. There's plenty of land round the hospital; I know the nuns will let us have the far corner." He gestures vaguely towards the rear of the compound. "You just need to dig up the grass and prepare the soil."

"That's a woman's job," sneers Joshua, turning away.

"And when we have no woman here…?"

There is a harsh note to Ouma's response, and Joshua lowers his head.

"Those nuns work hard to cure the sick, Joshua, and they let us live here for free. We must do something in return. Now that you're busy at school you can't earn for me anymore. If we grow our own food, we won't go hungry."

Since the parking enterprise was crushed, Ouma's savings have eroded and he cannot hope to live on the meagre offerings of passers-by. He wonders how he can even contemplate educating the boys. Or face his own son. For he is a beggar – the lowest of the low.

Maina and Musumba, his former henchmen, are earning more than he. They have found other boys to tout for the prostitutes, and sell stolen goods to stranded motorists gridlocked on the daily commute to work.

Ouma takes up position one evening under the street light outside the Five Bells restaurant. It is his special pitch, condoned by Alex Gomez who never fails to leave something for him. The patrons, especially those of Asian origin, are generous. Ouma bows his head and scrapes at every offering, hiding it between the folds of the sackcloth set out before him, while diners sit beneath muted lights in the rich ambience of the restaurant.

Maina struts up to him during a lull. The trade between the brothel and the drivers is unofficially tolerated now. Chauffeurs drop their passengers at the door, and then park the vehicles along the street two blocks down nearer the brothel. Maina waits outside, passing on the message whenever a waiter signals that a patron has called for the bill. The service is sleek, unobtrusive and lucrative.

Ouma reaches up to take an offered cigarette and waits for Maina to light it. He strikes several matches before one finally flares, and they draw together in silence, puffing clouds of smoke into the still night air.

"That girl," says Maina. "She comes here with her boyfriend. Do you want me to keep watching her? Musumba and I have started a detective business, but we'll do it for you for free. You gave us the idea, after all."

Ouma remembers the girl whose features make him think of his home village. Her association with Paul brings back thoughts of his former life. Will he ever be able to return to that world, he wonders, looking down at his foreshortened leg. But the service offered is free.

"So long as you never proposition her or use her in that brothel of yours."

Maina pauses in mid-inhalation and nods as a waiter catches his eye. He snaps his finger at a hovering *toto* and mutters in his ear. Ouma watches the boy scamper round the corner to deliver the message, and shuts his eyes.

There's one thing he could do to bridge the gap between the past and the ugliness of his present world. Why hasn't he thought of it before? The more he considers the idea, the more excited he becomes. But one step at a time. Ouma looks at his leg and laughs inwardly at the metaphor.

He remains at the annexe for days on end, sitting at the table overlooking the growing expanse of cultivated ground outside the window. He must get himself another notebook and refine the stories he has written. His talent has faded through lack of use, but with practice the articles will become good enough for submission to the national newspaper.

Meanwhile, the boys watch the wonder of nature as their seeds open, send down tentative roots, and sprout shoots to seek the sun.

"I've had another letter from Louise. She's planning to visit us."

Sister Brigid hands Ouma a cup of tea and passes the sugar. "You really must cut down on sugar, Ouma. It's bad for you."

He smiles mischievously and takes another spoonful just to spite her. His mind drifts to his Oxford days, when Louise befriended him as a raw fresher. He could never understand her obsession with sport. Her weekends were consumed with boring hockey and tennis matches, and he felt uncomfortable in the company of her friends with their flashy sports cars and hearty drinking habits.

That was over forty years ago. He wonders what she looks like now. She must have married; did she have children?

"How did Louise find you, Sister?"

"Some time ago our priest told us about this lady in England who wanted to make a donation to Africa. She sponsored the child of a prostitute who gave birth in this hospital. I think it might have been around the time Ruth came here to have your daughters, but of course no one knew the connection with you. Louise has sent us a Christmas card every year since then."

She brushes at a stray piece of hair, pushing it under her wimple.

"More recently, we had a church newsletter saying Louise wanted to find a man called Charles Omari Ondiek whom she'd met as a student in Oxford. It made me think of you. You don't act like a typical Nairobi beggar, and I've always wondered about your pure English accent. The name Omari – and you call yourself Ouma. Do you have a habit of changing your name, Ouma?"

He shrugs his head into his shoulders trying to hide his embarrassment, but the nun goes to the door.

"Louise has booked her flight, she arrives in three months'

time," she says over her shoulder.

Ouma regards his tattered clothing with disdain and tries on his only pair of decent trousers, hanging forgotten in the wardrobe. They are too small for him now. He wonders if they can be altered, then decides to buy another pair. His prosthetic leg, commissioned by Jackson in his days of recuperation, has been gathering cobwebs in the corner beside the sink. He tries it on. The cup fits over the stump of his thigh and a harsh unpleasant sensation shoots through him as he takes a faltering step. He reaches for his crutches. He'll have to practice more. Sister Brigid examines his stump and gives him some cream to ease the pain, telling him the best way to harden the skin is constant use. Ouma grits his teeth and makes a resolution.

Every day he straps on the leg, even if he only intends to sit at his table to compose stories for the newspaper. Magazines are starting to accept articles from him. He is becoming braver, pointing out the increasing gap between rich and poor, unveiling the sleazy side of Nairobi's underworld with its exploitation of the poor by the poor. He draws on his own experiences and tries to purge himself of past guilt.

But he continues to visit his old haunts once a week, discarding the prosthesis, telling himself that first-hand knowledge is important and he must keep in contact with his henchmen. News trickles through of the girl Emily and her travels up-country with Paul. As Maina gives his report, Ouma tries to picture Paul's mother Caroline in her house at the mouth of Mombasa harbour. It is over twenty years since he's seen her. The harsh African sun turns the skin of white people into dry freckled folds. He remembers his former attraction, firmly quelled by Caroline, and wonders how she has aged. Is she now a shrivelled stick of a woman, or have the years been kinder and plumped her out?

The day of Louise's arrival draws near, and Ouma doesn't understand himself. He is getting more nervous as the time goes by. The world she lives in is so divorced from his reality. He struggles to remember his carefree Oxford days. The last time he saw Louise was at a smoky staircase party, when he had to pay for a smashed light. But she doesn't live in Oxford, he reminds himself. Sister Brigid told him that Louise lives somewhere in Sussex.

He is scribbling away on his pad when he hears a call. He stands up and dusts his hand over his new trousers. The blue checked shirt he bought shows its creases. He glances at his crutches, but strides stiffly past them and goes towards the hospital reception area. He has practiced this walk often enough in preparation for the occasion.

Louise's eyes dance at him through the door, the same friendly blue eyes. She hasn't changed – only grown a bit wider.

"Charles! How wonderful to see you again – and I have heard so much about you…"

Ouma glances nervously at Sister Brigid. How much has she told Louise? And he hasn't heard his former name for years.

He is engulfed in a bear hug, and falters towards the wall, putting his hand out for balance.

"Oh sorry – I'd forgotten." Louise backs off, glancing down at his legs. "Sister told me – but I have so much to ask you. I know she's told you about my mission here."

Dear Louise, always impulsive, yet sensitive to others' feelings. He gestures towards an armchair as the nun disappears to bring them refreshments.

"I haven't been called Charles for ages. I'm known as Ouma here," he says. "And I am keen to know more about why you've come."

He feels guilty for not responding more warmly to her welcome, and he hands her a cup of tea. As she takes a sip, he studies her impeccably-styled bobbed hair. Her jaw has squared a little more than he remembers, but she wears a blue floral dress which matches her eyes.

She is talking about her home town and her project, but he has lost the first few minutes. Louise pauses and regards him with a quizzical smile.

"I'm sorry Ch – Ouma," she says. "Please forgive me. I'm forgetting myself. Sister has told me very little about you, really; except that you've taken some street boys under your care and they're nearly ready for secondary school. I'm here to help if I can."

Why is she offering to help? What can be her motive? Ouma chides himself for the thought, but is grateful the conversation has turned to the boys. She asks him questions about their background, and listens closely to his account of their life as parking boys and touts for prostitutes, their glue-sniffing and petty thefts. He is not ready to disclose his own involvement, and she doesn't ask him. Nor does she invite him to tell his own story.

"Have you found a school for Ken?"

"Yes. It is away from the temptations of Nairobi, and not far from my home in the western district. I went there recently, but the fees are expensive."

"I'd love to see your home village. My husband and I are going to the Kakamega Forest Lodge for a few days. Is it nearby? As I've just told you, the people in my town are looking for orphans to sponsor, and we are here as their scouts."

Ouma drops his head, shamed that he hasn't been listening properly.

"My village isn't far from that lodge, but it's too short notice to arrange anything now…"

He keeps his head low, suffering what he suspects are her piercing eyes boring into him. There is a pause, and Louise takes a long breath. He wonders if she has arranged to visit Amayoni village, where Ruth and his daughters live.

He glances up. There is a kindness in her eyes.

"That's okay – we can keep in touch through Sister Brigid. And now I must go, as there are people I have to see." Louise rises and takes his hand in both of hers with a meaningful squeeze. "It is good to see you again."

He walks to the car and opens the door for her.

Chapter 11

Louise had seldom been out of England. Her husband David had travelled to the Far East on business several times before his retirement, but she'd been too busy to go with him. Now, she stood and marvelled.

Tropical forest grew in great entanglements around her and its immensity engulfed her. It was denser than she could ever have imagined, with myriad shades of green and mystical shapes and forms, vibrant with life. Bursts of song filled her ears, yet she could see no birds in the thick foliage, which rocked and swished as the wind gusted through.

Suddenly a branch bent over with a crack, and something large and blue flopped partially into view. Her senses were filled with the glorious sight of a large bird, a flash of yellow on its beak, its blue-green feathers melding into the background. It stayed, majestic, still, for a breath-taking second, then crouched forward and hopped in smooth bounds up the branch.

"That's a great blue," a voice said at her shoulder.

"A great blue?"

"Turaco. You're lucky. They're a rare sight in this forest. The name of the village you're going to visit tomorrow is Amayoni, which means birds."

They were standing on a closely-cropped lawn gazing over the carefully cultured flowerbeds at a dense wall of trees. A stream raced between them and the forest, its bank smooth and inviting. On the other side, a disarray of broken sticks and branches trailed in the water. A tumble of trunks growing at various angles dissolved into the mass of trees, blocking off the evening sun.

She stooped to dip her finger in the torrent. It was icy cold.

She straightened her back and pulled her cardigan round her shoulders before following the manager into the Kakamega Forest Lodge. David beckoned her to join him beside a roaring fire.

"Well, what do you think?"

"I'm lost in wonder…"

Louise accepted a glass of wine in celebration of their arrival and sank into a soft leather armchair, allowing her face to glow in the warmth of the flames. She examined the room, its wooden walls decorated with mounted trophies, its floors spread with animal skins worn down by the feet of many guests. An African drum stood in a dark corner, its striped zebra skin pulled taut over the top and strings of hide decorating the sides. She smiled to herself, thinking of the political correctness at home, where people would throw their hands up in horror at the sight of such sacrilege. But, she told herself, animal products have offered available resources to the Africans for centuries. Besides, once an animal is dead, it's dead. Once the people have eaten their fill, why not use its skin for decoration and adornment? She reached out and fingered the sparse fur, her hand sliding in smooth strokes along the silky lie. She tapped it lightly.

"It's a fine piece, isn't it?" Her host lifted the drum and brought it nearer the firelight so she could examine the intricacies of its detail. "Of course, real African drums are made of cowhide. These zebra skin ornaments were produced to sell to tourists."

The manager settled his thin frame onto the drum and faced Louise.

"This one was offered as a gift to the lodge in days gone by. It doubles as a comfortable stool and a convenient side table. It won't last much longer. If you look closely you'll see the fur is wearing away in patches along the edge."

Despite herself, Louise could not help thinking of the poor zebra, and gave an involuntary shudder before turning to the matter at hand. She was looking forward to meeting the people.

The village of Amayoni was a stark contrast to the lush

tropical forest. Bright red soil stamped into smooth hardness separated clusters of houses made of sticks and plastered with mud and dried cattle dung. Rusted iron sheeting lay atop the walls, roughly bent over to provide shelter. Bedraggled clumps of banana plants growing at angles against each other rose from a mess of dried leaves. A woman raised a cloud of dust as she swept at the baked earth with a stick ending in a bundle of twigs. She paused when Louise and her party approached with the village priest, and welcomed them with eager deference.

"We are so pleased to see you," she said. "You've come to bring us schools and hospitals."

Louise tittered in embarrassment. All she wanted was an orphan to sponsor, and she was in no position to offer more.

"Aren't there schools?" she asked.

"There are free schools in Kisumu on the big lake – Victoria – but there are no books. The hospital is far away, and there are no medicines. We have nothing. The people are hungry, and there is no money for food."

As if to accentuate her words, a naked toddler tottered on skinny legs out of a nearby door, belly-button protruding in a bulbous blob from his swollen stomach. His nose dripped onto the fingers which were stuck in his mouth. Flies picked and flitted busily at the corners of his encrusted eyes.

The woman shouted, and a child no more than eight years old emerged from the hut, her dress of indeterminate colour draped nearly to the ground. She took her brother's hand and flicked at the cloud of flies, which dispersed only to return and settle again. With an expert swoop she swung the baby onto her right hip and stood watching in the doorway.

Louise smiled. "They're your children?" She gestured between them in the universal language of women.

The mother nodded with pride.

"Your daughter isn't at school?"

The woman looked towards the village priest.

"Most of the people in Amayoni can't afford to educate their children. They are needed to look after the little ones while their mother goes for water and feeds the family."

"And the father?"

The priest cast his eyes to the side, while the woman spoke rapidly.

"She says her husband is in Kisumu on business. She seldom sees him."

Louise looked at her more closely. Although she swept at the dust in a desultory manner, she was sturdy, her demeanour was alert and her eyes intelligent.

"You know English?"

The woman inclined her head and regarded Louise with interest.

"My name is Louise. I come from the UK. I used to know a man from Kenya – when I was at University in Oxford."

The woman responded. "I am Maria. I don't know my father, but my mother is educated and I have been to school."

The men turned away towards the main street, which ran between two ditches cluttered with debris.

"You go ahead, David," Louise called.

"Right – we'll come back for you," said David over his shoulder. "We're going to chat to some men in the village centre."

"Would you like me to show you round the village?" asked Maria.

Louise looked at the two children standing in the doorway.

"My mother will look after the children. She is in that house over there." Maria pointed her chin at a nearby brick house.

As the men disappeared up the road, an elegant middle-aged woman emerged, stepping past the children. She wore a simple cotton frock, clean, with bright red and yellow print. Her sandals scuffed up puffs of dust as she came to offer a limp hand.

"I am Ruth," she said. "Welcome. We have heard that you've come to help our village."

"We're looking for a child to sponsor. I expect you have some AIDS orphans here?"

Ruth nodded. "There is a clinic further up the road," she jutted her chin in the opposite direction from where the men had gone. "The HIV children are looked after by relatives and they attend the clinic regularly. They'll need help to go to school, but we have other needs here. Maria will show you."

Louise allowed herself to be led over the main street. They passed through a warren of narrow passageways between haphazard buildings in various stages of dilapidation. One stone house stood separate, beside a line of single rooms.

"Those belong to the landlord," Maria said in answer to Louise's question. "The wives of businessmen who can afford to pay the rent live there with their children. Some of them even have electricity."

"And the men?"

"These men have wives in other villages, too…"

Louise understood.

She noticed a brick building set back from the stone ones, its tin roof catching the light of the sun. A cross rose from the apex.

Children scrabbled in the dust and a hen scratched and clucked at her brood of chicks. Thatched buildings plastered with dried mud predominated as they penetrated further from the village centre. Women greeted Louise and chatted to Maria in their own language. Children watched, wide-eyed, and sidled up to Louise, taking her hand and touching her arm.

Louise bent down, stretched out her arms, and was overwhelmed by the response. This was so different from back home, where you were not allowed to touch a child for fear of reprimand. Forgetting the flies and the filth, she drew them into her arms until she was in danger of overbalancing into the dust. Maria spoke, and the children stepped back.

Louise followed her into the dark interior of a low building. A charcoal fire glowed to one side, and smoke filled the room. She paused, allowing her eyes to become accustomed to the darkness. A group of women squatted in a circle in the centre, their skirts caught under their thighs. Maria joined them, conversing in an incoherent gabble. Louise hesitated; she knew she would not be able to adopt the same pose.

A woman rose to her feet and prodded at the brazier, raising a glitter of sparks. Louise's eyes began to water and she went to the door for fresh air. Maria came towards her.

"This is my sister Naomi," she said. "She wants to show you something. Come."

Relieved to be away from the smoke, Louise followed the two women along a narrow path which crossed a bleak clearing. Sparse stalks of brown grass brushed against her legs as she trod between the cowpats. They stopped. Before her was a smouldering heap of ashes spread round an area about ten feet in diameter.

"This was the home of Naomi's daughter," said Maria. "Last night it burned down. She and her three children have to stay in Naomi's house."

Louise examined the burnt patch. How could a family live in such a small place?

"The children – was anyone hurt?"

"No. They got out in time, but there is no space in Naomi's house."

This was indeed an emergency, far more immediate than long-term education. A child peeped timidly at her from the door of a hut with a sparsely thatched roof. Louise could see daylight through the mud walls of another, which stood nearby. It was a wonder they hadn't all gone up in flames.

"What will she do?"

"She will make another house."

"Of the same material?"

Maria shrugged. "There is no choice."

Building another hazardous home was not the answer. Louise knew nothing about brick-making, but she remembered the church they had just passed, and resolved to talk to the priest.

As they left the scene a group of children started to pick at the ashes, spreading them out and jumping back whenever they touched a smouldering fragment.

"Those children should be at school," Louise muttered.

"They are needed at home," said Maria. "The mothers spend their time fetching water, and working in the *shambas*.

The older children look after the young ones."

Louise had seen no fields. The only plants in evidence were occasional clumps of bananas.

"They rent land from businessmen to grow food for sale in the market so they can buy things for the family."

"Can you take me to a *shamba*?"

Louise followed Maria along a path for a further mile through dwindling habitation. It was hot. She wiped her brow with her sleeve and her steps lagged. They passed a well where women and children were waiting their turn. A goat sipped at a muddy puddle. Brightly-coloured plastic containers stood in a cluster on the wet ground. A woman stepped back from the well and swung a large yellow container onto her shoulder, staggering slightly as the slops ran down her back. She turned along the path towards the village, and the line moved forwards a yard.

"There is only one well in the village," Maria told her as they moved on. "It is nearer than the river, and the water is cleaner."

Ten minutes later they stopped before an untidy field. Louise looked round in vain for somewhere to sit. Her shoes hurt and she could feel the beginnings of a blister. At least she had a bottle of water in her bag. She took a sip and stared at the field shimmering in the midday sun.

Patches of dry turned earth were interspersed with brown stalks of maize. Two women bent low, harvesting lines of dead-looking beans, throwing them into faded woven baskets. Further away, a figure wielded a large hoe-like implement, swinging it over her back and bringing it forcefully down onto the baked earth.

"We call what she is using a *jembe*," explained Maria. "She will plant maize there when the rains come."

Louise steeled herself for the return walk. She touched her nose, feeling the sting of sunburn, but her mind was a whirl of thoughts. There'd be much to talk about tonight. She wondered what David's reactions to his day would be. Most of all, she looked forward to a shower and a cool drink in the comfort of the lodge.

It was hard to imagine that the evening would be cold enough for a blazing fire, and she looked forward to the feel of a hot water bottle in her bed that night.

Over dinner, she chatted animatedly about her day, and asked their host if bricks were available in the village. He called over the head waiter, who told her that a youth had started making bricks after leaving school some years back. The business thrived when the church was built, but then he found a better job in town and nobody else carried on with the work.

"And the stone buildings?"

"Those were built by the *wabenzi*, Mercedes-owning businessmen and politicians in Nairobi for their wives and families. They rent out rooms to those who can pay."

"Where did they get the stone from?" asked Louise.

"There's a quarry along the road towards Kisumu."

Ideas tumbled round Louise's head as she nursed her hot water bottle beside David, who had fallen asleep the instant his head touched the pillow.

"Today you're going to meet someone with a strong connection to the village, although he's never lived there."

They were at breakfast, and their host gestured towards the buffet feast of fresh fruit and home-made muesli, followed by bacon and eggs. Louise decided to forego the latter.

Meanwhile, her body needed to recover from the ordeal yesterday, so they spent a restful morning motoring to the shores of Lake Victoria. But she couldn't dismiss from her mind that pitiful pile of ashes yesterday, where once there had been a family home. If only it had been made of bricks…

Maybe something good could come out of this tragedy. She would have to ask more questions. David had told her about meeting a teacher in the village, and she was looking forward to talking to him later.

When they got back to the lodge, the new visitor had arrived. A tall, elegant man with fine cheekbones greeted them. His pale brown skin and short cropped hair, thick with black curls, betrayed a mixed background.

"Good evening," he said, offering his hand. "Sam Ondiek. Our host told me you visited my village yesterday."

Louise controlled her surprise at his perfect spoken English, and David came up to introduce himself. The door behind Sam opened and a young woman came in, wearing a silky white evening dress which clung to her body, accentuating her limbs as she approached. Never before had Louise seen such a stunning African woman.

"And this is my friend, Emily. I imagine we shall find much to talk about. May I offer you a drink?"

Chapter 12

As she came forward to greet the other guests, Emily wished she had worn something more casual, but there was nothing she could do about it now. Sam should have told her. She glanced at his green neck scarf, grey pullover and slacks as he gave the orders to the waiter. He was perfectly at ease. She covered her bare shoulders with her hands and stared towards the glowing fire at the far end of the room.

"You must be cold, Emily," said Louise. "Here – you can borrow my jacket. Don't worry – I have this sweater to keep me warm."

Emily was grateful for the offer, and happy to cover the embarrassment of her evening dress. She studied Louise over her wine glass, noticing the square jaw which could most likely be set in obstinacy if the need arose. But clearly she was a woman with a kind heart. She had heard that Louise had come to sponsor a child through school.

Since her visit with Paul to the coast, Emily was convinced that help at village level was the best way forward. She didn't know exactly how she would follow the example of Paul's mining clients, but Nobel Laureate Wangari Maathai's advocacy for giving responsibility to the regions was a good idea. Inspired by Maathai, a vague idea had come to her mind. Whole communities, not just orphans, needed raising from the trap of poverty, but perhaps assisting AIDS orphans would be a start. She had intimate knowledge of that process, having gone through it herself.

She stood at Sam's elbow, listening half-heartedly to the men as they perched at the bar. Two uniformed attendants stood behind the counter. She noticed a third lounging against the door at the back, and caught a glimpse of his face in the shadows. He seemed to be scrutinising her intently.

Sam tried to include her in the conversation. What was his motive for bringing her here? There was certainly a spark of attraction between them. Paul had told her that Sam was thinking of settling down with a wife, and she hoped he didn't harbour any thoughts of her in that way. Her ordeal with the rapist at the coast still made her shudder.

Louise beckoned her towards the armchairs near the fire.

"Let's go and sit down," she said. "My back won't let me stand for more than ten minutes, and I had a long walk in the village yesterday. We can leave the men to prop up the bar!"

"The manager told us you've come to help the village," said Emily, sinking into the deep leather chair and stretching her legs to rest luxuriously on its footstool. She placed her newly-filled glass of wine on the side table. "I'm also here to see what I can do. I was brought up in an orphanage, supported by a wonderful lady called Caroline. She brought up Sam too."

"So you are brother and sister?"

Emily smiled. "In a manner of speaking, I suppose – although I only met Sam a few months ago. He's been away at Oxford University and is much older than I am."

"So that explains the way he speaks English," said Louise with a laugh. "Talking as one woman to another – he'll make a fine catch for somebody!"

"Did you find what you wanted in the village?" asked Emily, changing the subject.

"My idea is to sponsor a child through school, and I think I found one in Nairobi. He's a street boy who would do better away from city temptations. There are more potential donors where I come from, but yesterday I saw other areas needing help. It's difficult to know where to start."

"Perhaps it's best to start at the most urgent, and go on from there. Although the books will tell you to make a plan, set an objective, gather your resources and then take action."

"Are you a businesswoman too, Emily?"

"No. I'm not clever enough. But I've learned a lot from a friend, Caroline's son Paul. He's a chartered accountant who knows about such things."

"Really?"

Louise regarded her with interest, and Emily wondered what she was thinking. She liked Louise, who was friendly in a no-nonsense sort of way.

"Well, there was one urgent matter which was brought to my attention yesterday. Someone's house burnt down."

"That's awful. Was anybody hurt?"

Louise shook her head.

"But maybe that's not such a drastic matter," said Emily. "Was it a mud and wattle hut?"

Louise nodded.

"Then the owners will be poor with little to lose, and their relatives will take them in. It's the African way."

"But – "

"I know, Louise – may I call you Louise? They will have to build a new house, which will take them a week or two."

"That's what I'm concerned about. They'll build another one which will burn down again, and again; and the family will never better themselves."

"I see what you mean."

"Do you realise that practically all the buildings in the village are made of mud and wattle?"

"I haven't been there yet."

"The church was the first brick building."

"The people probably had what we call a *harambee* meeting – a traditional event where people pull together to raise funds."

Louise nodded. "I suppose so. Apparently someone made the bricks locally, but then he left the village. I wonder…"

"…If the family could build their house of bricks – like the parable in the Bible?" Emily laughed. "It would take too long. And they wouldn't be able to afford it."

"But if the bricks were already there – if somebody had the money to produce them?" Louise paused. "Emily, I believe I have an idea. What if one of my friends were to give money for a brick house?"

"That would be too late for the present family. But it's a

thought for the future."

"Why should it be too late? There must be a factory somewhere in the district. And after that, we could find somebody in the village to start another business."

"How would we do that, Louise? One man has already given up the idea, and it would be difficult to start afresh. You'll have to consult the people."

But Louise had a gleam in her eye. "You're right. One step at a time, and we must deal with the emergencies as they happen. I will email the UK tonight. I'm sure I can find a donor. How much will it cost?"

"That's the problem. I don't know. And surely the people would have to be involved in the solution. Somebody like my friend Paul would know how to work out the costs."

"You're right again. Why is life so complicated?"

But Emily had caught Louise's excitement, and she was looking forward to the next day.

"I've emailed the UK, and found a donor. Now we only have to work out the amount needed, and build that house!"

They were in the foyer after breakfast waiting for the men before going to the village.

It was difficult not to be affected by Louise's enthusiasm, but Emily wondered if she would keep up the momentum. She wondered who owned the land, and what the neighbours would think of a bright new brick house amid the mud huts. Maybe Louise would have to provide brick houses for them all. Did she have the resources? And was it a good idea anyway? Only the people would know.

Sam wanted to see his relatives.

"I need to get it over with," he said. "I haven't been here for several years. I know my aunt, Jackson's niece, has been saying it's time for me to settle down. Jackson told me she's found a suitable girl, but I want to make my own choice."

He glanced at her with a sheepish smile. An unfamiliar sensation of anger stirred within Emily.

"So you've brought me here to make them think I'm the one? Isn't that a bit presumptuous of you, Sam?"

"Well, at least I've given you fair warning…" His words tailed off and he gripped the steering wheel tightly as the car bounced into a deep hole, grating the sump. Emily clung to the strap above the door.

"I'm sorry."

Was he apologising for the jolt, or for his presumption? She didn't feel like giving him the benefit of the doubt. He drew the car to a halt beside the road and laid a hand on her arm.

"Surely you're aware of what's growing between us, Emily?"

He had not touched her before. The sensation of his fingers, vibrant with feeling, soothed her irritation. Yes, she did know. And at least he'd declared himself now. She closed her eyes and gave a little nod.

"Emily?"

She looked across at him.

"We'll talk about it later?"

He was right; this was not the time or place. But something else had been bothering her.

"Sam – you never mention your father. Is he…?"

Sam withdrew his hand and his face closed in bitterness. The transformation astonished her. He clenched his jaw and started the engine, spinning the wheels as the car skidded forwards.

"My father has nothing to do with this," he muttered, with a finality which brooked no more words.

He parked the car at the end of a narrow track which petered out beside a bank topped with strands of dry grass. Emily tried to open the door, but its edge caught in the soil and Sam had to manoeuvre the car before she could get out. They left it perched at an angle between the bank and the track.

"I'll have to reverse when we come back," he said, looking round at the way they had come. "There's no room to turn here."

He led her up a narrow path between rows of prickly sisal plants into a drab compound of huts with thatched roofs. One building with a rusted tin roof stood opposite the entrance. Emily stepped gingerly between goat turds and chicken droppings as Sam spoke to a woman wielding a brush made of sticks. They waited, and Emily studied her surroundings, noting a triangle of blackened stones around a heap of ashes near the building. No wonder huts went up in flames, she thought, and perhaps Louise had a vision worth pursuing. Emily recalled the Kibera slums where she'd lived when first in Nairobi. She hadn't thought of fire hazards then.

"I don't suppose you've been in a place like this before," said Sam. "When I first came here, I was horrified. It's a world away from our common background with Caroline. But this is where Jackson and my father come from, and even a half-African should never forget his origins."

"Don't worry, Sam. When I first came to Nairobi all I could afford was the corner of a room in the Kibera slums. Have you been there? It's much worse than this."

Sam shook his head, regarding her with wonder. "We have much to learn about each other, and I'm looking forward to the experience – are you?"

Emily looked into his eyes and a thrill of warmth passed through her. But she knew nothing about her own family, except that Ethel (who had lived with Caroline's father at the coast) was her grandmother.

There was a movement from the door behind them and a stooped woman shuffled into view, her face crinkling into a cautious smile. The smile widened as she recognised Sam.

"Simaloi?" Sam greeted his elderly relative. "*Jambo – habari yako?*"

The woman clasped her hands over Sam's.

"Greetings, Samuel. *Mzuri sana...* I'm very well."

It was clear to Emily that Simaloi's general outlook took a turn for the better at the sight of Sam, for she straightened her back and immediately looked younger, her eyes brightening as she and Sam traded questions and answers.

Emily left them to converse, and wandered towards a bench along the wall of the building. A small child stood on the threshold, bare from the waist down, his belly-button protruding from a swollen stomach. She offered a hand, and he toddled towards her, his face covered in a cloud of flies. She took a tissue from her bag and wiped at his nose. He wobbled, and his little legs collapsed under him. He looked up, chortling, and a fresh bubble appeared from his nose.

"Moses – where are you?"

A girl emerged from the house, stopping when she saw Emily.

"You're Moses's sister?"

The girl nodded, stooping to brush away the flies clustering round his eyes.

"I'm Emily. I came with him." She gestured towards Sam. "It looks as if we're going to be here for a while."

"I'll fetch my mother."

At their invitation, Emily pushed aside a curtain of sacking and entered the room, pausing to let her eyes get used to the gloom. Other women from different generations regarded her solemnly and greeted her. She noticed a figure sitting in the far corner surrounded by an assortment of gourds, bones and animal skins. She went closer. The woman's face was plastered with ash, and Emily felt a twinge of fear. But the woman smiled and beckoned. She said her traditional role as village sorceress was mainly to protect everyone and ward off evil. She showed Emily some herbs, and explained how to treat common ailments. Fascinated, Emily stayed listening until Sam called her.

"Hope you weren't too bored waiting for me?" he said as he led the way back to the car. "Simaloi and I had a lot to talk about."

"Not at all, Sam! I was fascinated to meet your family. I found out something about herbal potions and medicine from the village sorceress."

"That must have been Simaloi the elder. My family has a long tradition connected with magic and guardianship of the secrets of our ancestors, as you might have guessed when you met my uncle Jackson at the Magadi dig. Did Paul tell you about his second visit there?"

"Only that he was going to meet you again. But it would

be too hot and strenuous for me."

"He helped Jackson take some cave painting tracings to the Museum, and we'll be setting them up as an exhibition. The other reason for my visit today is to arrange for Simaloi to take over as custodian of the cave."

"So there's something more in that mysterious cave?"

"It's a sacred, ancestral place."

She could not help a mischievous thought.

"And the first reason for your visit...? I suppose you talked about me."

She laughed as Sam turned, denying it vehemently. "I did no such thing. I wouldn't dare – after what you said to me. But," he admitted, "Simaloi did raise the subject of my future plans, and asked if you featured in them."

"And?"

"I neither confirmed it nor denied it! But perhaps, having seen you, it will no longer be an overriding concern for her."

"So long as she doesn't cast a spell on us or something..." Emily joked, but afterwards she couldn't help feeling concerned. It would do no good to make light of such things.

They arrived back at the car.

"I think you'd better not get in until I've managed to put it onto an even keel," he said, as he unlocked the door and started the engine. He reversed down the track until there was space to turn round.

When they arrived in the village centre there was no sign of Louise or her husband. Emily saw the lodge car parked near the beer hall and Sam pulled up alongside. The driver was sleeping, his head rested against the steering wheel. Emily approached the window.

"Let's not disturb him. There's one more visit I have to make and we might as well do it now." Sam locked his car and stood in the middle of the dusty road. "I need to get my bearings... I have a couple of half-sisters on the other side of the village. I didn't know they existed until I was eighteen, and I haven't seen them for a long time."

He turned this way and that, before finally starting down a narrow passage between two buildings. "Come on – I think this is the way. You'll enjoy meeting Maria and Naomi, if they're at home. They are nearer your age than mine."

Emily struggled to keep up with him as he strode through shaded alleyways and across dusty open spaces. She bumped into him as he doubled back once, muttering that he'd gone the wrong way. He had to ask for directions, which meant prolonged stops to exchange greetings and trade news with the people who stood watching from their doorways. Emily scrabbled at the dust with her flip-flops, enduring long looks and inquisitive eyes while Sam conversed and struggled to memorise the route. Eventually, a *toto* led them the final few hundred yards. Emily wiped the perspiration from her brow, but Sam's steps quickened as they rounded the corner of a building made of brick into yet another open area. He stopped, and Emily did bump into him this time.

"There's Louise!"

She rubbed her head to ease the pain of the contact and peered round him. Louise and David were talking to a woman balancing a child on her hip.

"There you are!" said Louise. "We wondered what happened to you!"

"We went to visit Sam's family, and then lost our way." Emily turned to Sam. "I thought we were going to see the other half of your family?"

"We are, Emily. And we're here." He went towards the woman talking to Louise and David. "Maria – it's good to see you again, and you've met my new friends already. We've so much to talk about, and I want to introduce you to someone special. Emily?"

Emily came forward to greet Maria as Louise stepped back in surprise.

"Well, I never!" she said. "How did you know we met your family yesterday, and that we would be here this morning?"

"I didn't," said Sam. "But I'm not surprised. Our world is quite small, you know, and my family has connections with the lodge which sends tourists here from time to time. Isn't that so, Maria?"

Maria nodded.

An elegant lady in a red and yellow dress appeared on the steps of the brick house they had passed on entering the compound. As she approached, Emily noticed the wrinkles on her face which betrayed her age, but there was a spring in her steps.

"Sam, what a lovely surprise!"

"Ruth – you're looking wonderful, as always. I am sorry I haven't been here for so long."

"This really is a time to remember," said Ruth. "Did you know that your father came to see us not so long ago?"

Chapter 13

Yet another hot, dry day faces Ouma as he sits at his desk, gazing through the window while trying to produce an article for next week's newspaper. When will the drought end?

The country is sliding into disarray again after the euphoria of Kibaki's election as President. The cancer of corruption is ever near the surface. Ouma wonders at the recent concession to the Chinese to prospect for oil off the coast. Is it the beginning of something sinister?

More worrying is the arrival of thirty-five thousand Somali refugees over the border. The guns they brought with them are their only means of survival in the desert. Somalia has always been a thorn in Kenya's side.

Ouma remembers his happier days, when he went with Caroline, Paul and his new-found son Sam to visit Lake Turkana. Even then the Somalis were a problem, when armed convoys were needed to protect visitors to the area. He remembers his immense pride in having a son after all, and their delicious excitement as they got to know each other. Since then, everything has gone wrong.

Ouma gives himself a mental shake. He mustn't return to that dark place again. He takes a sip of water and wipes his brow with a piece of tissue torn from a toilet roll. Discarding the soiled paper onto the floor, he takes up his pen. Where to start?

It is hot. He wishes the window in front of him could be opened; it would at least offer a cooling through-breeze. Even Sister Brigid is showing signs of irritability, and her soothing creams cannot take away the brittle pain of his stump as it grates against the prosthesis. He procrastinates, reaching down to remove the offensive leg, then he starts to scribble. The hours slip away.

A tap at the window makes him pause. Sister Brigid gestures through the glass. She must be standing on tiptoe, for the ground dips steeply away on that side of the building. Why has she not come in through the door? He smiles through the smudge of dirt she has left on the pane. She's been tending to their *shamba* again. It's the boys' task, but they're not reliable, and she likes to make up for their shortcomings.

She gestures at him urgently and points towards the door. He can't understand what she's trying to say. There is a tap at the door and he looks round as Louise clears her throat.

"I've been standing here for ages, Charles!" she says. "I didn't dare interrupt, you were so absorbed in your work, but Sister Brigid said you've been at it all morning and it's time for lunch."

Ouma starts to get up, and then remembers to reach for his crutches. Dammit. Now Louise will see his vulnerability. He hates sympathy. But Louise chatters away about her visit to Kakamega and the people she's met. He sits there, trying to concentrate on what she's saying. How long is it since he first met her at Oxford? He's lost track of time.

"And our three-week holiday has come to an end. We're flying back home tomorrow, Ouma. I'm sorry I called you Charles before, the name just slipped out. It has been absolutely wonderful, and we've learned so much. I'm excited. Despite Emily's misgivings, I do believe we can start up something worthwhile in that village."

"Emily?"

Louise laughs. "I suspected you weren't listening. It doesn't matter. She's just a girl we met at the lodge, who seems to share our values. But what I've come to say is we'll sponsor Ken at secondary school when he's ready. And I don't see why we shouldn't be able to do the same for the others. I'm off to start up a charity, and Amayoni village will be the focus of our work. I have a feeling this idea will blossom into something special. It is important to address a problem from the grass shoots upwards."

"Grassroots, you mean?"

Louise hasn't changed, thinks Ouma. In the past he was never able to keep up with her incessant chatter, and this confusion of words is typical of her. She stops mid-thought and regards him with wide eyes.

"I do believe grass shoots is the right word for it! Thank you for drawing my attention... Grass Shoots. That's what I'll call my charity. It symbolises new growth from the basic unit of life – the family – which can, when nurtured under God's eye, spread to embrace a whole community."

"I don't understand a word you're saying."

"It's because you haven't been listening, Ouma. Don't worry, you'll learn soon enough. Your immediate concern is to ensure that Ken passes the entrance exam to the high school. And now, let's go and join Sister Brigid in the staff room. She's been waiting for us this past half hour."

"You go ahead, Louise. I'll follow shortly."

Ouma looks round for his prosthesis. The cream is on a shelf above the kitchen sink. It won't do for Louise to see him hobbling on crutches.

An hour later, he says goodbye.

"I'll be back when I've set up the charity and gained more pledges," she tells him through the car window. "Thanks to Emily's contact, I've already had valuable advice in Nairobi, and the next step will be to find suitable people in Amayoni village to form a local body."

"Emily's contact?"

"Yes – a man called Paul Clayton."

Ouma keeps his head low, but his mind is racing. How can she know Paul? And does she also know Caroline? There are too many intertwining links for him to manage all at once. He is afraid to respond. The silence between them lengthens.

She turns on the ignition, and with a spin of wheels on gravel, she is gone.

But he now understands her theory of holistic help to a single village. It is a logical progression from Wangare Maathai's focus on devolution of power to the regions.

Louise explained the concept over lunch, contrasting it with the tendency of large charities to focus on just one aspect, like health or education, and duplicate it throughout the country. But that's the second time Louise has mentioned Ruth's home village.

And Emily? There must be dozens of girls with that name in Kakamega, but he can't help thinking about the one he's seen with Paul over the past few years.

Louise is right about one thing: his focus should be on getting the boys ready for secondary school. They are due back any minute, and he must tidy away his papers before they destroy his morning's work.

The children enter the house chattering loudly and go straight to the fridge for something to eat.

A single sound like a muted bullet comes from the tin roof. Then another. Ouma glances outside as puffs of dust rise from the baked earth. The clatter above his head increases, drowning all thought. The boys rush outside, but return in an instant, hands over their ears, as a heavy torrent hits them. It settles into a driving downpour, and sheets of rain obliterate everything from sight. They gaze in awe as the garden turns into a swamp before their eyes.

It doesn't last for long. The boys change out of their uniforms, and Ouma breathes in deeply, savouring the damp earthy smell. He watches them play in the puddles before the water sinks back into the parched earth. The rains have arrived, and the country sighs with relief.

But the ensuing floods cut off the north, and Ouma wonders how the Somali refugees are faring in their makeshift camp on the Kenyan border. The papers have been full of those who fled the surge of political violence in their country. His journalistic instincts come to the fore, and he curses his incapacity.

A thought comes to mind. Maina has proved a promising investigator; perhaps it is time to use him for purposes other than stalking that girl, Emily.

The pavements are wet, and Maina has erected a

makeshift shelter outside the Five Bells restaurant. Ouma stands under an umbrella and holds a light to the man's rolled cigarette.

"I have news for you," says Maina. "That girl has been to Kakamega. She's left her white boyfriend and is now with someone much worse, a *nusu-nusu,* a half-breed. My informer got himself a job as barman where they stayed at the lodge in the forest. Do you still want her followed?"

Ouma raises his eyebrows. "There's no harm in keeping an occasional eye on her, Maina, but I want you to change priorities. See what you can discover about the refugee camp on the border with Somalia. I'll pay you this time."

More immediate events overtake the country. It is time for the elections, and Ouma is caught up with analysing the posturings between Government and opposition politicians. The elections have been postponed once already. However, the country goes about its business and the people are not unduly bothered by increased rumblings in the press, which many consider to be sensation-seeking.

Everything is in place for a peaceful transition.

Chapter 14

"I have to visit the museums in the country before taking up my new job," Sam said as they sat in the car on Upper Hill Road overlooking the lights of Nairobi. "I start on the north coast and will be staying with Caroline in Mombasa for a weekend. Would you like to come with me?"

A disturbing sense of *déjà vu* came over Emily. He had his arm round the back of her seat. His face was close, eyes searching hers, and their lips met. The tug of his passion drew her into submission, but as on many other occasions, she pulled back.

"I'm sorry, Sam." Tears pricked her eyes. "I don't know what's wrong with me."

"Nor do I," he said, frustration evident in his voice.

The last time she'd been to the coast was with Paul. Emily remembered the heightened sense of romance occasioned by that sultry climate. She also remembered, with a jolt, the man behind the bar at the lodge in Kakamega, who had studied her with such intensity. Was he associated with the one who had assaulted her at the beach hotel? She did not feel ready to go there alone with Sam.

"Why don't we ask Paul if he can come too?" she said. "It would be nice for Caroline to see us all. Shall I ask him when we next meet for lunch?"

Sam hesitated.

"If you think it's a good idea."

She sat opposite Paul at the Five Bells, enjoying her usual dish of prawn curry. Their meetings had lost importance for her, but she didn't want to hurt him by stopping them altogether. A niggling thought accused her of manipulation as she prepared her question.

"Sam and I are going to see Caroline next month while he tours the coastal museums. We were wondering if you'd like to come with us?"

The corners of Paul's mouth turned down.

"I would, but I'm afraid I can't get away from work." He paused. "But I've got another idea. Louise and David have been too busy up until now to enjoy our wildlife. Why don't I arrange a camping safari in the off-season? It would be nicer than a hotel, and we could invite Caroline too. I'm sure they'll get on well. What do you think?"

"I would absolutely love that, Paul!" said Emily. "Let's make a plan."

But in the meantime, she had committed to go to the coast with Sam.

They travelled by the night train to Mombasa on the Friday, Emily sharing a cabin with three other women, and meeting Sam for dinner in the dining car.

"I remember travelling with Caroline in the days when we had a three-course meal with silver service on this train, complete with damask napkins," said Sam.

Emily chewed with determination at a gristly piece of goat meat before swallowing hard, then reached for a banana. "It is a bit different now!"

At the station, Caroline was there to greet them. It was bustling with people, and Emily had to bump her way through the pushing crowd, using her back-pack as a shield. The humidity and heat were like a heavy load on her lungs as she gasped for air and mopped her brow.

"You'll feel better when we get to the sea breezes of Likoni," Caroline consoled her. "Throw your bag in the boot, and jump into the front seat with me."

The road to the ferry was jammed with traffic, and although the windows were wide open, sweat dripped in streams down Emily's face. The car crept forward in the queue, inch by inch.

"I think we'd better change plans. Do you mind dropping

us at Fort Jesus?" said Sam from the back seat. "I arranged to meet the curator there at 10.30, and I don't think we'll make it in time if we go to Likoni first."

Emily had an idea. "How long is it since you've been to the museum. Caroline? Would you like to come with us?"

"Not for a long while, and I wouldn't mind seeing it again, as there are bound to be changes. I hear they have a special ceramic collection on display. It would also save me a trip over the ferry to collect you later."

She swung out of the traffic, did a U-turn and headed towards the Old Harbour.

The ancient ramparts of the 16th century Portuguese Fort loomed above them. Sam bounded through the portals to make contact with Richard, Head of Coastal Archaeology. He invited Caroline and Emily into a back room away from tourist eyes, and showed them trays of ceramic fragments, carefully bagged and marked. Then he led them into the Museum towards the display cases.

"The local pottery was seldom decorated or glazed," he said. "But some crude attempts were made to copy the celadon glazing. The pieces imported from China, the East Persian Gulf and India are far more decorative."

Caroline's enthusiasm and Richard's explanations caught Emily's interest. She peered into the cabinet before moving on to the next one.

"And here we have European imitations, and imitations of imitations."

Going back and forth, they examined both displays.

"The message is so clear," exclaimed Caroline.

In the Laboratory, finds from a Portuguese sunken ship in the Old Harbour were being reconstituted. The sodden wood had been treated and made hard again. Rusty helmets and metal bits and pieces lay about on benches. In a corner, three technicians bent deep in concentration over a fragment.

"We're so privileged, having you to guide us round – I've learned far more than when I came before as an ordinary visitor," said Caroline, as Richard led them into the air-conditioned Library.

"This was plundered about twenty years back," said Richard. "But we are slowly building it up again."

Moving lightly from shady spot to shady spot, Emily dragged behind as they continued the tour. Ancient tramcars stood on narrow-gauge lines. From the battlements Richard pointed out the strategic placement of the Fort, and then led them into the dungeons, indicating the graffiti and the deadly cannon. It was near midday, and Emily needed a drink.

"We'll leave you two to enjoy a fresh lime on the turret overlooking the careening beach," said Richard, "while Sam and I go off to discuss business."

Emily turned her face into the sea breeze.

"The *Chini Club* is next door," said Caroline. "Would you like to have dinner there tonight, under the stars?"

"I'd love to, but only if you come with us. We'll treat you!"

"That's fixed, then. I'll book a table before we go home. The traffic will be clear by now."

Emily knew Sam was hoping to lower her barriers in this sultry climate, so evocative of love and passion. She hadn't the courage to tell him what held her back; he was not like Paul. She knew her fear of sex was the cause of her problem, but their relationship was special, and growing more profound at each meeting. Caroline had thrown her a lifeline.

They sat at a table for three overlooking the glistening waters of the Old Harbour. The soft lap of waves was muted by the gentle rustle of a date palm, and the ghostly shadow of Fort Jesus loomed over them. Dinner was a delicious lobster thermidor, and Emily didn't have room for anything else, although Sam and Caroline shared an enormous ice cream and fruit dessert. Strains of Strauss waltzes wafted through the loudspeakers, and several couples rose to dance. Sam stood, offering his arm to Emily. She smiled up at him and allowed him to hold her close as he tried to teach her the steps.

"Just relax into me, Emily," he whispered.

She tried, and although her toes sometimes got in the way of his feet, it was a wonderful feeling as she melted into the length of him.

"I think you'd better ask Caroline to dance now," she said as the music changed to a fox-trot.

For the remainder of the evening, he partnered them alternately, and never seemed to tire.

"You're a very good dancer, Sam. Where did you learn?"

"At University; I had a girlfriend who told me I had wonderful rhythm," he said, wriggling his hips and twirling her round his arm. "She taught me all the moves, and we went dancing every week."

Emily wanted to ask him what happened to his girlfriend, but it was none of her business.

The following morning Richard took her and Sam on a tour of coastal ruins. An ancient fishing and market gardening town stood on the banks of Mtwapa Creek. He led them on a shaded nature walk through a twenty-acre forest. The paths were narrow, and as Emily followed behind, she glanced upwards every few steps, for Richard had warned her to look out for green tree snakes. The thought of one falling on her head, even though the snakes were harmless, made her shiver with loathing. She didn't spot one, and wished he'd never mentioned them.

A rough drive along the secondary coastal road followed. The ruins at Jumba la Mtwana were preserved in open-plan fashion. Here, there'd been no Indian Ocean trade, Richard told them, because the beach was unsuitable for ocean-going ships. Emily rested in the shade while Sam examined the less-than-right-angled corners in the decoration of the *mihrabs*, a common feature throughout the coast. She tried out the rough foot-scrapers near a cistern, and observed distinctive joints at the apex of the arches, but she found the beautiful porites coral carvings the most interesting.

It was near midday, and although she'd been brought up at the coast, it was too hot for her. She preferred the higher altitude of Nairobi, and all this ancient history was becoming tedious.

"We'll travel via the main road to Gedi and stop at Watamu for a bite to eat," Richard told them.

Watamu? Emily had not realised they were going to the village where her grandmother stayed.

"Would there be time to visit Ethel?" she asked Sam. "You know that she was a housemaid in Caroline's home?"

"Was she, Emily? How—?"

"When Boney left his farm, he brought Ethel and me to Watamu, and I went to the orphanage there. Boney left her the house when he died. I haven't seen her for a long time. I told you I was an AIDS orphan, didn't I?"

"You did. And of course let's try to find Ethel." Sam glanced at Richard for confirmation. "Perhaps we can buy something for lunch at the *duka* and then call in to see her. But we have to get back to Mombasa in time to catch the night train for Nairobi."

As Richard drove down the sandy track leading to Ethel's home, Emily scanned her surroundings. Bush encroached onto the drive, and the bougainvillea which covered the old water tank had gone wild. It was clear that cars seldom came here, although bicycle tyres had left weaving imprints in the white sand.

The house seemed smaller than she remembered, and the paint on the doors and shutters was peeling. She got out of the car, motioning to the men to wait while she went to the back door. It was locked. She walked round to the front, stepping gingerly through the overgrown lawn, and a *shenzi* dog whirled round the corner, yapping ferociously. Emily stopped. Two more mongrels in varying shades of yellow and brindle joined the cacophony. A shaky voice called them to stop barking.

"Who's there?" It was her grandmother.

"It's me, *kukhu*. Emily. We've come to see you."

"*Karibuni!*" Welcome.

The dogs made way for her, sniffing at her hands and wagging their tails in uncertain greeting, as Emily climbed the veranda steps.

Ethel sat facing the beach, her frame spilling over a rickety chair. The stone floor was littered with leaves and other debris. The door to the living area stood open, swinging in the breeze and lifting the dust. Emily paused to wipe a mote from her eye before going to be enveloped in Ethel's arms.

"It is so good to see you again!"

The dogs bounded round them, anxious to be included, until Ethel dismissed them with a sharp word. They retired to a grimy corner, tails between their legs.

Emily told her about Sam and his new job.

"He's here with you now? Call him and let me see him!"

This was the signal for the dogs to come forward again, with yaps and growls and wagging tails.

They picnicked on the veranda, exchanging news.

"Are you here all by yourself, *kukhu*?"

"Esau looks after me – he stays in the servants' quarters and gets the milk and *posho* from the *duka* on his bicycle. He does the garden."

"And the house?" asked Emily, glancing into the dark rooms covered with dust.

"My legs are tired and my back pains me, and I've not been able to keep my old standards. But my needs are few."

"Otherwise you are well? Perhaps Esau can help you in the house?"

Ethel turned to quiz Sam about his job, and Emily slipped out to speak to Esau, suggesting he spend time cleaning every day. She gave him what was in her purse and promised to reward him in future, resolving to speak to Caroline and arrange something. She glanced at her watch. There might be time for a quick dip in the sea before they left.

She had put on a bikini under her clothes before leaving Mombasa. She returned to the veranda, pulled off her top and stepped out of her jeans, and threw an inviting glance at Sam. He followed suit, revealing a garish pair of boxer shorts.

They waved at Ethel and he slipped his hand into hers as

they skipped down the path to the beach, the dogs cavorting round them. Pausing on the bank above the crashing waves of the high tide, he put his arm round her shoulder, pulling her to him. They kissed, long and closely, flesh melding into flesh, as the sound of the rolling waters drummed in her ears. She felt him stir against her.

"Race you to the sea!" she cried, scrambling over the soft sand and diving through the seaweed into cleaner waters beyond. Sam followed, catching hold of her, his lips finding hers in a salty embrace. She clung to him, buffeted by the waves. His body was strong and muscular, speaking with an intensity which overwhelmed her.

Richard called from the shore – it was time to go.

"We'll just go for a walk to dry off," shouted Emily. "Be with you in ten minutes!"

By the time they'd raced each other along the beach, and then walked hand in hand up the path, the sun had dried them. But as she pulled on her clothes, Emily sensed a reservation in her grandmother. Her eyes were hard as she bade them goodbye, and a troubled frown creased her brow. But her words were affectionate, and she sent many *salaams* to Caroline, asking them to tell Caroline to come and see her soon.

The historic ruins of Gedi, a few miles inland, presented a completely different world. Emily wasn't sure about this gloomy place, hung with eerie creepers in the middle of a dark forest. Deep ditches crossed her path. Holes yawned at her feet as she clambered through the site, competing with the tangled undergrowth. It must be a nightmare keeping the place cleared, she told Sam, as he helped her over a broken wall.

Richard called them to examine the different levels of the walls, and Emily stood by as he discussed with Sam the problem of why the city had been abandoned in the 16th Century. Was it lack of fresh water, or even poison placed in the wells by enemies from Mombasa? Another theory was desiccation through widespread climatic change. This could only be proved scientifically, and had already been established in Ethiopia.

But they could not linger for long. Before Richard left them at the Mombasa station for their train journey back to Nairobi, he took them aside in the car park.

"Next time you come to the coast," he said to Sam, "you must go to Lamu, a wonderful place of Swahili history. You may be told about the Shanga Ruins. But please be aware that the claimed date in the 1st Century, based on ceramics found at the third level, has yet to be scientifically substantiated."

"What's he talking about, Sam?" asked Emily as they walked along the platform to their separate coaches. "I've never heard of Shanga."

"Nor have I, until this weekend. Richard told me that it's an archaeological site on Pate Island, part of the Lamu archipelago. Would you like to come with me when I go? We haven't set a date yet, but you'd have to allow several days for the visit."

"Maybe. I have other things on my mind. I'm seriously considering giving up my job in Nairobi and joining the Amayoni project. Paul has asked me to help him when they set up the new NGO. Louise and David will be coming from the UK to finalise everything, and I'm hoping there might be an opening for me somewhere."

He turned away from her, shoulders drooping.

"Let me know when the time comes," she called as he climbed into his carriage. She didn't want to hurt him, and a warm glow suffused through her as she recalled their precious moments on the beach.

Chapter 15

Louise surveyed the Belton Church Hall. She tweaked a jar of fresh flowers on the high table, and fiddled with the papers spread along its surface. She hadn't slept last night, her mind going over and over the preparations for this fundraising day.

She and David had devised a simple quiz with African connotations to exercise the minds of the guests, who were from various parishes, schools and associations in the area. Africa seldom featured in the sophisticated world of Sussex. Only when a disaster hit the headlines, like famine or revolution, did people briefly consider the so-called Dark Continent, shrug their shoulders in disparagement, and then turn back to matters nearer home.

A succession of preachers in the county had brought greater awareness of third-world poverty and a renewed sense of mission among the people. But the donors were becoming disenchanted with large international charities. Big budgets and unwieldy administration swallowed up a disturbing proportion of their donations. Government-to-Government aid invited corruption at the highest levels, and still the people suffered. There had to be a simpler way to help the needy.

The church band set up their instruments and harsh twangs of tuning cut through the silence. David stood ready at the refreshment bar with Laura. Louise regarded her daughter with pride. The gentle curves of her maturing figure and the long sweep of silky blonde hair reminded her of photos of her younger self. But Laura had David's brown eyes, and the high cheek bones of her grandmother. She would go up to Oxford in the autumn.

There was a commotion outside, and Laura went to the door.

"The mayor has arrived, Mum. Do you want me to greet her?"

Louise panicked. Only half a dozen helpers were in the room. Two people riffled through the literature on the welcome table, and prepared to make lists of emails and telephone numbers of the guests. Six tables stood pristine with their bouquets of flowers, each with chairs tucked tight underneath. She should have asked the mayor to come half an hour later.

She sent up a silent prayer, adjusted her hair and scurried out to the car park, leaving Laura to galvanise the welcome committee.

A tiny woman wearing a chain of office which looked too heavy for her stepped out of the mayoral car. Her escort, a tall thin man, towered above her. Louise came forward to introduce herself. Through the corner of her eye she saw a car disgorging passengers near the exit. Her prayers were being answered, but she needed to give God more time.

Exchanging platitudes about the weather only took a moment. The cobbled path to the hall entrance provided a means for further procrastination as the mayor wobbled on high heels over the uneven surface. Thank God it was sunny. They rounded a corner of the building and there were David and Laura waiting at the side entrance, wearing their best smiles. Louise ushered the mayor forwards, allowing space for the trickle of visitors to enter the hall behind them. David and Laura engaged their visitor in bright conversation, turning to admire the garden and the view to the distant downs. Louise glanced round, and another car arrived.

By the time the mayoral party entered the hall, a few people were waiting at the welcome desk, and Louise noticed her team of helpers dispersed casually among the tables, pretending to be guests. She saw musical instruments lying unattended in the front corner of the room. The band were sitting at a table nearby, engaged in animated conversation while they looked through the leaflets. Silently, she blessed them.

Leaving David to guide their guest through the display of literature and photographs at the back of the hall, Louise hurried to the welcome desk to chivvy the guests and urge them to their seats.

"Proceedings are about to start," she said. They could delay matters no longer; the mayor had patiently allowed herself to be informed for long enough.

Her speech struck just the right note. She was delighted to encourage their new charity, and remarked on the name, Grass Shoots, which so aptly described the desired journey from the grassroots upwards.

David's speech detailed the groundwork that had been done so far, and he appealed for help to take the charity forward. The band played their praises to the Lord, and by the time the first part of the afternoon was over, the hall had filled. David announced a break for tea, and the mayor prepared to leave.

Was the day a success? It was too early to evaluate. They had raised enough money to build the foundations of a new school for children who were too poor even to go to the government school. The problem would be to sustain the momentum of giving.

Half a dozen people had come forward to sponsor a child each through primary school. It was a start, and follow-up measures were in place. She and Maria needed to match the sponsors with their children, and had devised a plan for the families to write regular letters and send photographs, to forge a bond between the village and the charity. But Maria needed more help, and they had not yet formed a body to lead the project in Kenya.

Louise tried to stop herself from worrying. It was all she could do to keep up with events in the roller-coaster which had been started – by God, she told herself firmly. All this was in His hands. She and David were merely His instruments. But sometimes she wished she could just stand back and take a breather.

An email arrived from Paul in Nairobi. Legal papers had been drawn up to form a non-governmental organisation (NGO) for the Amayoni project. Louise and David would serve on the Board, and they needed to identify members in the village as leaders. It was time for them to visit Kenya again. The business should not take long to resolve, said Paul, who asked if they would then like to go on a safari?

"We shouldn't miss this opportunity," said David. "Let's take Laura with us. She deserves it after all the work she's been doing. And we can have a holiday while our volunteers in the office wade through the mountain of paperwork which has generated since the fundraising meeting."

Louise sat next to a Nairobi businessman on the flight to Kenya. Elections were due in December, he told her, and he was confident that Mwai Kibaki would get in again.

"He has done so much. The roads are improved, and although there will always be corruption, it is better than in Moi's day."

"What about security?" asked Louise.

"That's an ongoing problem, due to poverty and the gap between rich and poor. There are lots of hijackings, and lots of violence. There are too many people in my country, but business is thriving and Kenya is a good place to live."

Paul met them at the airport, and it took over an hour to negotiate the chaotic traffic into the city. Crooked lines of cars wove along the broken tarmac. An invisible code of push, shove and reluctant give way, made collisions surprisingly few, although Louise noticed that every vehicle had a dent or a scratch. The road undulated, the sharp sides of the tarmac falling steeply onto a third lane, where *matatus* bumped and bounced over the corrugations to gain three or four car-lengths before pushing their way back into line. Due to a recent Government directive, Paul told them, although people were still sardined into *matatus*, nobody actually hung out of the back door any more.

Shanty shops thrumming with activity crowded both sides of the road. Nairobi city merged into Langata, which merged in a seamless pandemonium with the suburb of Karen where they were staying the night.

Louise wondered whether there was indeed any scope for hijackings amid the chaos.

"I feel almost safe," she said., "The roads are so tightly packed, there's nowhere for bandits to escape."

"Not a bit of it." Paul laughed. "Karen is notorious for hijackings, especially in the evenings when commuters return home from work. Make sure you lock yourselves in and close the car windows wherever you go, for there's also the danger of theft."

The following morning after a restful night behind high security walls where night guards patrolled, they took a private minibus into town. Louise chatted in the front seat with the driver, a well-spoken youth, full of enthusiasm and appreciation for his country and his President.

"My name is John," he said in answer to her question, "and of course Kibaki will get in again. He's done much for Kenya in just five years. We no longer have rubbish or plastic bags spoiling our countryside, there's no smoking in public places, and no overcrowded *matatus*."

Louise smiled to herself. His definition of overcrowding clearly only covered people hanging out of doors and windows.

"We have free primary schooling, and free secondary schooling is on the way. People don't fear any more. We're not afraid to spend our money how we wish. We are proud to be Kenyan, and look forward to a bright future."

"What about security?"

"That will always be a problem, but it is being addressed. The police have been overhauled, and there are no parking boys now."

"But where does the money come from for all these improvements?"

"The World Bank has started payments again, and the money is going where it is meant to go. Even young people are being supported with new Government loans to groups to start up new businesses, and interest rates are coming down. Thirteen and a half per cent is still high, I know, but nothing can improve overnight."

"I am impressed," said Louise. She was also impressed by John's knowledge and enthusiasm, and wanted to learn more about him. But they were approaching the end of their journey.

"Have you been into central Nairobi?" he asked her as he negotiated the minibus round the large hospital roundabout and headed down the hill in the direction of Uhuru Highway.

"No."

"You must go; there are no more broken pavements, or broken signs. Everything is in good order and working well."

"And the traffic?"

He smiled. "Too many vehicles; thousands of reconditioned cars imported from Dubai are flooding the market. But there are plans for flyovers and by-passes."

Halfway down the hill, he turned right into a parallel road and they arrived at the Fairview Hotel. Paul was there to take them to Amayoni. With him was a familiar figure.

"I think you've already met Emily," he said. "She's coming to record our meetings."

Louise stepped forward. "It's lovely to see you again, Emily. One day perhaps I'll begin to understand how you, Paul and Sam are connected." She turned towards Laura. "I want you to meet my daughter, Laura. She's looking forward to seeing the village, and David and I can't wait to find out what's happened at Amayoni since our last visit."

Emily pulled some legal documents from her briefcase and laid them on a coffee table for David to go through, while Louise took Laura for a stroll through the hotel gardens. She pointed out a bronze sunbird with metallic feathers darting among the foliage. She told Laura about the exotic great blue turaco she'd seen on her last visit, and confessed that coming to Kenya had awakened a latent interest in birds.

"Here in Kenya they perch openly on the branches,

inviting attention; unlike the shy creatures back home," she said. "And the name of the village – Amayoni – means birds. I think it is such a lovely word."

They ordered a pot of tea and sat in a shaded spot until it was time to go.

The following morning at the lodge Maria greeted them with a wide smile, and accompanied them to Amayoni. There was a new brick home with a corrugated iron roof on the site of the previously burned-out hut, and Naomi's daughter thanked Louise profusely for her support.

"With your money, we bought the bricks from a town near Kisumu. And now, the factory in Amayoni has been started up again by a school teacher."

"You will meet Joram soon," said Paul. "He's one of the leadership candidates for our project."

On their way back to the church, they passed a rectangle pegged out in the dust.

"It's the start of our new school," said Maria proudly. "Already forty children are waiting to attend. As you know, it's for pupils whose parents can't afford the books, uniform, or food required by the government school."

The priest was waiting for them in his office, and after a short prayer, he let in the candidates one by one. Louise immediately liked Joram, an enthusiastic teacher who had been at the mission school for two years.

The candidates agreed to serve on the Committee for a trial period, and it was decided that the Project Leader would be elected after six months.

Joram told them the mission school was thinking of building boarding facilities. "In this way, there'll be scope for introducing more vocational activities to help those too poor to go on to further training." He turned to Louise. "Your protégé is one who would benefit, Mrs Louise."

"You mean Ken?"

Joram nodded. "He's in my class, a bright boy who needs to be stimulated and guided. He's waiting to see you outside."

"I'm so glad! I was wondering if I'd be able to meet him on this short visit."

"I've re-started the brick-making project in the village," said Joram. "It's a good way to occupy the youths out of school hours. Ken helps me organise the boys, but I don't have the time to supervise it properly. I'm hoping he might manage the project when he leaves school."

Louise nodded enthusiastically, pleased that her original idea had taken root.

They emerged into the blazing sun, where a boy, stiff in newly-creased grey shorts and green blazer, was waiting. Louise bounced up to him in delight.

"Ken! I'm so pleased to see you. How are you? I've heard good things about you."

The boy came forward to shake hands. "*Jambo, mama.*"

Louise beckoned to Laura. "I want you to meet my daughter, Laura. And Emily, who has come from Nairobi to help with the project."

As Ken and Laura shook hands and exchanged greetings, Louise noticed Emily taking a step backwards, then composing herself as the boy held out his hand.

"Ken was a parking boy in Nairobi when my friend Ouma rescued him," said Louise. "You must meet Ouma, Emily. He is quite a character. And we're getting two more street boys through him next year."

Louise drew Ken aside, bombarding him with questions, while Emily withdrew.

Later, when they were at the lodge, Louise took Emily aside. "I couldn't help noticing your reaction to meeting Ken," she said. "Had you seen him before?"

Emily shuddered. "Yes. I never forgot that face." She told Louise about the time when her bag was snatched from Paul's car in the middle of a traffic jam on Uhuru Highway. "He is no longer a scruffy *toto*, but the features are the same, and I know it's him. Luckily he didn't seem to recognise me, and I am sure he must be a reformed character."

"You're probably right, and I don't suppose he even

looked at your face when he grabbed your bag," said Louise, her eyes twinkling. "According to Ouma, Ken was involved in a multitude of dodgy activities in Nairobi before he took him under his wing."

Over the next two days Maria showed them round the village. Crops grew well during the rains, she told them, but the people had to learn about mulching, and to make good use of manure. They also needed to install guttering and storage tanks on the houses for times of drought. Louise would see what she could do about raising the funds. Ideas flowed, and the hours sped by.

"And now for the fun part," announced Paul on their last evening. "Emily and I have to go back to work, but the rest of you are in for a treat. I have booked you on a flight to Shaba Game Reserve on Tuesday morning. You've heard of Joy Adamson and the Born Free Lions?"

Louise nodded. "We've even seen the film."

"Well, you're going with my mother Caroline to a tented camp in Shaba, the Adamsons' old stamping ground, for three nights. Chris Trent, a friend of mine who runs a safari business, will look after you. Then we'll catch up with you in Nakuru."

"I just can't wait," said Louise. "And at last we're going to meet Caroline!"

Chapter 16

Louise dozed beside the pool, blocking her ears and trying to shut her mind against the throaty roars of the planes, which took off and landed on the runway nearby.

"You'll get used to the noise," said the manager of the Aero Club as a helicopter clattered past. With him was a diminutive woman, her deep blue eyes twinkling with merriment. Wild grey hair fluffed round her face, drawing Louise's attention away from the wrinkled folds of skin under her chin.

"You must be Louise and David. And is that Laura cooling off in the swimming pool? I'm Caroline. I've heard so much about you. No, don't get up."

She flopped on the grass beside Louise's sunbed, chattering about the forthcoming safari and her excitement at being reunited with her family. Louise warmed to her immediately, and Laura jumped out of the pool to be introduced.

The following morning, they boarded a private jet for the hour-long flight to Shaba. Louise had never been in a six-seater plane before. She clutched at the seat in front of her as it bumped through the clouds and swung northwards. By the time they passed by the Aberdare Mountains, she had grown accustomed to the steady thrum of the engines and the occasional sideways drift on currents of air. She gazed at the long outline of the range, which bordered the Rift Valley, remembering the story about Joy Adamson's lions roaming free. Their offspring must be somewhere in the forest below. Caroline touched her arm, pointing to the other side of the plane, where the jagged summit of another mountain poked through a white mass of swirling cloud.

"That's Mount Kenya."

Louise gasped. "I would have missed it if you hadn't shown me."

"I've never seen it so bare of snow," said Caroline. "Before global warming took hold, the peaks were always covered with white, even though we are near the equator."

"Really? I thought it was impossible to have snow at the equator."

The plane descended towards an expanse of brown scrub. Louise could see no sign of a landing strip. She screwed up her eyes and braced herself, wondering what was going to happen next. Caroline patted her reassuringly on the arm.

"Our bush pilots are among the best in the world," she said. "Don't worry."

Louise barely felt the touchdown. Clouds of dust caught up with the plane as the reverse thrusters kicked in after landing. She saw a herd of zebra scattering from the runway as they taxied towards a lone vehicle. A man in khaki shorts and sleeveless jacket stepped out, introducing himself as Chris Trent, their tour guide.

Louise had bought a bird book in Nairobi, and resolved to start making a list. On the two-hour game drive into camp, a pale chanting goshawk came at them, its light grey form flying low in attack mode, and then it perched on a thorn bush beside the track, squawking angrily in disappointment. David focussed his camera.

"We must have disturbed its prey," said Chris.

He stopped the car on the bank of the Uaso Nyiro River. They got out, and Chris pointed out a single crocodile basking, mouth open, on a rock.

Caroline beckoned to Louise. "Come over here."

The ground fell away into the river thirty feet below. The afternoon sun caught a clump of rocks in the foreground, transforming them into topaz jewels washed by the soft lapping water. A sandbar stretched into a small beach along the near shore. A fringe of trees covered the opposite bank, the green foliage failing to hide the hard baked earth beyond. Deep blue waters reflected the cloudless sky.

More rocks had appeared on the near shore, captured by the sun. She glanced across at the original clump, and back again. They had multiplied, and were covering the sand bar. They were moving...

"You've seen the elephants?"

Louise caught her breath and watched the ponderous giants emerge in ghostly fashion from the bush. The deep silence and the infinity of peace held her in thrall.

"Here, take a look through my binoculars."

The great beasts sprung close in her eyes, their immensity magnified. Their snaking trunks drew in the water and curled inwards into triangular gaping mouths. A calf sheltered under its mother's belly.

This magical scene by the river far below would remain with her, always. She took a photograph, spending time to include fringes of foliage in the foreground for artistic effect.

It was time to head for camp. Three men in dark green uniform lined up to greet them beside a large marquee which faced a swampy area, and Louise saw a line of tents strung out beyond.

"I'll take the one on the edge," volunteered Caroline. "I love being close to the *bundu*."

Laura hesitated outside the one allocated to her.

"Don't worry," said Chris. "I'll be on one side of you, and your parents on the other. *Askaris* will patrol all night, and you'll be quite safe."

Water trickled from a spring beside the tent Louise shared with David. She sat on a camp chair, bird book on her lap and binoculars round her neck. Hundreds of tiny brown quelea birds passed through, chattering and swirling from tree to tree, looking for seeds.

"The farmers hate them," said Chris as he came up behind her. "They steal the wheat heads when they're ripe for harvest."

A coal black drongo swooped to steal a morsel from the beak of a spurwing lapwing pecking at the water's edge only fifteen yards away, and she identified a lilac-breasted roller as it flashed by in a blaze of blue and purple to settle in a dead thorn tree on the other side of the swamp. A herd of sleek chestnut-coloured impala drifted towards her, and a tawny eagle perched on a dead branch, waiting motionless in the midday heat.

As they returned from their first evening game drive, a cheetah with four half-grown cubs stepped through the undergrowth alongside the road, their yellow and black rosettes blending perfectly into the dry scrub. Chris stopped the car, switching off the engine to absorb the silence, and they strained their eyes into the shadows until it was too dark to see.

In the morning a caracal skulked close beside the road, its sinuous body coiled for immediate spring, triangular tufted ears turned back over the tawny body.

"This is a rare treat," whispered Chris, and Louise forgot to take a picture.

They passed through the main Shaba Gate into Samburu National Park on the opposite side of the dirt highway leading northwards. A picnic breakfast awaited them on Champagne Ridge. They consumed large wedges of fruit, home-made muesli, bacon, eggs and sausages. Long-necked gerenuk and Grants gazelle grazed unperturbed nearby, their short tails flicking back and forth under white patched rumps. Giraffes peered at them over the thorn trees.

"You cannot leave without a dip in the famous Buffalo Springs pool," said Chris, ushering them back into the car. "I hope you remembered to bring your swimming costumes?"

He drew up beside a concrete tank and Laura went behind the vehicle to change while Chris slipped into the lukewarm water topped with green scum. Louise dipped in a toe, withdrawing instantly, but Laura dived in after Chris, surfacing with a shriek.

"Ugh – it's all sludgy and slimy!" she squealed.

Grants gazelle and shaggy grey waterbuck were grazing beside a swampy area about fifty yards away. David walked towards them, camera ready, and Louise followed. The animals lifted their heads, looking away at a fringe of scrub to the left. A large black shape emerged from the bush, eyeing them boldly. David raised his camera. The animal took two steps forward, tossing his head.

"Come back here, David – quickly. It's a buffalo." Chris was at Louise's side. "Run back to the pool, Louise, and get behind the wall."

A second buffalo emerged from the bush, and he shouted again at David, who started to run back.

Louise joined Laura and Caroline behind the wall, panting heavily with exertion and fright. She peeped over the top. As soon as the men retreated, she was relieved to see the buffalo lose interest.

On the way back to camp, Chris gave them a severe warning and a lecture. "You must never again go wandering away from your guide into the bush," he said. "Not even for ten yards. These animals are wild, and you are in their territory. Although you're safe enough while in a car."

On the evening drive, eight lions lazily flopped on some rocks in the dusk, doing nothing but raise the occasional head at them as they watched from the vehicle. They seemed so harmless and cuddly.

The food in camp was excellent. Full breakfasts, followed by tasty buffet lunches, and a three-course silver service dinner every day.

On their final drive, three klipspringers tidily tripped up some rocks near the lions' resting place of the previous day, and a serene family of elephants engaged in mock-fighting and mud-bathing in the river. Louise looked up at millions of red-billed quelea in quick silent flight; streams and streams of them travelling westwards into the setting sun, which formed a molten triangle between two hills, topped by golden-fringed clouds.

It rained during the long journey to Naro Moru where they enjoyed a fresh trout lunch beneath trees dripping noisily onto the canvass roof. It rained as they crossed the equator and arrived after dark at Maili Saba, their destination on the side of Menengai crater, seven miles from

Nakuru. The amenities were poor, the electricity flickered on and off, and the "succulent joint of Molo lamb" offered on the menu for dinner was tough.

"I think it's actually goat's meat," said Caroline as she removed a piece of gristle from her mouth. "I doubt a place like this serves Molo lamb as I remember it. It was a delicacy when the white highlanders farmed sheep imported from the UK."

"This hotel is run by a foundation which trains orphans," Chris explained apologetically. "We like our clients to see both sides of the coin when they come to Kenya. Over the next few days, you'll pass through some deprived areas, revealing the gap between the haves and the have-nots." He paused, pushing his plate aside. "But I must admit the quality of this meal is inexcusable. I'll complain to the management."

High concrete steps led up to the large double bed in the chalet Louise shared with David, and she tripped over a corner as she felt her way in the dim light.

"The health and safety people at home would throw up their hands in horror if they saw this," she said, examining her grazed shin with the light of a torch.

She awoke to a crisp morning. A panorama of desolate beauty lay far below, revealing a vast crater of black forbidding lava punctuated by bristly scrub, which disappeared into the distance. To her left a promontory sparsely fringed with trees jutted out, and a raptor rose and swooped in the thermals nearby.

"When I was a child," called Caroline from her nearby chalet, "that rim was covered with thick forest. It was a good place for lovers."

Louise beckoned her over. "What happened?"

"Deforestation. Over the years, the *watu* have taken the trees for charcoal, and not replaced them. It is the sad story of our country." Caroline pointed at a wisp of smoke on the near horizon. "And Menengai goes up in smoke every year as grass fires are lit to encourage new growth. There will be no trees here for the next generation to enjoy."

"The crater is impassable on foot," Chris told them at breakfast. "The terrain is rough, and there's no water or shade. An old colonial story tells of a farmer who murdered two girls, and hid one of them in the crater. Her body was never found."

"I remember that story!" said Caroline. "My step-father Boney told me he had to question the man throughout the night. I listened as a child to him describing the cold and exhaustion they felt, and the relief when he finally confessed. Then Boney and another farmer walked across the crater and back again, searching in the blazing sun for the body. But it was his description of that night of interrogation which I will never forget."

Louise shuddered. "When are we going to meet up with Paul and the others?" she asked. "I thought they were going to join us here."

"We'll see them later," said Caroline. "I don't think we've ever been all together, for the boys left home before Emily arrived. I'm looking forward to it – it's the main reason I've come on this safari."

"Now is my chance to work out the intricacies of your family," said Louise. "Yours must be a fascinating story."

"You must understand, that they are not my true family. Paul is my son. I became Sam's unofficial guardian after his mother, my best friend, died. Emily came along much later. She is not related to the others, although nobody knows who her father was. This is not unusual in Africa. Emily is the orphaned granddaughter of our house-girl, who came with Boney to the coast after he sold the farm. So I have three children who embody my ideal of Africa: a *mzungu* (white man), a *nusu-nusu* (a half-breed), and an African."

"And what about Sam's father?"

"He was a journalist who went missing, feared dead after the abortive coup of 1982. I'm afraid that was a traumatic time for us all."

The students cleared the tables and Chris stood over them.

"Sorry to interrupt you, ladies," he said. "But we must get moving. The others are waiting for you in Nakuru."

Chapter 17

Emily stretched and yawned widely, and as they topped a rise she gazed to her left at Lake Nakuru, its shores fringed with pink. They entered the town's expanded industrial area and the view was obliterated. The journey from Nairobi down the old escarpment had been more tortuous than usual, as they were stuck behind a slow-moving convoy of heavy lorries through the hairpin bends.

"I told you we should have taken the top road," Sam had grumbled.

"That's such a boring journey," said Paul. "I have to do it often on my safaris. It is quicker but more dangerous, as the traffic speeds along the new tarmac in both directions with no thought for anyone else."

It started to rain as they reached their meeting place in Nakuru. They dashed into the foyer of the hotel where the rest of the party were waiting. Emily headed straight for Caroline.

"How wonderful to see you again!" Emily gave her a big hug, and Caroline extracted herself with a laugh, holding her at arms' length.

"You get more beautiful every time I see you," she said. "Is it something to do with one of these two young men, I wonder?"

Emily was thankful that her dark skin did not show the blush she felt creeping over her face. She glanced at Sam as he enveloped Caroline in his arms, and their eyes met over her head. He winked, and a warm glow spread through her.

Caroline turned to greet Paul, and Emily stood at Sam's side, their shoulders brushing. He squeezed her hand. She closed her eyes, savouring the moment.

"I've ordered a second car for our visit to Lake Nakuru," announced Chris. "We'll go in convoy and I suggest we split the party into age groups."

Emily squeezed between Sam and Laura in the back seat of the hired car, while Paul sat up front beside the driver. They followed Chris through the industrial area towards the lake and stopped at the Park Entrance to present their tickets. Emily peered at the tall yellow thorn trees which crowded the narrow road. Several baboons swung through the branches and others gathered in a watchful group on the ground. She cringed as she studied the cheeky animals, glad that Sam and Laura were between her and the windows.

Chris opened the roof-hatch of his vehicle and signalled their driver to do the same.

"You can stand on the seats as we go along," the driver told them. "But it might be a bit of a squash if all four of you want to do that at the same time."

"I don't mind sitting down," said Emily quickly. She would feel vulnerable and exposed out there, and wasn't at all sure how she was going to enjoy the afternoon. They crawled past the baboons who reluctantly gave way, raising thin kinky tails and presenting their bare bottoms with rude haughtiness. They allowed the vehicles only just enough room to pass. Paul stood on the front seat and Laura poked her head through the roof behind him.

"Are you okay?" asked Sam as he crouched beside Emily, preparing to stand. "There's room for all of us if we keep still."

"No – I'm fine. I can see better through the windows now that you're both standing up."

She wriggled nearer to Sam's window and wound it up before pressing her face against the glass.

"I know what you're feeling," said Laura. "I was just the same in Shaba – until we came across some animals. You wait, it's so exciting, you'll forget all about the fear."

Emily wasn't convinced. The car rattled along the corrugated road behind Chris and the others, and there was nothing to see in the thick forest anyway.

"What are you looking for?" she asked the driver, who was scrutinising each tree as they came to it.

"Leopard," he said.

That made her feel more frightened. The driver increased speed through a clearing, and Sam's bare legs brushed against her as he struggled to keep his balance over the ruts. He lowered himself to sit beside her.

"We'll leave the others to keep a look out," he said, putting his arm round her shoulders. "Don't worry, you'll be safe with me."

She laughed, enjoying his closeness.

The car ahead stopped suddenly. Chris was pointing to a tree on his right, and David, Louise and Caroline stood in the hatch with binoculars raised.

"*Chui*," whispered the driver.

Emily slumped against Sam, a feeling of sheer terror paralysing her.

"Where?"

"There – on that branch sticking out to the left – that big tree. See?" he mouthed, pointing.

"I've got it!" Laura's excited voice sounded above Emily's head.

"Shusssh... You'll frighten it away. And don't move!"

Paul stiffened and focussed his binoculars. Sam stood on the seat again, trying to be as quiet as possible. Emily gazed through the closed window. She stared at the tree and identified the branch, but she could see no leopard. She didn't want to see a leopard. Suddenly, she sensed a movement; a stealthy shadow drifted faintly over the dappled branch, and the dapples disappeared.

Sam exhaled above her. "It's gone."

"Did you see it, Emily?" Laura sat down, quivering with excitement.

Emily nodded, catching her mood. "I think so." She felt better now that the animal had gone.

"You're very lucky," said the driver. "Even though there are lots of leopard in the park, not many people see them. They are more active at night."

He drove on, following Chris towards a large flat area of grass. Dirt tracks glistening with mud meandered to and fro. Beyond lay the shimmering waters of the soda lake. As they approached the flats, thousands of feeding flamingos paused, their heads raised.

The cars stopped, the group stared in wonder, and the strange birds resumed their scouring of the smelly water for algae, filtering it between the frills of their upside-down beaks. Wading in stately fashion on bright pink stilt-like legs and shedding feathers into the putrid grey filth, they emanated a shuddering crescendo of incessant murmurings.

A pod of pelicans performed a beautiful ballet with synchronised dives into the shallows. A pair of spoonbills shadowed them nearer the shoreline, swishing their bills from side to side to grab mouthfuls of fish.

"You can see they're spoonbills, Emily. Look at their beaks! Here – take my binoculars." Paul opened her door. "Come – there are other smaller waders too."

A tremendous flapping roar filled her ears, and the flamingos rose in flight, blotting out the sky. They whirled and swooped as she watched, then came back to rest in a clattering medley of sound and resumed their feeding thirty yards further into the lake.

Paul handed her out of the car. Emily took off her shoes and headed for the water, trying to get a closer look. She wasn't afraid of birds.

"I wouldn't do that if I were you, Emily," he said.

But it was too late. The slimy substance squidged between her toes and her feet sank deep into the mud. It hadn't looked that treacherous.

"I'm stuck!" she shouted, trying with arms flailing to keep her balance. Paul caught her before she fell and pulled her onto firmer ground, laughing. Her bare legs were covered with black, smelly sludge.

"You'll have a job washing that off when we get back," he said. "It will dry quickly into a hard white crust on your skin and itch like mad."

"White crust?"

"Yes – the soda, mixed with excreta and goodness knows what."

She tried to rub off the worst of the mud on the grass before getting back into the car, and placed her feet gingerly on the floor with an apologetic look at the driver. Sam had remained in the car. He inched away from her, holding his nose in mock aversion.

"Now you're most certainly not going be allowed to stand on the seat, Emily!"

She pulled a face, pretending to be devastated, and a feeling of sheer happiness pulsed through her.

Clouds were building up over the hill on the far side of the lake.

"We'll have a picnic lunch in Chui Camp at the far end of the park," said Chris. "We'd better get there before it rains."

A pair of Rothschild giraffe nibbling delicately at a thorn tree in a *donga* made them pause, and a herd of buffalo veered away from the track. The aggressive beasts turned to toss their massive horns and glare in hostile stance at this intrusion on their territory.

The convoy stopped in a grassy clearing. The twitter of birds and a soft sound of water falling replaced the clatter of the vehicles. The others gathered beneath a spreading tree, but Emily glanced fearfully at the thick bush surrounding them.

"Where are the buffalo?"

"There are no buffalo here," said Paul, handing her out of the car. "They only come to water early in the morning, and in the evenings."

The driver set out camp chairs and tables, and Chris heaved at a large cooler bag, emptying its contents. Paul strolled towards the sound of gushing water, binoculars dangling round his neck. Seeing him stiffen and stare intently into the bush, Emily followed. She touched his sleeve.

"It's a sunbird," he whispered. "See its bright red chest? Here – take my binos. Isn't it beautiful?"

The tiny bird flitted busily among the branches, but with

Paul's help she fixed on it for a brief moment and gasped in wonder at the iridescent feathers and intense red chest. It disappeared behind a twig and she handed back the binoculars. With the naked eye, she tracked its movements and it reverted to an insignificant flutter in the bush. She couldn't see any sign of red.

"Come."

She followed him to the far end of the clearing where the sound of falling water drowned the bird calls. Emily held back, remembering the last time they had stood beside a waterfall, when its thunderous roar and the sheer volume of the water had frightened her. Paul took her hand, cradling her arm against his, and gently led her forwards.

A little pool opened out before them, disappearing into a trickle through the bush. She raised her eyes to the cliff above. A soft skein of water fell lightly over dark rock between thick green foliage and chuckled into the pool at their feet.

This was more like it. Paul placed his arm around her shoulder and laid his head against hers as they watched the water. She felt safe and happy.

"There you are, you two! Lunch is ready – you'd better come while there's something left!"

Caroline was standing on the bank behind them. Paul handed Emily upwards, and she caught a friendly twinkle in Caroline's eyes and a faint nod of approval. Emily smiled back, hoping Caroline would not read too much into the scene beside the waterfall.

There was more than enough food to go round, and Emily hadn't realised how hungry she was. But Chris was packing up. He beckoned to the driver to put the chairs and tables into the vehicles, and gestured at the glowering clouds.

"You can finish your lunch in the car," he told her as he closed the roof hatches. They left the clearing and headed in convoy through the savannah towards the outline of Lion Hill.

The heavens opened. Heavy drops of rain thudded on the

roof and splattered against the windscreen. In an instant, visibility was reduced to a few yards and the track turned into a river. The vehicles slid and slipped, sometimes skidding sideways in the treacherous mud. Emily marvelled at the skill of the driver as his hands rapidly turned the wheel into the skid one way and then the other. Her sandwich fell to the floor. Louise and Sam were hanging grimly onto the hand straps. Emily clasped the seat in front, where Paul sat silently staring ahead.

The rain settled into a steady downpour. Bedraggled herds of dripping impala and gazelle stood with backs to the wind as they passed. A waterbuck raised its head, its thick grey fur an effective blanket against the weather. They came to an expanse of mud flats and Emily saw the lake again. Their driver turned off the track and led the way towards the shore line between banks of tufted grass. The car skidded out of control and she let out a squeal, thinking they would get well and truly stuck in the mud. Paul glanced back at her.

"The driver reckons the ground nearer the shore is firm," he said. "And I think he wants to show us something."

They were close to the lake and the car started to flounder. The driver spun the wheel back and forth, revving the engine. It looked to Emily as if he were going to take them right into the lapping waters.

"Stop!" shouted Laura. "We can't possibly go any further."

With a sigh of resignation, the driver complied. He focussed his binoculars through the windscreen towards a faint blob in the lake thirty yards away. A line of flamingos gave way to their left. The rain subsided into a heavy drizzle.

"What is it?"

Emily peered through the windscreen and Sam wound down his window, but quickly put it up again as the rain came in. The car steamed up and Paul wiped at the glass with his sleeve, trying to clear the view.

"It's a python," said the driver. "It's been trying to eat

that pelican for the past two days."

All Emily could see was a dark splodge in the water. Paul handed her his binoculars and she looked through the cleared window, trying to make out the thick coils of the snake. She saw the wide disjointed jaws half-smothering the body of a large white bird. Two pathetic webbed feet stuck out behind.

"It's swallowing the pelican head first."

The driver nodded.

Paul took off his shirt. He grabbed his camera and turned to Sam who followed suit.

"What are you doing?"

The two men got out of the car and Paul reached back for a towel, which he draped over the camera.

"You're absolutely crazy," said Laura. "And you'll catch your death of cold."

"We absolutely must take some photos," said Paul.

"And at least we can put on dry shirts when we get back," Sam explained.

"But the python…" Emily pictured them both being squeezed to death in the coils of the snake.

"It cannot do anything when it's swallowing its prey," said the driver. "It is completely helpless."

The rain hammered against the car. Emily couldn't see further than a few yards ahead and there was nothing she could do. She noticed her sandwich lying squashed on the floor.

"I think there are some leftovers in the box," said Laura, reaching over the seat into the boot of the car. "Here." She opened the lid and pulled out a pack of cooked meat. Emily munched on a chicken leg. The rain paused and she opened her window. Paul and Sam were on their way back, Paul carefully protecting his camera under the towel.

"Did you get good pictures?"

"I hope so."

She handed Sam a towel, and a weak sun glowed through an opening in the clouds. The men dried themselves vigorously before pulling on their shirts. Sam got into the car beside Emily, who inched away from him. He laughed, enveloped her with his arm and pressed her firmly against him, ensuring she shared his dampness, while Laura kept away from them both.

The following day more rain and mud awaited them after a tedious, bone-shaking journey westwards along atrocious roads through the tea country around Kericho. On the road towards Bomet they had a puncture. It was repaired by roadside mechanics, but delayed them further.

Two pillars stood in solitary grandeur astride a slippery track which could scarcely be called a road. Not even a fence demarcated the boundary of the Mara Game Reserve. Beyond, the track degenerated into a morass of gleaming black cotton soil, made worse by the onset of more rain.

The drivers wrestled with the wheels as they slid and slipped through the ruts, shifting from one set of tracks to another. Ominous clouds darkened the landscape, and thousands of wildebeest dotted the plains. Emily wanted to stop and marvel at this vast migration of animals, but dared not distract the driver. They had to get to camp before nightfall.

Ten hours after their departure from Nakuru, the cars pulled up. Glowing lanterns greeted them, and a delicious meal had been prepared, but all Emily wanted was to sleep. Her body, used to the swaying motion of the car for so long, teetered as she staggered out.

She and Laura shared a tent, but had to call the men to readjust the canvass so the zip could be closed against snakes. They finally dropped to sleep to the sound of snorts and grunts from hippo in the invisible river flowing a few yards beyond their feet.

A paradise of new experiences, punctuated by five-star meals over the next four days, blended into a rich collection of memories.

"That's Snaggletooth," said Chris, stopping the car beside two black-maned lions resting under a bush, bellies full. He pointed out the crooked tooth of the one nearest to them. "We heard them last night in camp."

They followed a lone lioness walking along the road, calling. A herd of zebra and topi crowded forward to get a better look, and then frisked away in fright when she turned her head towards them. She headed straight for an elephant with a tiny calf. The enormous beast faced the lioness in threatening mode, placing herself between the predator and her calf. The lioness stopped, changed direction and made a wide detour through the grass.

They enjoyed a picnic breakfast overlooking fire-burnt plains, and drove to the Mara river to see a dozen large crocodiles and numerous hippo basking, heads on each other's backs in the shallows.

"Look at that tiny baby!" exclaimed Laura. "It's just like a wood carving I saw in the Nairobi market."

On their penultimate day, as they were nearing the end of a game drive, Paul stiffened. What looked like a yellow piece of rope hung motionless from a tree. The driver manoeuvred the car so that everybody could stare at a dappled shape draped along the branch above.

He pointed higher up the tree. "There's a kill. It's a fresh one."

Paul trained his binoculars.

"I think it's a tommy," he whispered. "I can see the markings on its side."

The leopard looked at them, agitated.

"It wants to come down, but it's frightened," said Emily.

"Shusssssh."

A hyena appeared at the base of the tree, its heavy jaws salivating, waiting for morsels of meat to drop to the ground. The leopard looked at the scavenger and across to the vehicles, hesitating long enough for them to take more photos and videos. It glanced back up at the kill, then scrambled down the trunk, sidestepped the hyena in a couple of leaps, and bounded deep into the bush.

On the way to the airstrip the following morning, Emily stood in the roof hatch feasting her senses on the wide open spaces, picking out impala, giraffe and gazelle amongst the plains game, storing the sights in her memory. Sam, standing on the seat beside her, placed his arm round her shoulders.

"I'll never forget this holiday."

"Me neither," he whispered.

Their plane took off an hour later than scheduled, and they weren't allowed above a certain altitude because the Kenya Air Force was practicing for a public holiday.

"We have so many public holidays," groaned Paul. "No wonder nothing works properly in Kenya."

The flight through the clouds was unbelievably bumpy, and they all made use of the brown paper bags provided.

"Such a waste of a good breakfast," Emily said, pulling a face at Paul across the aisle, the greenish tinge to his face betraying his discomfort.

"Work tomorrow," he said before holding back as his stomach heaved. "And then we have the elections to face; not that we're expecting any problems."

"No," said Sam, sitting by the window on Emily's other side. "Kenya has learned her lesson, thank goodness."

Chapter 18

Ouma sits brooding through the window, staring with unseeing eyes at the figure of Sister Brigid stooped over a straggle of maize plants in the patch of ground outside. The boys are at high school, so she has taken over the garden and introduced home-grown vegetables for the hospital. Bean and marrow plants grow in between the maize alongside a bed of drooping cabbages, their leaves pricked with holes. She has a never-ending battle with the *dudus,* and insecticides only provide temporary relief.

But his mind is far away from the scene at his doorstep. What is his country coming to? How can it happen that shining hope and confidence in the future has shattered in the space of a few days?

The elections were conducted peacefully enough, as everybody proudly expected, and President Kibaki has won a second term. But murmurings of discontent are rumbling beneath the surface. It is not untoward. After all, it has been a hard-fought battle between the two main factions, and it is only natural that the losers should lick their wounds and harbour feelings of resentment.

But this?

All hell has been let loose.

In the aftermath the people have awoken to insane violence which leaves 1,500 dead. What is happening? Why have ordinary citizens living and working together suddenly gone berserk and started killing each other? It doesn't make sense; it is politics at its dirtiest. Are the opposition infiltrating thugs into government party areas to seek vengeance? Or is it the other way round? Rumours fly. Dissidents are trucked into regions round the country to cause havoc. They pop up in pockets of unrest, only to melt away, leaving the villagers shying away from each other in distrust. The strife escalates. People leave their livelihoods to re-group, and the dreaded word *tribalism* lies unspoken in their hearts.

The media, of which Ouma is now a part, rush all over the country, fanning the flames of havoc and dissent in their desire to chase down the latest conflagration and report it, complete with comment from anyone they can grab to say a few unthinking words. He reads of families fleeing rape and pillage, of villages burned down, of people killed. He fears for the boys, and his people in Amayoni.

Kenya is on the brink of a step back into chaos. The country holds its breath. We cannot degenerate into the terror of the Emergency. Surely we have learned from past lessons? Can somebody, somehow, talk sense into my people?

Ouma has only words. Cannot somebody do something? Pockets of conflagration flair in different places. Politicians work behind the scenes, tempered by unobtrusive mediation from overseas. Nobody wants Kenya to descend into civil war, but evil forces are at work.

An uneasy peace is brokered and a coalition government formed. To everyone's relief, reason prevails. President Kibaki agrees to power-share with his enemy, opposition leader Prime Minister Odinga, and multi-party politics is introduced.

Ouma wonders. If his country cannot survive the practice of healthy adversarial government, normal in the developed world, how can it hope to run itself as an efficient coalition? He fears for his people whose nascent instinct is an undemocratic attitude of survival of the fittest and winner-takes-all. His misgivings are compounded when the government fails to hold an investigation into the violence, and rampant corruption breaks through the surface like an ugly sore. The income from former President Moi's ill-gotten gains in vast overseas holdings is suspected of having supported Kibaki, but the report is suppressed and left to simmer below the encrusted surface.

People creep back to their former occupations eyeing each other warily, and it is a long time before there is again the semblance of peaceful co-existence. It is not helped by periodic threats from the International Criminal Court, and vain calls for witnesses to show themselves and speak out against the criminals who caused the chaos.

And who are the criminals?

Ouma asks himself, will this really mean peace? What he does know is that trust will remain a distant hope long after the power-hungry politicians have patched their relationships with monetary deals. Family lives have been disrupted in the villages, and friendships broken. It will be years before his country can recover its fragile harmony, if ever, but he must not fear the worst. History will show.

And there's always hope, he tells himself, as he turns his attention to the article he is preparing for a new series in the national newspaper.

Chapter 19

Louise has been in touch again. The sponsors' visit to Amayoni, planned over the past year, is finally coming to fruition. Is the time right, she asks Ouma in a letter – is it safe for them to come? She doesn't want to disappoint the half-dozen people who have been looking forward to their adventure. It has taken so long to come to this stage, and she fears more delay will jeopardise the project.

Ouma writes saying that an uneasy truce has been called, and the people, though still in shock, are repairing the damage and looking to the future. Her visit will renew their vigour and offer further hope. She must not cancel.

He ponders over Louise's ideas. She says a charity can bypass the red-taped government-to-government aid, which is vulnerable to corruption. Ordinary villagers need the most help, and it is best to receive it at grass roots level. The more he thinks about it, the more is he inclined to reconsider this approach which his people have for decades suspiciously associated with colonial missionaries. He must keep an eye on developments elsewhere, for Grass Shoots is not the only project in the country which seeks to experience the joy of giving at village level.

The problem is that each pocket of optimism is isolated. Perhaps that is the source of its hope? The villagers take responsibility for their own development until they can move on. It is a slow, fragile process, for mistakes are made and progress hindered.

It is tempting for large organisations to take short cuts and specialise by building schools and medical centres in different places throughout the country. Their work is good, but the areas in which they operate remain backward, and the gap grows between the haves and the have-nots.

He senses a quickening in his country. Dare he think it? A stirring of maturity, coupled with resentment against their leaders, who focus on the heady power of politics and the wealth it can bring. Corruption. An evil recognised by all.

Ouma addresses the blank sheet of paper in front of him. He's always preferred the physical act of putting pen to paper for the first draft. The framework for his new series takes shape, and he has a deadline to meet.

Chapter 20

Louise and David finalised their plans to visit Amayoni with the six original donors. The charity now had an office which extended over the downstairs floor of a building in Belton High Street. Louise liaised with the Kakamega Forest Lodge for accommodation. Email was the best method of communication, but mobile phones were more common now. She marvelled at the low price of communication in Kenya, and encouraged her contacts in the village to ring or text her, rather than the other way round. It was much cheaper.

Dates were fixed, but travel arrangements remained a headache. It made sense to organise a group booking, and there were questions about inoculations, visas and baggage as well as insurance. The donors didn't want just to see their children, they wanted to do something. What could they bring with them? Pens? Books? Uniforms?

"No!" emailed Maria from Amayoni. "We've got those here, although appropriate books would be welcome. Kenya isn't that backward, and the country does produce the basics. What we need is much more fundamental."

"What?"

There was so much, Maria wrote. And where to start? The election violence had left homes flattened, and the village community centre was a heap of ashes. The best thing the volunteers could do would be to help build new homes and repair the damaged ones, leaving the people free to fetch water, provide food, and look after their children. Absenteeism was a problem at the school; sometimes because the children were needed to guard the animals and fetch water, but more often because they were sick.

"Why are they sick?" queried Louise.

"Malaria."

It was the most frequent explanation for absences from school, and Louise wondered if it covered a multitude of illnesses. But malaria was not to be trifled with. Louise Googled it. The region around Kisumu and Lake Victoria was rife with the disease. The cause was the female anopheles mosquito, which passes the infection from person to person as it sucks their blood. They emerge in the evenings, and the best way to combat the deadly disease is to protect the people at night.

Mosquito nets.

"Do they make mosquito nets in Kenya?" asked Louise.

"Yes, but the material is no good. It tears easily. And the nets are expensive."

A sponsor volunteered to look for durable netting which they could bring with them as a trial, and Maria would find someone in the village to make the nets. Did they have sewing machines?

Louise wondered at the enormity of the task before them. How much could six people accomplish in one week?

They arrived at Jomo Kenyatta Airport with an excited group of English visitors who had never before set foot in Africa. Louise breathed in the hot humid air as she stepped onto the tarmac, and removed her sweater. There was not a cloud in the sky. She waited for the volunteers at the foot of the aeroplane steps and they walked to the terminal. She turned on her mobile phone. Paul had messaged her. He was outside with a minibus. She smiled. Such a nice man, and their finances were safe with him.

Louise and David claimed their baggage and waited near the customs tables for the remainder of the party. A mass of waving placards faced them in the arrivals hall. Paul stood near the car hire booths at the back, waving. A white minibus awaited them.

"The driver will take you to the Fairview Hotel for rest and refreshments," Paul told her. "Then you will go straight to Kakamega. You'll not get there until after dark, I'm afraid, but you're in capable hands and on the latter part of the journey there will be no traffic."

On the way into Nairobi, Louise noticed a row of roadside buildings bizarrely exposing their innards, complete with furnishings. They looked as if they'd been cut in two.

"What has happened here?" she asked the driver.

"Those buildings were illegally erected on the road reserve many years ago. The owners ignored notices to move, so the contractors for the new highway just cut along the demarcation line. You can see they've started clearing on the other side as well."

Louise stared at the brutal chaos around her, and remembered John, the taxi driver on her previous visit, who had boasted about the coming new highways.

The road down the Rift Valley escarpment was a nightmare of speeding traffic and dangerous driving. They took the bottom road and stopped at a viewpoint to stretch their legs. The volunteers gasped in amazement. The Great Rift Valley disappeared into the haze of the afternoon sun, the outline of the volcano Mount Longonot rising in stark contrast from the plains below. A clamouring group of vendors, with wood carvings and trinkets, swooped round them like vultures.

"You'll have plenty of opportunity to buy at Amayoni," Louise warned her friends, leading them back to the minibus. "The goods will be cheaper there, and your money will go to the project."

She steeled herself for the hazardous drive down the narrow serpentine road to the valley floor. Their driver was careful, but he had no control over the vehicles coming from the opposite direction, or the speeding *matatus* bent on passing them dangerously close to a bend, and more than once he had to veer onto the rough verge to avoid a collision. By the time they reached Nakuru, the passengers were pale-faced and quiet. They scarcely responded to the spectacular sight of the soda lake fringed with pink flamingos as they approached the town for a welcome tea break, and applauded the driver to express relief when they arrived.

"We've passed the worst of the journey," David told them. "There's little traffic on the next leg as we climb into the Mau hills on the west side of the Rift Valley. We should arrive at the lodge in time for dinner."

The great blue turaco was not in evidence. Indeed, Louise had not seen it since her first visit to Amayoni, and the undergrowth no longer seemed so dense.

"More people are living in the forest now," the manager told her over breakfast at the lodge. "They cut down the trees for charcoal and clear the ground to plant their *shambas*. We can't do anything about it. The politicians in Nairobi allowed it in exchange for votes. People go to live in the forest every day. And you'll find a change in Amayoni."

His words were ominous, but she was not prepared for the extent of the change when she and David led the party of volunteers into the village the following day.

Maria greeted them, seeming to have shrunk in stature since their last meeting. Previously there had been extreme poverty, but the people were filled with hope and laughter. Now, the people failed to look her in the eye. A toddler stood at the door of Maria's home, his face encrusted with flies. On impulse, Louise snatched up the thin body and held him close, wiping at his eyes with the hem of her dress, and smearing away the snot with her hand. His loud cries of anguish made her wince. She put him down.

"I'm sorry, Maria. I should have thought…"

"No matter, Louise, he has been through a lot since you were here last."

Maria called into the house for her elder daughter to see to the child. Why was the girl not at school?

The visitors shuffled in embarrassment, wide-eyed with pity and a touch of horror.

There was worse to come. Maria led them through a maze of narrow passages between derelict huts, many singed by fire. Some were reduced to pathetic piles of ash, and stone or brick buildings stood starkly empty, their walls gaping into a roofless sky.

"How did this happen, Maria?"

"The elections. I told you about the violence, and you must have heard in the press about the fighting and terror afterwards?"

"Of course you told me, but I never imagined... Who —?"

"We don't know how it happened. People who didn't belong to the village – suddenly everybody started fighting. Friends were frightened to stand up for each other. And a lot of villagers ran away. They haven't come back. Our friends haven't come back." Maria hung her head. "We are sorry and ashamed that this has happened."

Louise had read about the elections of the year before, and the widespread ethnic violence which followed. The world had held up its hands in horror and despair. And then something else had hit the world headlines, and Kenya was forgotten.

It was Louise's turn to feel ashamed. "I didn't realise Amayoni had suffered so much."

"We wanted to spare you the anguish, Louise. We're trying to make things better. The children you and your friends are sponsoring are doing well at school. You'll meet them tonight. And those who are left are coming to terms with life, but it is hard."

That was an understatement, thought Louise, as they continued their tour of the village. A few signs of rejuvenation were visible. They came to a cluster of newly-plastered huts, and a shy young mother no more than fifteen years old, with a child clinging to her skirt, offered a limp hand and a hopeful smile in greeting. Louise noticed that the roofs were made of tin.

"They have used the tin from the houses of the people who have run away," explained Maria. "There was no grass left to make the thatch."

A small gathering waited for them in the church hall.

This had escaped the devastation, although stains of blood showed on the floor where terrified families had sought refuge. Maria pointed out a large blot in front of the altar.

"We have scrubbed and scrubbed," she said. "But it never goes. We will never, ever let that happen again. Such senseless, evil violence against innocent women and children."

Maria introduced the sponsors to their children, shy smiling faces scrubbed clean and glowing with gratitude and happiness. The girls proudly wore spotless blue uniforms, and the boys were in khaki shorts and long grey socks. The hall buzzed with chatter as the visitors recognised their protégés from the photos they had been sent. They exclaimed at the tightness of the plaited hair, pulled smartly across the heads of the girls. It must have taken hours of painstaking dedication to achieve such perfection. The children smiled shyly, careful in their behaviour and nibbling politely at the European finger foods. Louise noticed grimaces of distaste as the younger ones took hasty bites and then tried to hide their dismay at the unfamiliar taste. Even the fizzy soft drinks were left half-consumed.

Maria called everyone to order, and the children sat quietly on the floor while Louise and her friends were shown to their seats on a platform in front of the altar. The village priest prayed for guidance over the proceedings which followed.

He formally welcomed the sponsors, and Maria introduced a new *Mia Moja* scheme. The Grass Shoots Charity would give the sum of one hundred pounds to each volunteer, to spend on a project mutually agreed with their designated family. The project, which would benefit the whole family, must be implemented within the course of the week while the sponsors were present.

"We have explained to our friends from the UK that we don't have small families like those in Europe. Our children whose mothers have died of AIDS, or whose fathers have gone away, are taken in by their aunts or their grandparents..."

"Ehhhh!" A ripple of enthusiastic assent spread through the building.

"...And the burden of feeding and educating the extended families is impossible to bear, especially when sickness strikes."

An even louder murmur rose among the people. The faces of the children glowed with hope.

The buzz of excitement grew as Maria explained the procedures and handed out money to each sponsor. She had spent time with the families, exploring ideas such as mosquito nets, mattresses, school uniforms, repairing houses, or even providing a pig or a cow to those committed to learning how to look after them. But the final decision rested between the family and the volunteer. Over the course of the week they would come to know each other, and hopefully reach wise conclusions.

Louise expected the exercise to help her volunteers appreciate the fundamental difficulties facing the villagers. It was a concept she was only recently beginning to grasp. The difference between the simple needs of a remote African village, and the complexity of modern western life, was vast.

While the volunteers worked on the *Mia Moja* project, Louise sat in on assessment meetings conducted by Maria. One AIDS orphan needed sponsoring through school. Maria brought out a check-list of questions which she had composed in consultation with the project leaders. The boy's aunt wore a welcoming smile and what was obviously her best dress of much-washed yellow material.

"I don't normally warn the families when I come to see them," Maria told Louise. "But this time I had to get permission for you to be here."

Louise sat with Maria on the bed, which she learned was shared at night by three small children. The boy's aunt squatted on the bare floor at their feet. There was no other furniture in the room, and Louise wrinkled her nose at the smell of urine which tainted the air. As the interview progressed, she shifted uneasily, conscious of a growing wetness seeping up from the blanket beneath her. Bed-wetting was a common occurrence, Maria had told her, as the children felt insecure and unwanted. Louise made a mental note to suggest that future gifts might include waterproof mattress covers.

The name of the child was confirmed, his date of birth compared with his stated age, and his level at school. Then the aunt's details were required. How old was she? Did she have a partner? How many children had she given birth to? How many had survived? Louise wondered what the woman thought of these intrusive questions, but there was no sign of reluctance in the answers. And Maria had assured her that it was necessary to double-check, to avoid future confusion.

There was so much to think about. Louise was grateful that Maria had such a good grasp of what was required, leaving her and David to grapple with the administrative problems of bringing the villagers and the volunteers together. Maybe it was time to think about delegating more tasks. Neither of them were getting any younger.

Chapter 21

Ouma greets Louise when she comes back from Amayoni, and quizzes her about the effect of the election violence. She is able to allay his fears about his family.

"Ruth is bearing up stoically, and Maria and Naomi are getting on with their lives," she tells him. "Maria is a tower of strength to the project, but there's so much to do, as everything has taken a backward step. We have to start from scratch again, and rebuild, but the volunteers are full of ideas, and looking forward to coming back. Hopefully, we won't lack for material help for some time to come. I want to introduce regular visits three times a year. Having the lodge nearby is convenient, and we need to make an agreement with them. We also want to encourage school trips. It will do our children good to see how those in Africa have to live. We're spoilt in England, with our material possessions and amusements, and I'm sure there'll be many life-changing experiences."

"Did you see Ken and the boys while you were there? They don't bother to communicate with me now."

"Briefly. The twins are near the end of their school days, and Maria has been encouraging Ken to expand the brick-making business, with guidance from Joram. You remember I told you about the teacher at the Mission School?"

Ouma nods.

"There'll be plenty of work if Ken goes about it the right way. David had a meeting with him before we left. He's an ambitious young man."

Ouma lets Louise chatter on while he allows his mind to wander.

He feels his life in Nairobi lacks meaning. He knows that

Jackson has retired from the Museum, but hasn't heard from him for some time. He wonders about Simaloi, and the cave of his ancestors. Louise and David do not have any contact with that side of his family, and even though the country has embraced the use of the mobile phone with astonishing alacrity, the new technology has left the older generations behind. He doesn't even have Maria's number.

What good is he doing, really, with his newspaper articles, fuelled by occasional reports from Maina and Musumba on the Somali problem and the Indian Ocean piracy which has been hitting the headlines? Handicapped as he is, he cannot hope to compete with able-bodied international reporters. Not that he wants that; he's too old. It's a sobering thought. And does anybody even read his philosophical pieces? Going by press reports, there's been no improvement in corruption, or any lessening of greed in Kenya's acquisitive society.

There is a pause in Louise's chatter. She is regarding him with amusement, waiting for an answer to a question, probably.

"You haven't heard a word I've been saying, have you, Ouma?"

He apologises profusely, pleading deafness and old age.

"I'm just as old as you are, remember! But I must admit David and I need to delegate more. Our daughter Laura is ready to take on greater responsibilities at home, and Maria and Emily are the backbone of the project in Amayoni. We're very lucky. I guess we just don't want to let go."

"And why should you, Louise?"

"I know, but the long plane journeys and the stress of trying to organise everything does take its toll."

"You love it really. Go on…admit it!"

They both laugh.

"It's time I left," she says. "Look after yourself, Ouma. You have a comfortable little place here with the nuns, but I guess it might not last for ever. Sister Brigid must be ready to retire to Ireland."

It is as if she's been reading his thoughts.

PART III

2009-2015

Kenya's new Constitution limits Presidential powers and grants devolution to the regions. In 2011, Kenya suffers the worst drought in 60 years.

The ICC facilitates a Truth Commission, paving the way to Mau Mau veterans claiming damages, and Britain apologising for torture in the detention camps.

Somalis raid Kenya's coast, and Kenya retaliates. Somali piracies in international waters peak, and the refugee camp in Dadaab on the border with Kenya continues to grow.

Uhuru Kenyatta narrowly wins the Presidential election against Raila Odinga in 2013, and Al Shabaab terrorists attack the Westgate Shopping Mall in Nairobi.

Chapter 22

Poor, battered Kenya.

While the west shouts and screams at international terrorists and vows bitter revenge, her people bow their heads, pick each other up and carry on. They have demanded recompense from Britain for its past sins during the Mau Mau emergency. Ouma watches while the world gnashes its teeth in futile objections against this humbling of Great Britain, which might lead to a succession of similar demands, and he smiles. In war, nobody escapes punishment.

But he needs to stay in touch with his roots. The barrage of current affairs and crises is clouding his judgement. The confines of his hidey-hole with Sister Brigid and her hospital are suffocating him, and the boys are no longer here to keep him anchored.

The last time he spoke to Jackson, who is now retired with the family in Kakamega, his brother expressed a wish to be with his ancestors in the cave overlooking Lake Magadi. It is time to go there again. Ouma is stronger now, his depression kept firmly in its place. The new prosthesis is part of him, blending into his limb and allowing him to walk with the ease of constant use. He flexes his leg muscles, remembering the agony when he last left that cave, the stumbling trek down the mountain through the arid plains, gritting his teeth at the pain, the frequent stops and the enormous effort to get going again.

This time, he will make the journey comfortable for Jackson. It will be tough transporting his brother across that terrain, and it needs people more able-bodied than he. Simaloi, the latest in the family of sorcerers, is ready to take up her duties at the cave, but he needs at least one other person. It has to be someone trusted, part of the family.

Sam, his son, is the obvious choice.

His mind cringes away from the idea. He let Sam down, abandoned him a few short years after that joyful day when, thanks to Caroline, they met in the grounds of the museum.

No wonder Sam is full of resentment at being kept in the dark over the disaster which befell Ouma during the attempted coup of 1982. Reconciliation will be complicated and difficult, for Ouma doesn't know how or why he should take the blame for what happened in the aftermath of that uprising.

He tells himself he is stronger now, both physically and mentally, and these things must be resolved. More pleasant thoughts are of Ruth and his daughters, Sam's half-sisters Maria and Naomi in Amayoni.

Preparations don't take long. All he has to do is gather a change of clothes into a bundle, and inform Sister Brigid. He will leave tomorrow.

He shrinks into an insignificant huddle in the rear corner of the *matatu* which takes him up-country. It is crammed with people and their chattels, and he closes his eyes as the vehicle travels on the wrong side of the road to avoid potholes. He can do nothing about it.

Night has fallen when the car leaves him at the junction to Kericho, a hundred and thirty miles north of Nairobi. Carrying his bundle, he stumbles towards a roadside shack and settles down, pulling a thin blanket round his shoulders. It takes time to get used to the stillness and the silence, and the biting cold of the highlands penetrates his bones. He sets his mind against such distractions and wills himself into a deep sleep.

The thin light of dawn creeps over him. He opens an eye and massages the stiffness out of his neck. Jackson steps from a clapped-out car and greets him. His brother has shrunk in size since he last saw him, and there is little flesh on the frail bones. But his eyes are bright.

"You shouldn't have slept out last night, Ouma. Why didn't you send word?"

Ouma smiles. Why should he bother to send word, when the African bush telegraph and mutual intuition does the job far better? Jackson smiles knowingly back.

"You knew I was coming."

Jackson nods.

"Simaloi?"

Jackson shakes his head, and Ouma understands. He knows his brother has the strong vision of a seer, concealed beneath the veneer of academia. It will be good to commune in this alternative world for a while, to feel the touch of his roots and allow his own gift some freedom. For how else could he have known that Jackson was ready to go to the cave, and needed his help to get there? As Ouma takes a seat in the ramshackle car, the thought occurs to him that his brother may not be aware of this imminent event.

Ouma greets the younger Simaloi in her hut, surrounded by the chattels of her calling as the village sorcerer. Jackson follows behind, and Ouma sees this knowledge flash in her sombre eyes. But she has another message.

"You're going to see your family while you're here?" she asks. "Sam is with them."

"Yes. Perhaps it is a good time for you to talk to each other," says Jackson. "You need to reconcile."

Things are moving too fast for Ouma.

"Wait a minute," he declares. "I've only just arrived, I need a break, and I came to see you first. There'll be time enough to visit Ruth later."

"But Sam—"

The vibes from Jackson and Simaloi are strong in their silence.

"How do you know Sam is there? And why all this urgency…?" Ouma's words falter as he faces his implacable relatives, then with a sigh he succumbs. "Tomorrow?"

They nod in acceptance. The tension disappears and the family gathers round to exchange news. Food is lovingly prepared, the children come forward, and the men retire to relax and chat far into the night. There is a strange look about Jackson as he sips at his home-brewed beer, and Ouma discerns a paleness in the skin around his eyes. He locks gaze with Simaloi, and understanding flashes between them. Their beloved brother is not long for this world.

Ouma would rather stay here, but at their bidding he steels himself for tomorrow. He's not prepared. How is he going to handle Sam? What is he going to say?

On his way to Amayoni he remembers Ken. Turning onto the track leading to the high school, he stops at the new brick-making factory.

A dozen women are labouring in the mud, slopping the red stuff into pre-prepared moulds and passing them on to others for setting in rows to dry in the sun. Another group extracts dried bricks from their cases and lays them in piles, ready for sale.

He goes towards a hut in the centre of the open-air factory, and Ken rises from his desk to greet him.

"Ouma – it's you! I'd heard you were coming."

Ken has filled out, and he exudes an air of importance. Gone is the sly ragamuffin and thief of Nairobi days.

"Sales are good. Soon this village will turn into one of bricks and mortar."

Ken calls out to the supervisor of the team stacking the newly-formed bricks. "Come here, Joseph – let's show Ouma round our factory!"

Joseph has also changed. Ouma marvels at how a boy can grow into a young man in such a short time.

"I left school this year," he says. "I don't want to go on for further studies when there's money to be made in business – do you blame me?"

Ouma understands his desire, knowing that although Joseph is reliable and loyal by nature, he lacks Ken's intelligence. But he can't help thinking that Ken's talents are wasted in this remote place.

"Joseph will take over the running of the factory when he's learned every side of it," says Ken. "And I'm already talking to builders. All they need is me to organise them into a viable contracting business, and we can upgrade the whole region."

Ouma nods, regarding Ken with respect.

"And then, who knows, we may even buy some land, build on it and sell the houses. Just think – a whole construction empire from start to finish! You didn't know that Louise sponsored me through a business course when I left school?"

Ouma didn't know. What else doesn't he know, he wonders, looking at the humble beginnings of the brick factory and trying to envision the future through Ken's eyes. What it is to be young. The boys don't need him anymore; it is a good thing, but he can't help feeling sad.

"The twins?"

"They can join us if they wish when they leave school in a couple of years' time. Our ready-made family will stay together, maybe, and prosper."

"Who knows?"

There is a shout from the stacked wall of bricks, and Joseph turns aside to investigate.

Ken leads Ouma back to his office, hesitates, and offers him a cup of tea. But Ouma sees that his former protégé is anxious to return to the papers on his desk.

"No, thank you, Ken." He shakes hands. "I have another meeting to go to, and I'm already late." He wipes his eye. "It's good to see you doing well and looking forward to a bright future." He opens his arms, and the men embrace.

Ouma returns along the way he came and doesn't let himself look back. Ruth's home is a long walk away, and he must find transport to take him there. But he needs sustenance before facing his son. Why is Sam visiting Ruth?

The temptation to join the men idling outside the beer hall is too great. That is the trouble in his country. The women scrape a living at home, spending days cultivating meagre crops from the scorched earth and fetching water for their families, which increase every year. And men make more babies from other women in other villages, get drunk and talk about finding work. They think up excuses and look for the easy way out, and the women bear the burden of bringing up the children. Ouma knows he shouldn't generalise; he should be ashamed of himself. There are exceptions, and Ken is one of them.

He drains his bottle and steps aside to signal towards a bank of motorised bikes on bare ground at the junction of two tracks. These *boda bodas* have appeared from nowhere, overrunning the country in the space of a few years. They are cheap means of transport, faster than a bicycle and a way for the less lazy of men to earn a few shillings at a time.

One pulls away from the parking area, its rider wearing a flamboyant yellow jacket and green beret, and with a flourish and a spin of wheels draws up beside Ouma. He levers himself stiffly over the seat behind the driver. The tortuous ride rattles the breath out of his body, and banishes all thought but the grim necessity to hang on. He is a shattered bundle of nerves when he finally eases his aching limbs off the machine in front of Ruth's home.

Maria comes to greet him, holding out both hands.

His good leg buckles under him, and the prosthesis cannot compensate. He goes down heavily, thinking he's put on weight over the years and this will be painful.

The world goes blank.

Chapter 23

Sleep, blessed sleep, and a peaceful blackness surround him. Faint voices sound, laughter and the rustle of movement in the background. He doesn't open his eyes, but tries to will himself back into oblivion.

A blanket is tweaked over him and a hand lightly touches his brow. Is that a kiss he feels brushing gently on his cheek? His lips widen into a faint smile and he turns his body away from the dim flicker of light which glimmers behind his closed eyelids.

There is a feeling of freedom in his right leg as he brings it over. Somebody has removed the prosthesis. The vague thought is lost as he sinks into a deeper sleep.

Chapter 24

"What made him want to come here in such a hurry, I wonder – and on a *boda boda* of all things? I could have sent the project car to collect him if he'd only asked," said Maria as she slapped a pot of deliciously-seasoned groundnut stew on the table.

Emily helped herself to a portion of mashed beans and sweet potatoes to go with the stew, and savoured the rich spices. Her hand brushed against Sam's as she reached for a second mouthful. She smiled at him as the vibrancy between them came to life, but he didn't respond. His eyes were troubled, his mouth a firm line across his face.

"I didn't know he'd lost his leg," was all he said.

"Nor did we, until he came to see us not all that long ago," said Ruth. "We didn't even know he was alive."

"He must have suffered so much, all these years," said Emily. "I wonder why he didn't contact you earlier, Ruth. After all, you are his family."

Sam shifted uncomfortably beside her, and she put an understanding hand on his knee, remembering his former angry words against his father.

"I can answer that question," said Ruth. "We were estranged, and it was my fault. I ran away after our baby son died. I brought you, Maria, with Naomi back here." Ruth turned away, and Maria tried to console her, but Ruth shrugged her off. "You have to know," she said. "I lost the will to live and remained in depression for a long time. Your grandmother looked after you both. I refused to speak to Charles whenever he came to see me. I suppose he gave up in the end."

"And then he discovered me."

Sam's words hung between them, and Emily held her breath. She could sense a new awakening in this man she was growing to love more as the months went by, but there was something wrong. Perhaps it was her own hang-up over sex, but she felt that he was also troubled. Sam had a mission and a sense of urgency. His work at the museum filled his life, sometimes at the expense of their relationship, and he harboured a deep resentment against his father. She had never summoned the courage to ask why.

She reached for a second helping and they ate in silence. Sam wiped his mouth on his sleeve, and went to stand over the sleeping form of his father.

"My mother was Caroline's best friend," he said, returning to the family circle. "I can't remember much about her, as I was young when she died. But Caroline took me on, and Paul and I were brought up as brothers." Sam jutted his chin over his shoulder towards Ouma. "Caroline had promised my mother not to tell him of my existence. But when Jomo Kenyatta died, she changed her mind."

Sam stopped, and held his head in his hands. He stayed sitting in silence while they cleared away the meal. The afternoon sun penetrated the room and he looked at his watch.

"It's time for me to go," he said, "or I won't be any good at work tomorrow morning."

Emily went with him to the car and he held her close for a goodbye kiss.

"Isn't life wonderful," he said, "the way you've ended up here in the same village as my half-sisters."

"And I've never been happier, Sam, I'm doing the work I've always dreamed of, and it is bringing me closer to you. You'll come and see us often, won't you, especially now that your father is here?"

"I don't know about my father. We enjoyed a few good years before he disappeared; I thought we'd become close. I can't think why he didn't contact me. He must have suffered greatly and I could have helped him…"

Sam hugged her closely, got into the car, and Emily

watched him disappear into the night.

Her love for him had undergone a subtle change over the past year. It was no less intense, but had developed from the original disturbing sexual attraction into a deeper, almost filial feeling of harmony and understanding.

Chapter 25

The stillness and the silence penetrate his mind. Ouma stirs, tuning in to his surroundings. He is facing a rough brick wall, a thin blanket draped over his body. He senses a vacuum below his right knee, and wonders where they've put his prosthesis. Is there a stick nearby which he can use? Can he even get up? He is alone in the house.

He stretches, flexing his muscles one by one down the length of his body while his eyes grow accustomed to the dim light. His right arm aches near the elbow. He turns gingerly onto one side and winces, then quickly falls onto his back to wait for the pain to subside. Carefully he raises his left leg, flexes his knee and wiggles his toes. He lifts his stump from the hip, gently testing the joint, grateful that it moves at his bidding, although he is reminded of the pain. He raises his head and turns it from side to side. No problem there. He can see to the other side of the room now, beyond the half-closed curtain round him. But his eyelids close and he sinks back to sleep.

By midday he needs to empty his bladder. There is a movement nearby and Ruth comes to his side with a crutch as he manoeuvres to sit on the edge of the bed, protecting the pain in his buttock. Remembering the time when he broke his hip when hit by a car on the streets of Nairobi, he is thankful this is only a bruise.

"Where did you get the crutch?" he asks.

"Maria's boys made it," she says. "I've sent for yours from Simaloi. I told her what happened. She doesn't expect you back until you're better."

"There's nothing wrong with me," he says, levering himself up. He hops a few paces, but the movement irritates the bruise. His stump is tender to touch, and he knows that wearing the prosthesis will be impossible until it heals.

Ruth ministers to his needs while he indulges in a period of rest and recuperation.

His grandsons haven't forgotten his parting challenge when he was last here. "How do you like the crutches we made, *kuka*? We've been practising, and we're ready to race you!"

Ouma laughs, ruffling the tight curls on their heads. "You'll beat me easily, I know. I'm too old for such things now."

He jots down thoughts in a notebook. Maria tells him that Louise will arrive in three weeks' time, and perhaps he can stay here at least until she comes.

He is intrigued by the concept of the Grass Shoots Charity and what they are trying to achieve. What makes the English want to spend time and money on a poor village like Amayoni, when there is no obvious benefit for themselves? It would make a good topic for his newspaper column. And if he digs deep, he might uncover a motive.

He quizzes Maria in the evenings when she returns from work, and she shares with him the everyday problems and activities of the project. As his bruise heals and his confidence in using the prosthesis increases, he goes with her to the office and makes suggestions regarding administration, for her work entails a mountain of record-keeping.

"Follow-up is the key to the success of the project," she tells him. "I have to report everything to the sponsors, for those people in the UK are anxious for news of the children they sponsor, and they want ideas on how to help the families further."

Ouma doesn't fully understand her reasoning.

"Why don't you come with me when I do my assessments?" she says. "I use a basic questionnaire, which probably needs amendment. Circumstances are always changing, and you could help with that. We don't just offer free schooling; sometimes we help the grandparents who are left to look after orphaned children. It's difficult to decide what is best for each family, and of course the wishes of the donor also need addressing. There is a fine line between people pulling in different directions, and we don't always get it right."

"It sounds intriguing, Maria. I might as well help while I'm here."

"You'll want to see what Emily is doing at the project as well."

"Emily – I've seen her around this past fortnight, and our paths crossed briefly in Nairobi. But who is she, and where does she come from?"

"She's another protégé of Caroline – didn't you know? After Paul and Sam left home, Caroline took on Emily. She's the reason why we see so much of Sam nowadays. He arrives like clockwork every fortnight. Mother is hoping that she and Sam will eventually marry, but sometimes I think Emily is more comfortable in Paul's company."

"Why do you say that?"

"I don't know – perhaps it's my imagination, but I've seen Paul regarding her with more than brotherly warmth."

Ouma laughs. "You women and your romantic notions…" He pauses, remembering the first time he saw Emily walking down the hill from the Kibera slums. "Where does she come from? It can't be far from here."

"I don't know. Why do you ask?"

Ouma shrugs his shoulders. "There's something vaguely familiar about her face."

"Now whose imagination is running riot? You can ask her this weekend. Sam usually brings her to see the family before he goes back to Nairobi on a Sunday evening. Mother has a soft spot for Emily."

Ouma is not ready to meet Sam. Guilty thoughts and fears jump around in his mind, and yet he knows it is important for them to reconcile. He needs Sam to help with Jackson, but that is not his immediate worry. Ruth has told him of Sam's intense aggression whenever his name is mentioned.

"What have you done to him that he appears to hate you so much?"

"Why don't you ask Sam?"

"I have. He doesn't answer – he just sets his jaw and stays silent. You must find out, Charles. Find out, and make up. And perhaps you'd better decide who you really are – Ouma or Charles. Why can't you be known as Charles again? You could always retain the pseudonym Ouma for your work as a journalist – can't you?"

He hasn't thought of that. It would make his life simpler, and there's no longer a reason for dissembling, he tells himself. Is he ashamed of his life as a beggar? The thought hits him and takes root. His family doesn't know about that, but Emily knows; he's seen a glimmer of recognition in her eyes on the occasions he's crossed her path this past fortnight. So do Ken and the boys. He's been using the disguise lately as an undercover for his journalism. Perhaps it's time to revert to his true identity.

He shies away from the embarrassment of disclosure and immerses himself in Maria's project, allowing the days to drift by until Friday arrives.

Chapter 26

Maria meets him for three assessments in one morning, having told the families that Ouma will be present.

"I've said that you're my *baba*, and want to learn more about the project," she tells him. "And of course, they know about your connection with Ken and Louise. Two of the meetings are follow-ups with people whose children are already sponsored by the volunteers. I treat each application separately, as it gives me a chance to check if they give the same answers as before. At the third home, the volunteers have put a tin roof on the new brick house, with guttering and a tank to hold the rainwater. We don't just help with schooling."

"How did you start the building projects?"

"When Louise first visited the village about three years ago there was a fire, which destroyed the home belonging to Naomi's daughter. Louise didn't know that Naomi had a connection with you, but she found sponsors to build a brick house. The practice has grown wherever the need arises. We believe that God has a hand in all that's being done here."

"So, I am doubly indebted to Louise – not only has she helped my protégés, but she's also stepped in when my family is in need. And yes, God is very much present in all this, although I know I often forget to give Him credit."

As he follows Maria on her rounds, Ouma understands that there can be no other conclusion. How else to explain the concept of charity – doing something for nothing – which is alien to the African mind? His people are convinced that the first explorers and missionaries had an ulterior motive, and this distrust still prevails. The white missionaries want to take our children and teach them the English ways, and there is nobody left to help in the *shamba* and with the goats; we are being forced to change our customs. Why? Could it be trade, or a buffer against Muslim extremism? Ouma considers today's threat of *Al Shabaab* from the border with Somalia, and nods sagely to himself. Perhaps his people are not far wrong.

The scent of urine pervades the first home they visit. A cotton garment droops over the shapeless figure of the mother as she studiously ignores him. One boy still wets his bed, she admits to Maria, and she beats him for it.

"My own child used to wet his bed," says Maria. "But I encouraged him to help wash and iron the clothes. I didn't scold him, and his problem was cured within a month."

This is clearly a new concept for the woman, who looks half-convinced. Maria opens her folder.

"You remember when I first came, I asked you questions? The sponsors want to know about the children and the homes they live in, so that we can find other ways to help."

Ouma has his own copy of the form and makes notes as the interview progresses. It is two pages long, and he is surprised at the detail required and the repetition in some of the questions. As he listens, he admires Maria's skill in revealing the woman's half-truths, and her ability to pick up on discrepancies such as income earned versus rent paid. A full disclosure is demanded of those who live in the shabby home, and Maria points out that there are two extra children here since her last visit.

She physically checks each room, asking who has a bed, who has a blanket, who has a mattress and who has a mosquito net?

The woman does not earn any money for herself, but she grows vegetables for the family in her *shamba*. Her husband works as a night guard for a land owner in the village.

In response to a final question, she confesses that her worst fear is being beaten. A brave admission, as the curtain behind her tweaks, and her husband reveals he is listening. His hands tremble as he emerges to have his photo taken with his wife. It will be sent to their sponsor as part of the ongoing records. Ouma notices fresh wounds on his face. Afterwards, he asks Maria if she knows him, and does he drink?

"Yes to both your questions," she says. "But what is most disturbing is the beating. Do you know that many husbands in this village beat their wives? And the violence is passed on to the children."

He cannot deny knowledge of the problem; it is well understood that wives have to be submissive to their husbands. Ouma stares back at Maria, who is gearing herself up for an outburst. He can see it coming.

"It all boils down to our backward traditions. There should be a program in this district against circumcision of women, or Female Genital Mutilation as it is called nowadays! It should be made illegal. Why do you think wives are afraid of having sex with their husbands? It's not because they don't want children. It's because of the awful pain."

Ouma doesn't know what to say. He hasn't seen this side of Maria before, and it is not usual for sex to be discussed between father and daughter. But he understands her concern.

"But—"

"I know what you're going to say! I know our Luhya people are better than most in the country in this matter. But the problem is still there, and should be dealt with!"

He holds his hands up in surrender, and Maria smiles.

"Well, now that I've got that off my chest, let's go to our final interview. The lady's name is Esther."

A beautiful woman in her thirties greets them with a shy smile. Her hair is braided and she wears a striking red dress. Ouma sits on the bed, letting his eyes feast on her luscious curves as she squats on the floor at their feet.

Her three children sleep on the floor of this single room, she tells them, and Maria makes a note that mattresses could be considered for future donations. The sponsor of her elder children has also paid for a new cement floor, together with a tin roof and guttering.

Hers is a familiar story. She married young, had two children and then her husband moved on. She found another partner who wanted her to live with him at his place of work, but when their own child was born, he refused to take in her two older daughters, so they were left with Esther's mother.

"I tried it for a week, and then left him because I missed my other children."

"Does your second husband contribute for his child?"

"No," she says. "And I have bad news for you. The landlord has seen the improvements to this house, and he wants me to leave so he can sell it. I've been given one month's notice."

Maria is visibly flustered. "It is not your house?"

Esther shakes her head.

"Where will you go?"

"I'll have to find another place to rent, but I can stay with my mother for a short while."

"And does your mother's house belong to her?"

Esther shakes her head.

Maria invites Esther outside with her baby and takes a photograph, telling her that Louise must be told the bad news.

On the way back, Ouma is lost in thought.

"Perhaps I can help you devise some more questions for future assessments, so that this won't happen again? You'll need to make sure that people own their houses before improvements are made. Not only that, but do they have a land title, or agreement."

"It's not as simple as that, *baba*. You must know that the land question is complicated. And isn't there a difference between owned and inherited land? This will be a blow to the charity, for I know several people in the UK are ready to give money towards improving the houses. Quite a few brick buildings have been started by the project. The money will be wasted if the titles are not secure, and now absentee landlords will take advantage."

"I'll think up a few more questions for you anyway," he says. "It would be wise to make an inventory of each home before putting a family forward for sponsorship. Even things like: does the home have a water tank, or a good outside toilet? I can see there could be no end to the questions."

"You're right. We learn as we go along. But I expect you need something to eat now; I'm certainly hungry. And then, if you wish, I can ask Emily to show you round her side of the project. Paul brought her here to help with the business side of things, and she's already made a difference. I expect she'll be glad to get away from the office. She finds it difficult to concentrate on a Friday before Sam arrives."

"Tell me more about Emily," says Ouma. "And, by the way – I think you were right earlier on. I have nothing to hide anymore. It is time I went back to my old name."

"I didn't know you had anything to hide?"

Charles laughs. "I'm not about to enlighten you, my dear – it is all best forgotten! Now – who is Emily?"

"I don't really know; I met her when Sam brought her here. She's such a caring person, and Sam likes her a lot. I'm surprised they haven't got married. I know *mama* is still hoping."

"But where does she come from? Her features show she might be from around this region."

"Nobody knows her. Nor does she know who her family is. She's an AIDS orphan. Let's invite her to share lunch with us, and then you can have all afternoon to get to know each other."

Emily joins them in the shade of a tree outside the project office, which is tucked behind the new primary school. She and Charles acknowledge each other, and with Maria they buy a snack of small *mandazis* from the school shop. The ladies sit on the grass, and Charles glances round for a bench.

"I'll fetch you a chair, *baba!*" exclaims Maria, getting up and running into a nearby classroom. "Here. You walk so well that I keeping forgetting about your leg." She settles back onto the grass and turns to Emily. "What time are you expecting Sam?"

"He comes late in the night. It is a dangerous journey, and everybody wants to get out of Nairobi in a hurry for the weekend. I'm never happy until he's arrived safely."

"He must love you very much, to brave all those hazards every fortnight!" Maria gets up and dusts the crumbs from her jeans. "And now I will leave you together. Emily, I thought you might like to show my father your side of the project this afternoon. It will take your mind off your loved one, and make the time go by more quickly perhaps?"

"Cheeky!" retorts Emily with an embarrassed titter, but she gets up quickly. Charles watches her lithe young figure skip up the steps to return the chair to the classroom. Her flip-flops scrape along the dust as she leads him away from the school compound, and he is reminded of the first time he saw those elegant legs, teetering above ridiculously high heels on the muddy path leading down from the Kibera slums.

"I expect you've realised by now where we first met," he says.

She glances up at him and nods. "Your name is Ouma, isn't it?"

"Yes, it is. Sorry, Emily. We've never been properly introduced."

He stops to take a breath. He is feeling stiff after the lunch rest. A couple of *boda bodas* chug by and offer them a ride, but he quickly declines.

"I hope you don't mind walking slowly, but I never want to ride on a *boda boda* again." She waits for him to draw alongside. "Would you mind calling me Charles? Ouma was an abbreviation of my middle name, thought up on the spur of the moment. It was at the lowest point of my life, long before you gave this poor beggar a coin on the streets of Nairobi. I'm trying hard to put it all behind me. Besides, most people here know me as Charles Omari Ondiek, and I want to stop confusing them."

He knows he's made her feel awkward, but is glad he has confessed. She smiles shyly, gesturing at him to follow her past one of the four boreholes built by the project. Several *bibis* and children are waiting to draw water, and they greet her warmly. She points to an electricity pylon.

"The village elders will tell you that the coming of electricity was a turning point," she says. "Paul arranged for the Kenya Power and Lighting Company to put in a branch line. It took ages to organise, but now it has attracted new business and raised the price of the land. I won't take you to the brick factory, as it's too far for you to walk, but that was Louise's first project. It's doing very well.

"I've already been there. Ken, the manager, is my protégé. I am proud of him."

She stares at him, wide-eyed. "You know Ken?"

"Yes. He was a street boy in Nairobi, and Louise sponsored him through school."

Emily nods with a firmness which surprises him. "I know Ken was a street boy. I'll never forget him. He stole my handbag from the car once, when Paul and I were caught up in traffic on Uhuru Highway, and I recognised him as soon as I saw him at the factory. But don't tell him. I don't think he even looked at my face when he took the bag, and he's obviously a changed person now."

"On the contrary," counters Charles with a smile. "I think you should tell him, when you get to know him better. People ought to be reminded of their past sins when it's done in the right spirit. I expect you would both be able to laugh it off, and what's more important, he'll be forever in your debt."

"You have a point there! And support from such an astute person may come in handy one day, you never know. But Ken wasn't nearly as frightening as the sinister men who used to follow me a few years ago."

"Oh?" His throat becomes parched.

"Yes." Emily fidgets at her skirt. "One of them used to leer at me, and worse. I don't want to think about it. He even appeared at the lodge when I first came here with Paul, but I haven't seen him for a few years now, thank goodness." She avoids his gaze.

Charles hasn't heard from his henchmen for a while, and he doesn't doubt that Emily is referring to Maina, the rogue with an eye for women. He wonders what is happening at the refugee camp on the Somalia border where he sent Maina and Musumba, and resolves to get more news. Tales of Somali pirates hijacking ships in international waters off the coast have been dominating the press recently.

They approach two low buildings half-hidden behind long grass.

"This is our piggery. Have you heard of the *Mia Moja* Challenge?"

Charles shakes his head, and Emily tells him that the Grass Shoots Charity in the UK organises groups of volunteers to visit the Amayoni village project for a week at a time. They stay in the lodge, and meet the families of the children they sponsor, to work out how best to use the £100 spending money allocated to each volunteer. Sometimes the help is in the form of practical gifts, which is Maria's domain. But sometimes a donor provides long-term, sustainable help, such as when households receive animals. The project uses a model for this exercise which takes time to develop.

Emily wrenches open the waist-high door of the nearest shed. It creaks inwards on its hinges, and she wipes away some cobwebs as Charles steps gingerly after her. Piglets scamper along a dividing passageway in front of them, and his ears are bombarded by a rising scale of demanding grunts and squeals. Enormous sows are trapped in the sties on either side. Emily pushes the door shut before anything can escape, and Charles spots a toad lurking in the corner as he sidesteps to avoid a curious piglet.

"The pigs in each sty belong to different families," Emily shouts, as they lean over a separating wall. She reaches down to scratch the shoulder of a sow, and Charles notes the leathery skin with sparse hairs sticking out of it like long bristles. He has never been this close to a pig before.

"They are responsible for their own animals. When they've gone through a training course, they take the animals home to generate an income. But the project monitors them regularly."

The piglets have overcome their initial fright when the door was opened, and snuffle round Charles's legs. He sidles backwards and Emily follows him out, fastening the gate. Immediately the cacophony subsides and he can hear himself think.

"A training course?"

"At first, experts came from the Egerton University in Njoro, and the project sent students there to train. Now we have our own qualified people in the village."

Charles nods approvingly.

"The next phase is the most exciting," she says, leading him towards some open ground. "All piglets from the first litter are given back to the project, and sold to sponsors through *Mia Moja* for the benefit of other families. Thus, the gift is passed on, and the original owner keeps subsequent litters for generating an income."

"Like a contagious disease, but in a positive, good way!" says Charles with a laugh. "Who devised this cunning plan?"

"The idea was thought up by the project Trustees," says Emily proudly.

Her focus is always on her local project, Charles notices. Emily never mentions Louise's charity, which is quite natural he supposes. He wonders if the Grass Shoots volunteers in their turn also perceive it as "their" charity. How do the two sides work together?

"Paul has invited Maria and me to the UK when he goes on leave later this year," she says, as if reading his thoughts. "And Louise thinks it's a good idea for us to learn what goes on in the Grass Shoots office. We're very excited."

"You'll certainly have a big culture shock, Emily! But it will be an unforgettable experience for you both."

Emily turns through a maze of passages between buildings, and he quickens his steps to catch up with her. She waits to raise a strand of barbed wire for him while he clambers into a field.

"I'm now going to show you our model *shamba*. We've been using quality seed, and teaching the villagers how to intercrop with maize, beans and squash growing simultaneously. See how the seeds have been planted three or four feet apart. Then we prune them down to one plant and mulch heavily."

She shows him a compost heap, telling him how it is turned regularly and finally reduced into their own home-grown fertiliser. "So now we don't have to buy expensive chemicals. And we have plans for building a maize mill in the village, which will provide employment for the men…"

"…Thus avoiding the expense of transporting the grain and buying it back as *posho* through middlemen," says Charles with a smile.

She nods and grins.

As they make their way back to the office, negotiating the uneven ground in the field with his prosthetic leg, he notices the distinctive humps of Somali cattle grazing on open ground. Idly, he wonders how long it will be before the project introduces a European breed, favoured by white highlanders in the past.

It is as if Emily has again read his thoughts. "Do you know anything about cheese-making? Would it be a suitable occupation for women, I wonder? We're trying to find commercial jobs for women, so they don't just produce stuff for family consumption."

"I don't. But I can find out for you. I'm beginning to understand how the village works, and it is an exciting concept. I admire the enterprise and imagination of your project. This is worth supporting."

She gives him a lovely smile and then goes to prepare herself for Sam's impending arrival. Charles takes stock of his day's experiences. The village homes touched by the charity are sparsely scattered over the area, and he wonders how long it will take to achieve a cohesive community.

Some people will be suspicious; they will wait and watch, and wonder at the motive behind the offered help. In time they might acquiesce, or turn away. Others will grab what they can and then sit back and see if they are offered something else for free. And the wise will embrace the help, take ownership and run with it. It reminds him of the Parable of the Sower in the Bible. It will take time. It's barely a hundred and fifty years since Kenya saw its first missionaries, and it's taken the UK since Roman times to get to where it is now. Perhaps that's the secret: patience and collaboration. And implicit trust in God.

But how will the volunteers benefit? It should not be perceived by either side as a one-way exercise, with the volunteers providing cash for projects, education, and livelihood. What does Africa offer to them? The concept of giving and receiving must be transparent to all. Is that the secret of Amayoni?

Maybe Maria and Emily will find out when they go to the UK. The faithful know the joy and fulfilment of giving. But the layman stands back and wonders why crazy people should want to offer their hard-earned cash for "nothing" in return. Altruism is an alien concept.

The weekend flies by, and Charles only comes face to face with his son for a few hours on Sunday evening. Is Sam also feeling reluctant about their meeting?

Ruth rushes to greet Sam when he arrives with Emily, and smothers them with fuss and kindness, setting out a lovingly-prepared meal. It is evident that she thoroughly approves of the match, but nobody is in a hurry. Charles considers that the couple are well suited, and wonders at the delay. But it is not his business to ask.

Nor is it a good environment for ironing out past differences, and father and son maintain a polite reserve throughout the evening. At least Charles can discern no outright hostility, which is a relief.

"I heard from Simaloi while you were out this afternoon, Charles," says Ruth. "Jackson has been asking after you. She was wondering if you've spoken to Sam?"

The room goes still as Charles holds his breath and glances at his son.

"What's all this about?" says Sam, avoiding his father's eyes and looking directly at Ruth.

So, there is still resentment simmering under the surface. Charles is not surprised, given the extent of their estrangement. It will be easier if he takes the blame.

"It's my fault, Sam. I should have made a point of contacting you long ago, but it's not been easy. It is time we had a heart-to-heart talk." He pauses as Sam visibly recoils. "However, we need to focus on your uncle. He's not well, and talks of returning to the cave of our ancestors…"

Sam pauses, and the family waits.

"You're right about the heart-to-heart, I suppose. But I have to return to Nairobi tonight." He turns towards Emily. "Emily has told me you've been learning about the project this past week. It's a cause dear to her heart." He puts his arm round her and draws her to him with a squeeze. He takes her to one side and the family averts their gaze as the couple embrace. Then Emily pulls away.

"When are you expecting to go back to Nairobi, Charles?"

He regards her with surprise, and the tension is broken as the family laughs.

"I mean…" Emily glances from Charles to Sam, "…if you're thinking of returning, would it be a good idea for Sam to give you a lift home?"

Her words hang in the air as Charles grapples with this new thought. It is a clumsy, spur-of-the-moment idea, but it has its merits.

"Tonight?" Sam's voice is edged with a tinge of horror, which causes Ruth to smile.

"Why not?" she says. "It would be a good way to resolve your differences, and neither of you will be able to escape. What is there to stop you from going now, Charles? You've been here several weeks."

Charles cannot help smiling at her impudence, and before either of them can voice a coherent argument, he and Sam have said their goodbyes, and are driving across the floor of the Great Rift Valley towards Nairobi.

Chapter 27

Charles reaches over to move his meagre bundle of belongings from the cramped foot well onto the back seat, and massages his right leg above the prosthesis.

"Mind if I take this off, Sam?" he asks.

"Of course not. Go ahead."

There is no antagonism in his voice. Progress has been made, thinks Charles, as he searches his mind for an appropriate opening. He was in a similar situation years ago, when he puzzled for hours on how to approach Sam as a schoolboy that first time they met. The best way is merely to say what comes to mind.

The road is empty and straight. The night is black, and the headlights of the little car strain to penetrate the darkness. The right beam reaches further down the road than the left. Charles glances across at his son. Sam's face in the light of the dashboard is a deadpan effort to keep alert.

"You need to get those lights realigned at the next service, son."

Sam grunts. He widens his eyes, turning his mouth into a yawn and falls back into more determined concentration.

"Would you like me to tell you my story? You can stop and question me whenever you wish. Or not. I don't mind."

Sam grunts again. Charles peers out of his side window seeking the stars, but the glow from the headlights spoil his vision. He forces his mind back. Where shall he begin? From his frantic efforts to catch up with the boys on that fateful night in 1982? Or when he awoke in a hospital bed?

He starts talking, reliving the pain, the fear and the confusion.

"What I don't understand," Sam says, "is why you didn't

contact us when you were recuperating in hospital? Jackson knew. Why didn't he tell me? We were looking for you everywhere, and I wouldn't let Caroline stop asking questions. Eventually we gave up. We thought you were dead."

It is complicated. How to tell Sam of the clash within him, between his faith in God and the primeval terror of the evil powers of witchcraft? He doesn't understand it himself. But whenever he thinks of Mwangi, his body shakes and his mind goes numb – even now that Mwangi is dead and the curse is broken. But the healing has begun, and now he is encased in this car with Sam, hurtling along an empty road – to where?

"With all my heart, I wanted to protect you from the evil. I had to keep you away from me while I battled with those terrible forces. Jackson was there at the worst times. I wouldn't let him tell you or Caroline. It was my battle. Mine alone."

Charles pauses, remembering. His voice falters as his mind brushes over those dismal days of his depression.

They reach the lights of Nakuru, and Sam pulls the car off the road. "Let's stop for coffee."

Charles fumbles for his prosthesis and prepares to strap it back on.

"Don't bother, *baba*. I'll bring it to you."

He senses a hesitation from Sam, who appears to make up his mind.

"I never knew you'd lost your leg."

That had not occurred to Charles. Of course, it must have been a shock for Sam to see him as a cripple. And it is the first time Sam has used an endearment when addressing him. A sense of warmth and relief trickles through him.

"How could you have known? But it is of little consequence, son."

He watches Sam cross the road, enter a wayside café and return with two cartons of steaming coffee. Charles burns his mouth at the first sip. His hand shakes, and liquid slops onto his leg. He dabs the hotness into his trouser and Sam reaches into the side pocket of the car for a cloth. There is a softening in his demeanour, a sense of apology. But Charles does not want sympathy, and his son must not be made to feel guilty about his previous anger.

He reaches for the remains of his coffee and takes a sip. It has cooled, so he gulps it down. Sam turns on the ignition and pulls back onto the highway. The silence between them is companionable.

Charles continues his story, warming to a subject nearer his heart as he speaks of his newspaper column. He is concerned about the problems Kenya faces, both internally and on the wider international front, as its fifty-year anniversary approaches.

"I've sent people to the Dadaab refugee camp on our border with Somalia to keep an eye on things there. It is a hotbed of terrorism, and the acknowledged source of guns into our country, but the government can do nothing about it. I expect you're aware of the pirates in international waters, causing mayhem to shipping?"

Sam nods. "And frightening tourists away from the coast, too. Our museums have suffered a drastic fall in revenue."

Sam turns into Naivasha town. "I like to avoid the top road," he says. "Even though it is wide and smooth, it's too remote at this time of night – there are many *mwivis,* and car-jackings are on the increase."

The car groans up the gradient towards Mount Longonot, and Sam accelerates down the valley to gain momentum for the tortuous climb up the Aberdare escarpment. Charles can see lights from lorries and tankers snaking towards the top. The authorities have not yet succeeded in enforcing the night curfew on this up-country route.

"But what's this about Jackson, *baba*?" Sam pulls in behind a behemoth as it creeps round a succession of hairpin bends. "I confess I haven't seen him since he left Nairobi."

"Your uncle is ailing. It is why I went home to Kakamega three weeks ago. And then I got caught up in the Amayoni project. Your Emily is quite a force to be reckoned with, there – and Maria, of course." Charles struggles for a moment, trying to recall his reason for going to Amayoni. "When I heard you were at Amayoni, I hurried to meet you…"

"…And you fell. Why did you want to see me?"

"I needed you. We needed to talk, but I was afraid."

"Afraid of what?"

"Of facing you. I knew you were angry with me."

Sam accelerates past four floundering lorries on a brief stretch of open road midway up the escarpment.

"I need you to help me with Jackson, Sam. He is ready to return to the cave of our ancestors, and I can't do it by myself."

Sam's eyes flicker towards his leg, but Charles does not want sympathy.

"No one else but Simaloi can come with us, and I fear that Jackson will need carrying at least part of the way. He has helped me in the past, and I don't want to let him down now."

"Of course I'll come. Emily and Maria are going to the UK with Paul, and we can arrange it while they are away. Can Jackson wait that long?"

"I'll find out. Once he knows the journey is arranged, he will prepare himself. Thank you, Sam."

Sam is peering through the windscreen wipers as a heavy drizzle settles over the forest.

"I think it best if Jackson comes back to Nairobi, I can bring him down in my car after one of my regular visits, and then we can take him on to Magadi. Leave it with me."

Charles settles into the seat and closes his eyes. It is a comfort, knowing that Sam has taken control. It will be an ordeal getting Jackson to the cave, but it will be no more arduous than when his brother transported him there after he'd lost his leg.

Charles's lips twitch into a smile. He will merely be returning the favour.

His mind dwells on the mysteries hidden in that ancestral cave – mysteries he has yet to uncover. Perhaps more of them will be revealed over the next few months.

Chapter 28

The place was as arid as ever. Sam stood on a hillock beside the track savouring the thin, dry air. To his right, the sands of Lake Magadi panned out in symmetric blocks. The soda factory had been there ever since he could remember. He looked to the south. The faint outline of Ol Donyo L'Engai shimmered distantly in the heat. Somewhere on his left lay the disused dig. The termite mound would have disappeared or changed shape many times, but he didn't need a landmark; he knew the area intimately.

A bell tinkled in the undergrowth and a dappled outline appeared in stilted movement behind a bush. He watched a narrow mouth tug sharply at a leaf, and a faint bleat heralded the arrival of a kid. Who was herding the goats now? Sam had been herdsman once, keeping watch and ferrying messages to and fro, making sure the scientists working on the dig didn't stray beyond reasonable limits in their desire for further knowledge. Before him, Jackson had guarded the place.

His father never did fulfil those tasks. He remembered the days they'd secretly planned to explore the distant cave when he was a youth, when Charles was a man with a mission consumed with ambition. Now, he was almost as helpless as Jackson. He must stop thinking of his father in a formal way, now that they had made their peace. His continued use of the intimate name of *baba* since their journey to Nairobi had helped to ease the tension between them.

Sam turned full circle on the hillock of sand, letting his eyes sweep over the horizon. What a wonderful last resting place. He almost envied Jackson, who had shrunk into a wizened shadow of his former himself. The worst part of the journey was yet to come. They had to take him across that hostile terrain to the haven of the ancestral cave.

A *toto* emerged from the bush, tattered garments barely covering his nakedness. He slapped at an inquisitive billy goat with his *rungu*. Sam admired the sheer maleness of the animal, its gleaming white coat and defiant response as it turned away in haughty disdain as the weighted stick glanced off its rump.

"You want to go to the cave? I'll show you the way."

"Thank you. What's your name?"

"Amos. I will take you to my brother."

Not waiting for Sam, the child disappeared down the track. Sam returned to the car and started the engine. Jackson was sleeping on the back seat, his head resting on Simaloi's lap.

Charles shifted position beside him. "This place depresses me," he said.

"Does it, *baba*? But I suppose your memories aren't good. Mine are different. For me, it's like returning home. I'm looking forward to a rest and the chance to delve deeper into my roots. Perhaps we'll uncover more mysteries of our ancestors, and I may even take a spell at herding the goats again."

Jackson stirred behind him, and an amused grunt told him the gruff old man was not asleep.

Amos waited for them where a path left the lakeside track. Chivvying the goats before him he ran into the bush, coming to a halt in a clearing which had overgrown considerably since Sam was here last.

"Here is Rueben, my brother," said Amos, turning aside to water his animals at a rusty trough. A red plastic container stood half-empty beside it.

Sam eyed the youth striding towards him, wielding a long spear. The red blanket draped over one shoulder revealed glimpses of a pair of boxer shorts as he moved. The youth's arm muscles rippled, his legs glided over the ground in perfect harmony with his surroundings. They greeted each other, and Sam knew that getting Jackson to the cave would not be the impossible ordeal he feared.

Rueben prepared tea for them. At his uncle's bidding, Sam moved the car to a low hillock fifty yards away from the dry river bed.

"We're not expecting any rain," said Jackson, who had found new energy. "But you never know."

Sam nodded, remembering the flood on a dramatic day years ago when he, Paul and Caroline were stranded on the far side of the river. If it weren't for Jackson, he would have drowned.

They settled for the night, dispersed among the bushes. Sam drew his blanket tight round his body. Covering his head, he lowered his breathing rate, closed his eyes and melded into the sand.

Rueben woke them for an early morning start, and Jackson insisted on walking with Charles, who resolutely jerked along the uneven ground with the support of his crutches. Sam and Simaloi followed behind, swinging a stretcher between them with a tumbling burden of backpacks and witchcraft chattels. The crisp air turned translucent as the morning sun penetrated the valleys. They paused atop each rise to soak in the warmth and take a breather, but it was not long before Jackson faltered. Rueben handed Sam his spear and picked up the old man, effortlessly hoisting the feather-light body onto his shoulders.

"Like a child!" called Jackson in delight, and they walked on.

Sam settled his limbs into a rhythm and the miles sped by in companionable silence. The escarpment never seemed to get any closer, but he saw a dark shadow where he knew the cave opened, and a glimmer of light flashed at its corner. Simaloi paused to recover a torch from the stretcher they carried between them and sent a return message.

Charles stumbled, and Sam reached forward to prevent him from falling. They paused for a drink and pondered the next move. Jackson's face was a picture of resigned misery as he lay in the dust where Rueben had lowered him, eyes closed and refusing refreshment.

Sam made a bed for him between the bundles on the stretcher. "He is so light, we can carry him between us, can't we, Simaloi?"

She simply nodded at the stretcher.

Charles took off his prosthesis, and Rueben hoisted him into a piggy-back, finding it awkward to balance the foreshortened leg. He braced himself under the heavier weight, found momentum and set off. Sam and Simaloi followed, with Jackson lying like a rag doll on the swinging stretcher between them. Every hill seemed to be steeper, every valley shorter. Sam called for a pause when he saw Charles slumping at an awkward angle along Rueben's back.

They had less than half way to go, but it might as well have been a hundred miles. The task seemed impossible and the early afternoon sun beat down.

"We'll stay here for an hour," said Rueben.

They laid protective blankets over the still forms of Jackson and Charles, and Sam dropped his head against a backpack. Simaloi said she would keep the first watch.

Sam stirred at her nudge and glanced at his watch. The hour had passed and he felt no more refreshed. She jutted her chin towards the escarpment, and it was a long moment before he could gather his wits.

A light flashed, moving with uneven jerks below the looming escarpment.

"It's my grandmother – she's coming to help us."

How did she know? A secret smile glimmered on the girl's face. Sam did not understand this psychic link between the members of his family. But he appreciated its value, especially in times like these.

"You take a rest," he told her. "It'll be at least another two hours before she arrives, and I'll keep watch."

Finally, the crone arrived and chivvied the party out of their languor. "You mustn't wait any longer. We have to get to the cave before daylight fades."

Sam marvelled that such a bent old lady should have covered the distance so quickly. He squatted opposite Rueben and they joined hands, making a cradle for Charles to sit with his arms around their necks. They rose together, slowly bracing themselves under the burden. His father was no lightweight.

"This will be more comfortable than bumping around on Rueben's back," he said, grinning broadly.

They started off, Jackson walking ahead of them, with the women on either side. Simaloi had strapped the stretcher to her back, pointing to the sky like a ladder, but several pieces of baggage, including Charles's prosthesis, lay in the dust.

"We can come back for those tomorrow," said the crone. "They'll be safe here."

As the women stooped to conceal the remains of their belongings beneath a pile of stones, Sam and Rueben detoured round Jackson. He lifted a frail arm to them as they passed, his eyes bright and a smile on his lips.

The men turned with their backs to the sun and strode on in silent unison for an hour.

"Let's change places."

They stooped to lay Charles onto the earth. Sam flexed his tired muscles and looked back. The stretcher which had been jerking along the skyline above Simaloi's head was no longer visible in the low scrub.

"I can't see them anymore."

"They are carrying him now," said Rueben. "Wait here while I go back to check."

Sam got out his water bottle and offered it to Charles before taking a sip, and both men stretched out in the dust, closing their eyes. The sun had lost its heat and they fell into a pleasant doze.

"Come." The others had caught up, and Sam forced himself into a sitting position. The sun's rays caught the distant escarpment, the terrain between was in shadow, and a large red moon rose through the haze on the horizon.

Rueben pointed to a pile of hyena spoor near the path, and Sam searched the bush in vain for a sighting.

"We can complete the journey in the full moon, but we should aim to reach the escarpment before nightfall. It will be safer."

Again, they made a cradle for Charles and the women stooped to pick up the stretcher.

"We must keep together," said Rueben.

The crone quickened her steps and Sam strained his eyes to left and right as they crawled towards the foot of the cliff.

The dim line of a narrow ledge wound steeply above them in the moonlight.

"I can lead now, I am fresher than the rest of you," said Charles, as Sam and Rueben lowered him to the ground. "I know this place intimately, and the clock has turned back. Remember, Jackson?"

The old man smiled, nodding. "Together we can move up the mountain on our backsides, Charles; you can show me how," he said.

"It will take hours."

"But the night is young and the moon is bright."

"I'll leave you," said Rueben, turning to Sam. "You take the rear and keep a look out for that hyena."

"You'll be all right?"

Rueben rattled his spear and thrusted the end into the ground with a smile and a flourish.

"I must get back to Amos. I'll bring the rest of your baggage in the morning."

He melted away into the bush.

Sam shared more of his water with Charles, and persuaded Jackson to take a sip. He sat with his back to the cliff, watching the sun sink below the horizon. The grey cloud turned violet and orange; it briefly lit up with an outline of blazing light, and the flaming orb sank out of sight, leaving a pink wash in the sky. The dark closed in to swift African night, and the evening star pricked the sky. More stars appeared, and it was tempting to stay here. But the low whoop of a hyena from the shadows to his right made Sam stir. The others had heard it, too.

"Time to move on." Jackson rose, steadied himself, and took a few faltering steps. "I will lead the way while I can."

Sam took up the rear, grasping the *rungu* Rueben had left with him. The soft light of the risen moon bathed the wilderness, and his eyes scanned the ground as they traversed the cliff, ears attuned to the shadowy scrub for tell-tale signs of movement. He fingered the *panga* in his belt. Even as they reached the narrow ledge leading to the cave, he knew that the predators were following, and the knife-edged machete would serve as a last-ditch weapon.

Jackson stopped for breath and Charles discarded his walking aids, handing them back to Simaloi. "The ledge is too narrow for such things," he said, lowering himself to a sitting position. He grinned at Jackson, his single leg dangling over the sheer drop.

"Here we go – like old times."

He started shuffling sideways inch by inch on his backside. Jackson followed him, leaning against the cliff for support at each step. The women called occasional encouragement, and Sam let himself relax. His task of being vigilant was easier now that the hyena could only approach from behind. As time passed, he could sense the menacing presence. He lagged further behind and threw a stone at a dark shape, evoking a yelp of pain; then he lay in wait, *rungu* and knife at the ready, and hurled the knobbed stick into the darkness. There was a howl of anguish, then soft thumps of running pads retreated into silence.

The night cold took hold, and they quickened their efforts. Jackson joined Charles in a sitting position, and Sam saw the crone sidle past the two men shuffling sideways along the ledge.

"I'll get the fire going," she said.

They reached the warmth of the cave in the early hours of morning and collapsed onto the floor.

Streaks of dawn fingered the undulating plain below, picking out the hillocks and highlighting the mist rising from the valleys. Sam glimpsed a shy dik dik through his binoculars and spotted the mottled back of a slinking hyena, head turning from side to side as it approached its den, making sure not to betray the entrance.

He focussed on the sand river. A tiny figure sprang into view, the sun's rays briefly catching the tip of a spear at his side. Rueben was on his way to collect the rest of their baggage. Sam tweaked the mirror fragment at his side, sending a message.

Behind him, the women stirred. Jackson had retired deep inside the cave, refusing all sustenance.

"His time has come," said the crone. "We must respect his wishes."

Charles lay collapsed in a pile of rags beneath the rotting sackcloth which protected the precious rock art. There was work to be done, and Sam had brought the necessary tools.

In the days that followed, he worked on the rock face, uncovering the paintings once more and gently scraping further to reveal the beginnings of new treasures. Charles helped him, making ready fresh earth for a protective barrier, and holding firm the tracing paper. Sam's heart quickened as he settled into a daily routine. This was what he was born for – to explore the origins and history of his country, following the footsteps of his revered uncle. He started designing a new display for the museum.

"Jackson wants to see you both."

The crone led them behind the inner veil of the sanctuary and laid a hurricane lamp on the floor. Jackson sat against the rock, his body shrunk to skin and bone, his eyes alert.

Sam panned the inner cave with his torch. He had never been allowed this far in before. Half-buried in the sand lay dozens of fossilised bones. He could not begin to calculate how many skeletons they represented, or how old they were. His heart rate quickened as he stepped in for a closer look. These were not animal bones; nor did they seem to be entirely human. He saw a portion of skull protruding from the dust.

"Don't touch!" The strong voice of his uncle rang out.

Sam stepped back. "Of course not, Jackson – but what an incredible find. How long have you known...?"

"Long enough." The old man's voice weakened. "It's now your turn to take this further. Can I trust you both to do the right thing for our country, and our world?"

The skeletons nearer his uncle were clearly hominids, but

Sam eyed the more ancient fossils at the periphery of the circle of light. He was already forming plans in his mind to extract specimens for research in the museum laboratories. This could be an important breakthrough in the search for man's origins.

Jackson beckoned, and Sam came with Charles to sit at his side.

"The longer I live, the more I realise that what we scientists have been working at all our lives does not really matter. It is interesting, yes – and furthering our knowledge is a good thing. But is it important in the grand scheme of things?"

His voice was steady, settled into a rhythmic tone, and it was clearly a rhetorical question.

"God is spirit – there before the beginning of time. Why should God not have created man just like that, breathed life and spirit into a body, a human body made by him out of bones, not unlike those scattered in this cave? For man is physical, but also of the spirit – each one of us knows this in the inner core of our beings.

"And God is spirit. But he also made himself man, for the space of a few earth years, and left his own unique essence in each one of us whom he has graced with knowledge of him.

"That is why you and I enjoy a new dimension. We can't explain it logically, any more than scientists can bridge the evolutionary gap, or penetrate to the very core of the universe with mathematics and theories. There's always more to discover. But is it important?

"All this scientific emphasis on the evolution of man might be taking us nowhere. You and I, Sam, have made successful careers out of research and dissertation, but haven't our efforts led us up enough different branches, always leading outwards, away from each other; never finding that legendary missing link?

"We are men and we are of the spirit, held in the heart of God before time and out of time, and the spirit never dies, even after the physical body crumbles like these skeletal bones. And who's to prove that God can't raise dead bones like these and breathe life into them once again?

"Who am I? That's what's important. I'm an old man, ready to rest my bones with those of my ancestors, and to make peace with God. I have rejoiced in the wonderfully intricate world we live in, a world that I can never wholly understand. I am not God. But I know his spirit resides in me, and I know that spirit had no beginning, nor will it have an end.

"Spirits commune, and the spirits of our ancestors are present in this cave. Can't you sense them? My world has come full circle."

Sam stared unseeingly into the darkness, absorbing his uncle's words. He could sense the spirituality of the ancestral cave, and perhaps in time he would grow into a better communion. He glanced at Simaloi, sitting with a soft stillness beside him. Perhaps she would teach him. But in the end, it all came down to God. He started to pray.

Jackson cleared his throat. "You have work to do, Sam, for the older rock paintings in this inner cave must be traced and reproduced for the museum. There are many more to uncover, and we owe a duty to our ancestors and our country to further the cause of history and enlightenment."

He turned to Charles, a faint smile on his lips. "Some in their hot-headed youth have been driven by desire for fame and fortune, which is why I kept you away from here for so long, Charles. You can't deny it. You even infected Caroline and the boys with your misplaced obsessions. But you know better now, and your talents are needed to spread the word. Continue with your writings, exposing concerns and good news in equal measure, and God will do the rest.

"I am of no use to you anymore. I am a burden. You can leave me here to depart in peace where others have already laid their bones."

Sam stirred, but Jackson forestalled him.

"It should not be such a strange conception for you. Less than two centuries ago our forefathers went alone into the wilderness when their time came. I will neither eat nor drink until the end. Simaloi will keep watch."

He slept.

Simaloi went to join the crone at the cave entrance, and Sam stretched out his legs. Deep silence filled the place with an aura of heavy intensity, and he closed his eyes in an effort to commune with the spirit world. Tears pricked at his eyes and again he started to pray.

"There is much wrong with our world…" The words were faint.

"What did you say, *baba*?"

Sam whispered, too, in deference to the old man slumped between them. They rose to stand together by the veil which marked the inner cave.

"Jackson has made me think of other things, Sam." Charles's words were uttered with quiet fervour. "Of course you must carry on with your museum research, and I'll be at hand to publish whatever you think fit. But there are more immediate concerns on the international and political front, while the weighty matters of man's origins will no doubt continue through centuries to come."

"What do you mean, *baba*?"

"Maybe you can help me. Those two henchmen I told you about are collecting information in the Dadaab refugee camp on the border with Somalia. It has always been a hotbed of crime. I have heard talk of a link with the pirates hijacking the ships off the east coast. There is a branch of your museum in Lamu, isn't there?"

Sam nodded. "Of course I'll help you. What do you want me to do? In fact, I'm planning to go to Lamu. It was left out of my itinerary when I made my inaugural tour of Kenya's museums several years ago, and it's been on my conscience ever since. Emily is going to come with me when she returns from the UK."

"You and Emily?" Charles hesitated. "I have purposely not asked you any questions."

"I know, *baba*, and I appreciate your tact. Emily and I love each other, and we may have news for the family after Lamu."

Jackson stirred in the cave behind them, and they went to take their leave. Lingering in the shadows as he settled into the pile of rags which surrounded his frail form, they renewed their vigil.

Chapter 29

The plane dipped its wing and Emily pressed her face against the window. Through broken puffs of cloud, she saw neat patterns of green fields separated by hedgerows and trees. Changing direction, the plane descended from the holding pattern. A density of buildings of various heights and sizes filled her horizon.

She touched Paul's shoulder. "There's the Shard," she said. "It's exactly like the photographs!"

"And I can see the River Thames," said Maria.

"But can either of you identify the bridges?" challenged Paul.

The plane steadied and touched down at London Heathrow.

Endless corridors of slowly-moving walkways led to the main terminal. Emily and Maria left Paul at the immigration check to queue at the *Other Countries* gate with their new Kenyan passports. It was good to be on her feet after the flight, but Emily felt weary. She leaned on her trolley as if she had walked twenty miles, and waited in the crowd at the carousel.

At last, with their luggage intact, Paul led the way out. Emily raced her trolley alongside his.

"How do you know where to go?"

"Follow the signs."

There were so many bright flashing signs, so much noise and bustle, she didn't know where to look. Paul pointed to a plain black-and-white board high up on a wall indicating the coach station.

"We'll take the shuttle to Gatwick. It's better than trying to cram into the tubes with our luggage, and then we'll catch the train to Sussex. That reminds me…" He paused to bring out his mobile phone. "I'll text Louise to say we've arrived."

The coach pulled away from the terminal and joined a stream of traffic four lanes wide. Emily looked at her watch, and then at the mass of cars keeping pace with them along the M25, sprays of water spewing up from their wheels. It was two hours since they'd landed and she hadn't seen a blade of grass. The gigantic wipers on the coach windscreen groaned at each swipe. She fiddled in her seat beside Paul, feeling a tightening in her chest. So much activity, so much tension, it was quite exhausting.

Disgorged into the covered parking area at Gatwick, they bounced their baggage across the lanes and up corridors into lifts crowded with people, and then marched hastily along another lengthy passage to a platform. A sleek train pulled silently in, its doors opening automatically.

"Quick."

Paul pushed her forwards with the surging crowd and grabbed her case, swinging it with his onto a pile of others. He prodded her along the narrow aisle into a vacant seat, taking one for himself on the opposite side. Emily looked round. Maria sat three rows behind her, a bemused expression on her face. She glanced across her neighbour towards the window. The rain had stopped. And this was the first time since landing, nearly four hours ago, that she'd seen clear sky. The wheels chattered busily along the track as the coach swayed and Emily closed her eyes.

The tightness didn't go from her chest until long after Louise met them at the station and drove them to her home, a double-storey building covered with ivy. Similar houses crowded on either side. Louise stopped the car at the front door and Paul leapt out to offload their luggage.

Emily stretched her arms wide and yawned. Some low hills rose in the distance.

"Those are the Downs," said Louise, before showing Emily and Maria upstairs to their room. "I hope you don't mind sharing?"

Two single beds, with matching covers in pastel shades,

stood on opposite sides of the room.

"I hope you'll be warm enough with those duvets," she continued. "If not, just tell me and we'll turn up the central heating. I know you'll find our weather trying until you get used to it."

"Duvets?"

"Yes." Louise sat on one of the beds and patted beside her. "Try it."

Emily sank into the softness, feeling the feathery lightness, and marvelled. "We are going to learn so many new things."

"Your bathroom is opposite. You'll have to share it with Paul, I'm afraid. We're putting him in David's study at the top of the stairs. I'll leave you to get settled. Come down when you're ready, and we'll have a cup of tea."

Emily went to the window, but she couldn't open the lock. Below her, a garden the size of a maize patch was enclosed in a dense hedge. A close-cut lawn with immaculately trimmed edges lay between tidy flower beds. A tree stood at the far end, its branches straining in the wind. It was laden with large green fruit, and some had fallen to the grass; they looked like apples.

A sea of roofs spread into the distance, the different shapes and colours making a motley patchwork. Each building had a chimney and antennae with numerous wires strung haphazardly between them. Beyond rose the Downs, blueish in the distance, fading into a dull grey sky heavy with unshed rain.

She gave herself a shake, trying to raise her energy levels, and looked forward to that cup of tea.

The following day, an introductory afternoon was planned at the offices of the charity. Emily, Paul and Maria relaxed in the garden during the morning, then walked along Belton High Street to join Louise and David who had gone ahead to prepare for the meeting. Five large round tables crowded the room, each bearing a vase of fresh cut flowers. There was scarcely space to move between them. A screen dominated the far wall.

Louise hovered near a tea urn to one side. Paul went to join David, who was chatting to two people sitting primly at a corner table.

"Emily – welcome!" Louise came to greet her with a hug. "And Maria – it is special having you two here with us this afternoon." A nearby couple turned round. "You remember Sheila and Chris, who went to Amayoni last year?"

It was a relief to see familiar faces, and as more people crowded into the room, Emily and Maria helped Louise dispense cups of tea. The guests drifted towards the tables.

"Do you mind sitting separately during Laura's presentation?" said Louise. "You can give first-hand information about your village. We're hoping some will go out as volunteers, and maybe even sponsor a child."

Emily stiffened. "So long as you don't ask me to stand up and speak," she said. "I'm terrified."

Louise looked to Maria.

"I don't mind, Louise – I've done it often enough at home."

Emily turned away in shame, but Louise took her elbow and led her to Sheila and Chris's table, introducing her to two other couples sitting with them.

"Emily works at Amayoni," she said. "She's here to answer your questions and tell you what she does."

"Let me ask you something first," said Emily turning to Sheila. "What is your best memory of Amayoni?"

Without hesitation, Sheila opened her arms.

"It was a life-changing experience," she exclaimed. "And my best moment was hugging those children. I loved the way they clung to me so I could hardly walk, lots of them on both sides holding my hands, every time I passed through the school!"

"You said that with such fervour, as if you've been starved of love for years!"

"We have, Emily – with our idiotic stringent child protection laws, we're not even allowed to touch children here."

David stood up to introduce Laura, who started the

presentation, then Maria gave a brief summary of her role in the project. Conversation flowed as the guests refilled their teacups and read through pages of distributed notes. Many questions followed.

"What is your model?" asked a late-comer standing at the back of the room.

"We don't have a model," answered David. "Grass Shoots works closely with the villagers. We listen to their wishes, and don't impose our ideas on a culture of which we have little knowledge or experience."

He turned to whisper in Emily's ear. "Would you like to expand on my answer?" he said.

Emily did not have time to refuse. She got to her feet and, warming to the subject, explained how the villagers had taken ownership of the project.

"The people are included in every discussion and they help make decisions," she said. "There is joint representation from Amayoni and the Grass Shoots Charity on the Board, but we in the village regard it as *our* project, in much the same way as your charity probably regards it as *your* project."

"God is in command here," said Louise in affirmation. "It is all that's needed. We help this single village. There is no urgent compulsion. Just gentle, positive suggestion, then a step back to allow the message to sink in, be savoured, mulled over, and eventually – maybe – followed up. It all takes time."

"And there is plenty of time in Africa," said Emily.

Amid the general laughter, which warmed Emily's soul, a lady put up her hand.

"You say the volunteers physically do the building. Don't the villagers build their own homes?"

"The people do not have time to build," Laura answered gently. "Their time is taken up with ordinary living, like walking for miles to fetch water, and looking after children. There are few able-bodied men in Amayoni."

After the success of this first meeting, Emily knew she would be happy to stand up and speak again, but the level of detail and planning required to send a group of volunteers to Kenya astonished her. The English were bound by many rules and regulations, spelled out in pages and pages of terms and conditions, including how to behave and how to work in a team. She was particularly puzzled about a ban on sponsors offering private personal help to the people.

"It seems so harsh," Emily said to Maria said afterwards. "Surely there's no harm in personal transactions between sponsors and the families? Why does everything have to go through the charity?"

"I know, Emily. It's natural for us in Africa to ask for things – we know that if you don't ask, you don't receive, and we need so much. But the English don't like to be pressured with individual requests for help. We've found it's better to do everything through the project. So many things can go wrong with misguided attempts to help. Take, for example, the expense of re-roofing that woman's house earlier this year, only for the landlord to evict her."

"I suppose you have a point," admitted Emily. "And I remember another widow complaining recently that her maize *shamba* was taken from her by a greedy landlord before she could harvest it."

"Even sponsoring children through school is like walking a tightrope. There are so many factors, like uniforms, books, sickness, even brothers and sisters. And by sending a child to be educated, we are depriving the family of a hand at home to fetch water, tend the goats and look after the young ones while the mother tries to earn a living."

Emily wondered at the dedication and enthusiasm of Louise and her family in the face of such challenges, especially as the values, beliefs and world views of the people were so far apart. Not better, not worse, but just different.

As they were walking to the charity office one afternoon, she noticed barriers placed around a man mending a piece of uneven pavement. She'd also seen road repairs flagged by obtrusive warning signs, arrows and red markers. This emphasis on health and safety was a strange concept. Wasn't it natural to look out where you were going? And if you had an accident, surely it was due to your own carelessness? If a man had to mend a roof, of course he would ensure the ladder was secure before stepping up; it was his own fault if he fell. And passers-by would be careless if they didn't avoid an obstacle in their path. Risk assessments and glaring warnings around everyday hazards seemed unnecessary to her.

And why shouldn't the volunteers be allowed to wander through the village by themselves? Surely that was the best way to get to know the place. What was the danger? But they might get lost, she was told; there were unfamiliar hazards like snakes; in their ignorance they might fall victim to inappropriate invitations and requests; they must be protected. Even the villagers themselves must be protected. Emily was shocked to discover that every volunteer had to pass a criminal records check before being cleared to travel. These people were coming to help her people to a better life. What did it matter if they had been convicted of an offence? Nobody was completely innocent of wrongdoing. What a convoluted world these people lived in, compared with the simplicity of her home country.

And then there was the matter of fundraising, insurance, and seemingly endless extra payments for this and that. She wondered how the charity managed to find any volunteers at all for visits to Amayoni.

Why did they spend all that money and come out in their dozens three times a year? Why did some of them go back again and again, willingly giving even more money? The schools had started sending students on holiday projects, and she was told that some children returned home to change the whole direction of their lives.

Emily examined herself. She had left her job in Nairobi to work for her keep in Amayoni because of gratitude for the help Caroline had given her. She wanted to pass on her luck, so that others could experience enlightenment and progress. Was that all? It was enough for her. She understood the joy and fulfilment of giving, but she knew that some villagers wondered why people should spend their hard-earned cash for nothing in return. They claimed the *wazungu* wanted to further their own ends by forcing the villagers to change their ways.

They were nearing the end of their three-week visit, but before going with Paul and Maria to see the sights of London, Emily went to a meeting at a church hall, where a lady was reporting back after visiting Amayoni for a second time.

The congregation were shown a slide of an old mud-and-wattle house with a thatched roof, and in contrast, several more slides of new brick houses with tin roofs, the proud owners posing at the front door. The lady remarked on the "tidy" and "untidy" inhabitants, telling the audience that beds were a new concept for the villagers. One grandmother was shown using hers as a place to put junk. However, mattresses on the floor were better appreciated, and the people had learned to value mosquito nets as a weapon against malaria.

Emily squirmed inwardly at this depiction of her village as backward. But it was true, she told herself, compared with life in the UK. She lowered her head in shame.

"We give help at every level of village life," said the lady. "The main emphasis is on education. There are enormous classes and they have few resources, but the children work hard."

She told the story of a teenager who had become pregnant. As a result, she lost her sponsor and forfeited her schooling. That was a harsh lesson, but since learning about reliable contraception, teenage mothers had dropped remarkably in number.

"We also teach nutrition, and volunteers like to contribute towards a healthier diet, which includes eggs."

"Don't they have chickens?" asked one elderly gentleman.

"Yes, but they're kept for eating – not for the eggs."

"How much do the people have to live on, and what do they earn for themselves?" asked someone else.

Emily, who had made herself known beforehand, offered to answer that question. She stood up. "There is no social service or system of benefits in Africa," she said. "We have to fend for ourselves, and we learn to be resourceful. The government only provides basic utilities, and some health and educational needs."

This was clearly a shock to the audience.

Another lady shuddered. "I wouldn't dream of going to Africa for fear of creepy-crawlies," she said.

In London, Emily was amazed by the Underground. She marvelled at the sophistication of the country, its ancient history, its organisation and immense wealth, its quality of life. Here, people cycled and walked for pleasure; they spent hours growing flowers which you couldn't eat, and tended lawns on which maize could have been grown. In the supermarkets, she was shocked to see wide aisles given over to food for pets.

"You have a beautiful, well-organised and very blessed country, with much vegetation and very smooth roads," she told Louise, when it was time to go. "I have learned so much during this visit, and on behalf of Amayoni and everyone there, I thank you with all my heart."

"And you," said Louise, "give us a salutary reminder of our starkly opulent life styles, that we take so much for granted."

Perhaps that was the missing ingredient, Emily thought, as she prepared for the flight back home. An over-excess of riches and a lifestyle of indulgence could well account for a sense of guilt, or at least a modicum of shame on the part of the *wazungu*, and trigger a desire for redress. She knew her people were in their turn ashamed that they should have to be taught by strangers from overseas how to feed and care for themselves.

She discussed it with Paul on the plane home. They had been so busy that there had been little time for private talk.

"That's the beauty of Amayoni," he said. "It's a shining beacon, a true collaboration that stands out in the sorry mess of misplaced government-to-government aid in our world, and the corruption it invites. It's what you've always wanted, isn't it Emily? And now you are part of it."

"Thanks to you," she said, smiling into his eyes. "I'm sure you mean it in a congratulatory way, but from the African viewpoint, doesn't Amayoni stand out like a sore thumb? Already, greedy people have been quick to take advantage of the good that has been done. Shouldn't we dissipate that light, spread it further across the country so that other places can grow and counter the forces of darkness and greed?"

"You think your idea is better than battening down the hatches and surrounding our brilliant light with protection so it doesn't get snuffed out?"

"Yes, Paul, like fire, we should allow it to spread all over the country."

"But those little flames can easily be snuffed out."

"And isn't the steady glow of Amayoni bright enough to survive such onslaughts? Strong enough to spring up again in other places? Maybe the people of Amayoni should be allowed to experience more consequences of their actions, which is the best way of learning lessons in life, building character and strength through adversity. The brilliant jewel that is Amayoni may be too easy a target for the forces of evil, where they can concentrate on one place. I believe the concept must now grow outwards, adapt and spread so that the grassroots in different places may grow into more communities which become self-sufficient."

"My – you're quite the philosopher! Have you spoken to Charles? I'm sure he'll be interested in your ideas."

"Do you think he would? He was very interested in Amayoni when I showed him round the project."

"I'm sure you got on very well together, you seem to have much in common. You may even devise a plan to educate the developed world into this new concept where villagers take ownership, and volunteers turn into tourists, the source of Kenya's wealth."

"You mean a mutually-beneficial circle where the western world can break from complicated laws, politics and health and safety, and revert to the simple basic needs of mankind on which the principles of life are founded?"

"And Africa, which is on the cusp between dictatorship and democracy, can take the final step…? Now we're really dreaming!" Paul laughed uproariously, causing nearby passengers to raise their heads. He signalled a passing stewardess to bring them drinks. "But when we get back, and before you make any arrangements, shall we pay Caroline another visit? It'll be a good way to wind down, and we have a few days' rest before returning to work. We've had little time to ourselves while in the UK, and I want to show you a beautiful plot of land I've bought on the Nairobi-Mombasa road."

It sounded a good idea. She'd missed her regular meetings with Paul since going to work at Amayoni.

Chapter 30

Several miles after Athi River, Paul turned his car off the main highway past a roadside lodge, onto a narrow trail which disappeared into the wilderness. A few miles on, Emily saw houses set back from the road, each with its own large area of bush. There were no fences or hedges.

"This area was opened up a number of years ago by some Nairobi residents," said Paul. "They wanted to get away from the city at weekends and create their own haven of *bundu*. Nobody is allowed to put up fencing. So the game can roam free, and the birds here are amazing."

He slowed down and turned the car towards a gate made of rough wood, and hooted the horn. A Masai wielding a spear emerged from a tin hut to open the padlock. The distinctive outline of Mount Lukenya rose in the distance.

"That's where the Mountain Club do abseiling training," said Paul, letting out the clutch. "Remember, you met them before we climbed Ol Donyo L'Engai?"

She nodded.

Two faint tracks disappeared through the long grass down a slope towards some trees. He stopped at a clearing.

"This is where I plan to build my house." He took her hand. "Come, I want to show you something."

Emily followed him through the long grass, treading gingerly in his footsteps while she tried not to think about puff-adders.

"Look."

They had come to a lone thorn tree, and at its feet lay a tiny dam, brim-full of water. At the far side a herd of gazelle were drinking, but they skittered away. Emily could see the head of a giraffe nibbling at the top of a tree beyond the dam wall. And in the middle of the water rose a cone-shaped island fringed by a clump of papyrus, beside which a grey heron stood sentinel, watching for food.

"This is wonderful, Paul."

He put his arm round her shoulder. "Yes, it is. Maybe when my house is finished, you can come for a weekend, or two?"

"And Sam?"

Paul gave a long drawn-out sigh. "Yes, and Sam, too – I suppose. But I'm wondering how serious you two are, considering the time since you met. When was it – about eight years ago?"

He drew her gently towards him, and Emily pulled a face. "Is it really as long as that? I hadn't realised," she extricated herself, laughing. "I've been quite comfortable with things as they are."

"That's what I'm trying to say, Emily."

"Our feelings for each other are so wonderfully intimate, Paul, that sometimes I think they must be too good to be true. There's something holding me back. I've not discussed it with Sam, but I'm sure it's to do with that awful experience I had at the coast – remember?"

"How could I forget? I should have swept you off your feet before that ever happened to you!"

Emily smiled knowingly into his eyes. "You're such a wonderful person, Paul, and I'm glad you and I and Sam are good friends. Anyway," she tossed her head, "Sam and I will be doing something about it soon. He's asked me to go on a trip with him to Lamu. He needs to go there on business, and Charles wants us to gather information about Somali activity in the Indian Ocean. He thinks that the pirates might be operating from one of the islands."

Paul turned away.

"You know what my feelings are for you," he said. "They haven't changed." He went towards the car. "We'd better get back on the road, or we'll be late arriving in Mombasa."

She followed him, feeling guilty. She hadn't meant to hurt him. After all this time he should have come to terms with her relationship with Sam. To an outsider, it must seem strange that they hadn't married before this. Perhaps next time Sam approached her intimately, she should make more effort to respond.

She tried to remember when that had last happened. It must have been a long while ago.

She couldn't sleep. The howling gale battled at the warped shutters, billowing the open curtains into the room and brushing them over her face. The distant crash of breakers tumbling onto the beach reached her in regular surges. It must be high tide.

She sat up in bed. Caroline's security lights had gone out, and the night was pitch black save for a few stars. Her door was ajar. She always liked a through breeze in her room. As her eyes grew accustomed to the dark, she discerned a faint brightening from the passageway. Was that a shadow moving through – and could she hear a nearby tinkling, a scratching, between the thump of the waves outside? She held her breath.

It was unmistakeable. *Mwivis* had broken into the house. Better to let them take what they wanted and go. She cowered beneath the sheets, praying that Paul in the next room had not heard them. She knew that Caroline kept her bedroom door locked.

Paul's door clicked open. A sickening thud filled her ears and she heard his breath falling away along the passage in heavy grunts. Then silence. He must be dead.

They would come for her next. She got out of bed and hid behind the dressing table to the left of her bedroom door. They would go for the bed first, then she could duck out and escape.

A wild shriek split the air outside and frantic cries faded away into the night. It must be the night watchman trying to raise the alarm.

Subdued noises came from the sitting-room downstairs. "Hurry up. People will be here soon."

The whispered words reached her straining ears. Then

silence. The silence was worse. What were they doing? Had they gone, or were they preparing to burst into her room? She tiptoed to the door, closed it gently and turned the key in the lock, then went back to crouch behind the dressing table.

Her hands began to shake, her knees wobbled, and she buckled over. Her mind tried to take control, but her body cringed and collapsed onto the floor. She imagined them approaching her door, *pangas* raised. They would slice through it in seconds, then they would see her.

A sliver of daylight streamed through the window bars and touched the wardrobe. She hurried into it, burrowing among the clothes, pulling them around her as she cowered in a corner. She reached out to pull the door shut and closed her eyes, trying to control the shivers of utter terror which tremored through her body, and waited.

"Emily?"

The call was faint. Had she imagined it?

"Emily?"

She creaked open the cupboard door and tiptoed out. Streaks of dawn illuminated the room. She waited, listening to the deep silence, then padded towards the door and slowly turned the key, opening it a crack. She switched on the corridor light. Paul was lying face down in a pool of clotting blood which smeared along the floor.

"Paul – are you okay?"

Quickly, she caught hold of him and turned him onto his back. A red gash on his brow leaked down his face.

"Paul – we must stop the bleeding."

She ran to the bathroom for water and towels, slipping on the bloodstained floor, calling to Caroline and banging on her door.

The gash was deep. The robbers must have been lying in wait at his door, then when he opened it, they had clobbered him and left him for dead. He groaned and tried to get up, teetering against the wall. Somehow between them Emily and Caroline managed to get him downstairs and into her car. It took an age, but he remained conscious. The ferry was half a mile away and they finally arrived at the hospital on

Mombasa Island. A young emergency doctor rolled him into a bleak operating theatre and started to suture with painstaking calm.

"Aren't you going to use anaesthetic?"

"He can't feel anything – there are no nerves in the skull."

Emily glanced at the wound, then turned away. Caroline sat beside her, head bowed, lips moving in prayer.

She took Paul's hand, grateful to feel a faint answering squeeze. Her heart lurched. She loved this man, with a special solid love, nothing like her ecstatic feelings for Sam. And he was going to be all right.

Chapter 31

"Sam, you'd better postpone your trip to Lamu," Charles says. "I think our country has learned its lesson from the 2007 elections, and that our leaders will accept the results without a fuss. But you never know."

"I hope you're right." Paul raises his glass at the bar of the Five Bells restaurant, while they wait with Emily for their table. "But the government is entrenched in corruption and self-interest, and power is a devilish thing. Violence simmers below the surface. We shall see."

The emergency surgeon in Mombasa has done a remarkable job on Paul's head, Charles thinks, looking at the fading scar hidden in the wrinkles above his eyebrow.

"How are you feeling, Paul?"

"Much better, thank you, although the tinnitus in my ear is annoying."

"Did the police ever find the robbers?"

"Of course not. What do you expect?"

A waiter shows them to a table near the window, and Charles surveys the familiar dining-room. Alex Gomez has kept the décor in perfect repair, and his curries never fail to please. His son is now the manager, but the old man always comes to greet his friends. He places a hand on Charles's shoulder, leaning over to enquire if everything is satisfactory.

"As always, Gomez! And much better from the customer's viewpoint than sitting outside your door as a beggar."

"You've had a long association with this restaurant, haven't you, Charles?" says Emily, who has postponed her return to work until after her visit to Lamu with Sam.

"Longer, and perhaps more unseemly, than you can imagine, my dear," he replies, as Gomez leaves them for the next table. But although she raises an eyebrow, he does not elaborate.

Sam takes a gulp of beer. "What exactly do you want us to do for you in Lamu, Charles?"

"I'm hoping you'll explore the archipelago. Pate Island has some ruins on its eastern side, which you'll find interesting from a professional viewpoint."

Emily savours a spoonful of prawn curry, then dabs at her mouth with a damask napkin.

"Didn't the Head of Fort Jesus mention something about a village called Shanga that time we went to the coast, Sam?"

"Yes, and we're still conferring about the dating of the ceramics sent from the site."

"I don't know about ceramics," says Charles. "But my contact in the Dadaab refugee camp tells me that the Somali pirates operating off the coast have used Shanga as a base. It would be nice if you could find out what you can, and maybe take some pictures for me? It would make a good story."

"Of course we'll help you, Charles, won't we?" says Emily, turning to Sam.

"It's a pretty remote place. I hear the island is surrounded by mangroves, but the archaeological site is an important one. Yes, I could make it part of my official visit."

"I may be able to arrange for my contact to meet you in Shanga, but it will be a hard trek for Emily," says Charles, giving her a wink.

"I don't mind. Remember, I've climbed Ol Donyo L'Engai and survived, haven't I, Paul!"

"You're a remarkable lady," says Paul, calling for the bill. "And Sam is a lucky man."

The March elections are a nail-biting event for Kenya. Once he has placed his vote, Charles stays glued to the internet. The Kenya elections Twitter feed is alive with pleas for calm as the results come trickling in throughout the day, and the fight between Uhuru Kenyatta and his rival Raila Odinga, openly supported by overseas influence, is too close to call until the bitter end.

Odinga challenges the result, and vast numbers of young Kenyans renew their frantic calls on social media for peace until the challenge is finally dismissed. The country holds its breath, exhorting Odinga to accept defeat and let Kenya move on.

"We've done it without violence. We've come of age!"

They are at the Five Bells again, and Emily cannot contain her pride.

"It's monumentally significant," agrees Charles soberly. "We've had the best election turn-out ever, and demonstrated the power of youth and social media into the bargain."

The restaurant is full of patriots. "We are Africans and Kenyans," they chant. "We don't need anyone out there telling us who or what to vote for."

"And now that credible and peaceful elections have taken place, Kenya has redeemed herself!" shouts Sam, raising his glass.

"But there's work to do yet," warns Charles. "Democracy can go too far. We can only be trusted to govern ourselves for the good of all to a certain extent. Decisions based on the wishes of the majority can be misguided, or subject to apathy."

"Come on, Charles, don't be such a spoilsport in this hour of our victory."

"I'm just being realistic, Sam. Democracy can be disastrous when it swings out of kilter; we all know that from experience. By the same token, benevolent dictatorship compensates for the ignorant masses, but it must not degenerate into tyranny. There's a fine balance, and it is not easy to keep."

"Of course we'll make mistakes, but they will be our own mistakes," says Sam. "We have freedom of information and expression; the right for everyone to learn what he wishes and do what he wills."

"Another recipe for disaster, for no two people think alike." Charles smiles. "And those in Government must refrain from self-interest and keep to their promises."

He notices Paul silently observing from his corner of the

table, while Emily smiles at him and then closes her eyes, visibly soaking in the atmosphere of euphoria and joy. She is right to feel proud to be Kenyan; their country has turned an important corner. But Charles knows they must not be complacent.

In the days that follow, he senses a vibrancy within the community, a buzz in the air which refuses to be suppressed. He feels it on the streets, it speaks of life, of the refusal to be quelled even by the terror attack on the Westgate shopping mall only a few months later. *Al Shabaab* claim it is vengeance for perceived wrongdoing, but Kenya in her turn says her attacks on Somalia were in self-defence. And thus incessant hostility occurs, in a cycle impossible to break.

Adversity brings cohesion. He can see it clearly in Nairobi. Behind the corruption, the crime and the acquisitiveness, lies the stream of ordinary people determined to work out their destiny in hope and optimism, which fosters righteous anger against wrongdoing.

Kenya has that spirit in abundance, and the country will not be bowed. Grass shoots of hope and resilience will spring from the ashes of the Westgate disaster. It is God's country; its citizens know that, it is why they never give up. They come together and burst forth in a paean of irrepressible might. Their spirit will not be crushed, and never again will they tolerate manipulated violence.

Charles reaches for his notebook to jot down the words before he forgets.

Chapter 32

Emily gazed out of the window onto a flat expanse of sand as the plane touched down on Manda Island. On the landing strip she found her luggage, and Sam grasped her hand to run the gauntlet of porters towards the ferry crossing to Lamu. The curator of the Museum met them on the waterfront.

She side-stepped a donkey with two people on its back. She almost fell into an open drain in the narrow street, and, wrinkling her nose in distaste, hurried to catch up with the others. An ancient saloon car blocked their way, its horn blaring in protest.

"We're campaigning to ban cars in Lamu Old Town," said the curator as they waited patiently to pass. "It is now a World Heritage site, and the donkeys will soon have right of way, like old times."

On the flat roof of their lodgings, Emily lifted her face into a cooling sea breeze. An expanse of steaming concrete housetops spread before her, blanketing out the streets. She'd changed into a red sleeveless top over blue cropped trousers, eschewing a bra as it was too hot and sticky, and anyway she preferred the freedom. Sam stood beside her, communing in quiet companionship before it was time to go for a tour of the museum.

She draped a *kitenge* over her head and shoulders and the curator led them through the streets. The well laid-out museum galleries depicted the lives of the Swahili people in fine detail. In the plush bedchamber their guide lingered lovingly over explanations of the rituals of the marriage bed.

"Do you think he suspects something about us, or is this his usual spiel?" Emily whispered to Sam as they followed him through the rooms.

He squeezed her hand. "Does it matter?"

"I suppose not," she said, wondering once more at her own private reluctance to reveal their relationship. Would she ever get rid of her hang-up concerning sex?

But she became absorbed in the story of the coastal people, who were a mixture of many nations. There was a strong sense of aristocracy among them, born of lineage rather than wealth, and each person knew 'who' he was.

A tight schedule lay ahead, and they went along the narrow main street for a few hundred yards to the Fort, which had been converted into a Community Centre. Emily marvelled at the varied shapes and sizes of the archways. One of the rooms had the original hardwood ceiling beams. People were sauntering around the courtyard, seeming to ignore their awesome surroundings.

Leaving the Fort, they wound through a labyrinth of streets too narrow for anything but a donkey, walking under several bridges between the houses. Emily admired the unique carved doorways for which Lamu was famous, and exchanged greetings with the people lounging on the *madaka,* while dozens of cats disdainfully prowled the area.

The sun beat down with relentless monotony, and it was a relief to enter the sheltered 18th Century Swahili House. They paused inside a bathroom with beautifully embellished plasterwork. Fish swam peacefully round a basin of clear water while a cat lurked in the corner. A coconut cup lay nearby.

"Why the fish?" she asked.

"To keep away mosquitos and bacteria."

"And the coconut?"

"For scooping up the water," their guide said, demonstrating.

The bedchambers were delightful, with their decorated plaster niches and spotless linen. An intricately-carved cradle stood against the wall, and wooden clogs rested together on the floor. Sam crept an arm round Emily's waist as they listened to an explanation of the ritual of washing the feet before getting into bed. In the kitchen stood a clay oven flanked by the numerous utensils needed for the preparation of Swahili food.

Emily sought out a pocket of shade in the courtyard before they returned to their accommodation through the maze of Lamu streets. She was wilting fast, and longed for a cool drink and a good night's rest.

Her alarm went off well before the first *muezzin* call to prayer, and Sam was waiting downstairs. Their new guide, Sheikh, knocked at a makeshift box on the waterfront as Emily raised her head to savour the soft aroma of fish. A sleepy figure emerged to call across the water, and a muted reply came from the museum boat. She heard the rattle of an anchor and the craft slipped towards the pier. In the half-light they embarked for a three-hour journey to Pate Island. The glassy waters chuckled peacefully past the bows as they chugged between bushy islets, and the boat finally ground to a halt at the end of a narrow mangrove-lined channel.

"This leads to Siyu Village on Pate Island," said Sheikh. "It is just past high tide, and we have to hurry."

Emily could see nothing but the trunks of crooked mangroves towering around her.

"You have to get out."

She peered over the side at the heaving tidal waters. How was she going to keep her balance among the tangled roots which reached in tentacles just beneath the surface? A small canoe slid alongside and Sheikh handed her in, nearly capsizing it as he and Sam joined her. The boat boy fended them off, and paddled precariously towards a rickety pier.

Emily teetered against Sam before finding her land legs and Sheikh ushered them in unexplained urgency through a miniature market place where vendors lounged beside their home- made sandals, belts and stools. Two *totos* stood nearby, holding donkeys by their rope bridles.

"Who told you to bring them here?"

"A man, *bwana*." The boy looked round. "He is not here. I think he's gone on to Shanga."

Sheikh shrugged.

"It might have been my father's contact," said Sam.

"Charles did mention somebody in connection with his newspaper reports."

Emily examined the thick sacking on the swayed back of the nearest donkey, remembering her previous ride with Paul.

"How far do we have to go?" she asked, raising her camera to take a photo.

"You can try it for a short while."

She clambered onto its back. The donkey boy jumped up behind her and then demanded ten shillings for the dubious privilege. She wasn't sure she liked sharing with him, and the animal staggered with the added weight. But he was paid and they moved off, her feet nearly touching the ground.

They paused at a well on the outskirts of the town.

"Do you wish to take the donkey with you to Shanga?"

"How far is it?"

The reply was a vague forty minutes or so.

The palm trees provided mottled shade, although the sand was too hot and loose for comfortable walking. Emily decided to stay mounted, but she persuaded the boy to get off and lead the donkey. Sheikh strode purposefully off in front and disappeared. The animal's swaying back tipped her from side to side on the insecure sacking, and after half an hour she had had enough.

The meagre palms gave way to short scrub. It offered no cover, but at least the sand was firm, and her legs moved in a rhythm beside Sam's easy loping strides. An hour later they reached the bedraggled huts of Shanga village, and crossed a trickle of water to take a faint path towards their goal on the east side of the island.

The ruins came into sight, and Emily wilted. The entrance to the makuti-roofed building which preserved them was firmly barricaded. Sheikh broke it down and she hurried after him, anxious to stay as long as possible in the shade while they examined the site. They were on the floor of the upper level, facing the *mihrab*. Below her, distinct in the deep excavations, lay the previous two levels. The wall of the second level was arranged in alternating layers of different-sized stones, and the third level (on which they stood) was set at an angle from the other two. She listened half-heartedly as Sam and Sheikh discussed the finding of coins unlike anything else ever discovered – perhaps they had been minted here in Shanga? A line of post-holes presented a mystery, and Sheikh showed them evidence of leather tanning. Dates were vaguely mentioned, although he assured them that this was the earliest Muslim site south of the Sahara.

They went outside to examine some graves near the palace, and Emily waited by a well while Sheikh and Sam differed over the purposes of some store rooms. She admired the pretty pirites coral carvings, and then followed the men down a path to the rugged sea front, by-passing a rubble of broken pottery. Standing on a small promontory, Sheikh pointed out a ruined battlement, expounding on why it was so difficult to invade Shanga.

"You've already experienced the mangroves to the west," he said. "Now observe the unfriendly coast on the east side. See – it is shallow and covered with coral. It can only be broached by boat on high spring tides. A little further along there's a tiny beach which is exposed at low tides. We can't wait to see it now, as we have to hurry back."

"Why?"

But he was already trying to chivvy them up the path back to Shanga, and went ahead. Sam poked in the thick undergrowth and moved off the track. Emily followed him, stepping gingerly down the treacherous rocks towards the sea.

"Is this where Charles wanted us to look?" she said, pausing to stare out to sea. "There's absolutely nothing here."

There was nowhere to sit and rest.

"If it's so difficult to invade, it must be impossible to escape from," said Sam. "Do you think this is where Somali pirates might have kept their hostages while waiting for the ransom? Nobody would think to look for them here."

She faced the ocean, hearing the swell of the waves forming in regular bursts of spray on the unseen rocks beneath her feet. She imagined a bobbing ship's boat trying to land, its prisoners cowering between fierce Somali pirates. She shuddered, reliving the stark memory of her cowering from the robbers at Caroline's home.

Sheikh had come back for them, and he now turned inland off the path. "You're looking for this?" he asked, showing them an empty clearing in the scrub. Emily came closer and saw indentations in the sand and a scrap of cloth swinging forlornly from a twig. A tiny patch of ashes and charred wood could have been a cooking fire, and a broken-down shelter of sticks drooped to one side.

"How recent is this?"

"According to the village *mzee*, the pirates used to come here with foreigners, but they were stopped. I don't think this has been used for a long time."

Emily raised her camera. "Well, I'd better capture the evidence for Charles," she said. "But I don't think there's much of a story here."

The men went back to the path, but she lingered behind, hoping to find a scrap of paper, or anything which might be evidence of kidnap. A loud caw made her jump, and a black crow flapped out of a bush to her left. She watched it fly into a tree further away.

Something brushed her shoulder and pressed along her back. Arms grabbed at her from behind. The pirates – were they still here? But no – that smell of stale sweat, that heavy breathing. She would never forget…

Her body trembled. With violent shudders of revulsion, she wriggled and ducked, throwing herself to one side. She fell, grazing her knee on the coral path, and glanced up into eyes which she had never forgotten. Hard, black orbs filled with raw lust. She even remembered his name. Maina.

He grabbed at her, catching at her shoulder strap, and ripped away her top. Shouting with all her might, she fended him off, bashing his face with her camera and her fist, buffeting against the muscular chest, slimy with sweat, and thrusting her knee at his legs.

He backed off, still holding her torn garment. And out of the sudden silence she heard the sound of thudding feet. She slid to the ground and her world went blank.

"Emily?"

The tinkle of goat bells sounded faintly in the blackness of her mind. Behind closed lids, she felt the sun's brightness beat onto her face and she turned her head, remembering in a flash what had happened. She jerked into a sitting position and her *kitenge* fell from her shoulders. Reaching for it, she clenched it tightly to cover her bare breasts.

"You've woken up? I'm so glad!" Sam came to kneel beside her. "I'm so sorry – it's all right now."

He held her at arm's length and looked into her eyes. She gazed in deep communion with this man who was an intimate part of her very soul. He had saved her.

"You're all right? Emily – you have to be all right. We must hurry."

Emily smiled. "I am all right, Sam."

She opened her arms and lost herself in his embrace.

He pulled away, bringing her to her feet and she tied the *kitenge* tightly under her arms.

His eyes dropped to her legs. Her knee was dripping blood from the coral graze, and now it began to sting.

"We'll see to that later," he said.

They reached a well, beside which lay a pile of coconuts. He broke one for her, and never before had coconut water tasted so refreshing. Emily scraped at the soft flesh until pleasantly satiated. She went to douse herself at the well, but Sheikh did not let them linger for long.

The donkey waited nearby, and Sam helped her onto it. "We have to hurry back."

"Why?"

"It will soon be low tide, and the museum boat has had to anchor far out in the channel. If we don't get to it before the tide turns, we'll have to wait another twelve hours."

Her head was still muzzy with sleep and shock. "I don't understand."

"Trust us – you'll understand soon enough."

She bounced around on the loose padded sack of a saddle

as the donkey trotted forwards, the *toto* sitting behind her forcing it faster with shouts and a brandished stick. His urgent body leaned into her back, and even though this contact was innocent, she remembered with a shudder that other rapacious body which had pressed against her a short while ago.

The animal swerved round a corner and she tumbled off. She brushed herself down and remounted, trying to grip more tightly with her knees. After that, Sam loped beside her, holding her steady.

They followed the winding trail back through the village, where Sam paid off the donkey boy. The pier where they had disembarked many hours before loomed forlornly over a mass of mud and mangroves. A trickle of water ran deep between the roots. Emily followed the others to the end of the jetty and Sam eased himself over the edge, holding out his arms.

"Come."

She hesitated, searching the horizon. In the far distance glimmered a faint strip of sea.

"We have to get there before the tide turns. Otherwise the current will be too strong against us. If that happens, not even the canoe can reach us here."

She looked back. A tall figure was approaching the pier. Was it Maina? She didn't wait to find out, but threw herself into Sam's arms, making him lose his footing. They tumbled into a tangle of thick roots.

"Heyyyy…"

Emily lay sprawled, enjoying a brief moment of refreshment as the feel of water and mud cooled her skin. The coral graze on her knee started to bleed again, but there were more urgent matters on her mind.

Maina stood on the shore, watching them.

"Sorry, Sam – it's that man again."

He scrambled to his feet and offered her a hand. "He won't follow us, Emily; I'll look after you. We have a head start on him, and a boat waiting out to sea."

She levered herself up, balancing for a foothold between

the mangrove roots. Slowly, carefully, she trod in Sam's footsteps as he manoeuvred along the faint channel winding before them. The sea bed sheered gradually away and it became more difficult to keep balance.

The thought of Maina standing on the shore behind her diminished in importance. As she floundered and tripped over the roots in a race with the tide, she realised her feelings had changed. With her eyes on the rippling muscles of Sam's bare back, she followed his lead and smiled into his soft brown eyes whenever he turned to give her a hand. Where was that shudder of revulsion at the thought of sex which had haunted her for years? As they paused together in a tiny pool of clear water, a tingle of desire thrilled through her. The fear had gone.

Stretched out before them was a wet, winding creek flanked by squidgy mud and mangrove roots, dotted (as she found to her cost) with evil jags of coral lurking in unlikely places.

Sam pointed. Their canoe bobbed in the shallows, half-hidden behind a clump of reeds.

Eagerly, she made for it, bracing herself against the fast tidal trickle. The tide had turned. She fell twice, nastily grazing an ankle, and almost disappeared into the mud near some thick mangrove roots.

When they finally reached the canoe it was still only the beginning, for the water was not deep enough to float with all of them aboard. They had to pile in and out again countless times and push, before the *toto* could at last wield the pole and aim for the museum boat far away by the reef.

It was after dark when the lights of Lamu finally greeted them over the bows.

After a blissful shower, Emily treated her coral grazes and changed into a flowing coastal dress. She became a new person, ready to sample the delights of a Swahili dinner at the curator's home.

Clad in traditional *khanzu* and *kofia* Sheikh led them once more through the narrow maze of Lamu streets, to be greeted ceremoniously by their host, dressed in flowing robes and a decorated fez. His wife, a handsome woman with a striking profile and almond eyes, honoured them with her presence.

Reclining on the roof top, they sipped fresh tamarind juice and enjoyed rice and lamb in a spicy sauce, fish in coconut sauce, potatoes, *bhajias*, and sweets. Their hosts retired. The sky spangled with stars, and a fresh sea breeze stirred against her face as she leant against Sam's shoulder.

"Will you marry me, Emily?" he said, enfolding her in his arms.

Her heart thrilled as she reached forward for a consummate kiss. "This is our betrothal dinner," she whispered.

Tomorrow, they would tell Caroline. She had messaged some sad news for Emily on her mobile, but for now, they would enjoy the moment.

Chapter 33

It was as if she were a child again. The familiar place, the wide sands of Watamu, the pure waters behind the reef twinkling with many shades of green. As a toddler Emily used to live in the big house where the *bwana* smoked his pipe and sat on the veranda, gazing out to sea or dozing off, head nodding onto his chest. He would call out, and her grandmother Ethel would run to do his bidding. *Bwana* Boney would always have a treat for her; a sweet or a toy to play with.

When he died, Emily had a large bedroom all to herself.

Each morning, when she could still see the stars, the *muezzin* would blast his first call to prayer and fasting. She became used to the endless insistent calls. The Muslims were not allowed even to swallow their spittle between sunrise and sunset during Ramadan, and she wondered how they coped. Caroline would often come to visit, and as Emily grew up, Caroline was there to guide and encourage her. They would walk down to the beach together, negotiating the uneven steps leading to the fine white sand, disturbing the *bhang*-smoking beach boys who waited to pounce on unwary tourists.

Now life had come full circle, and Ethel's health was fading. The old lady sat for hours on end in Boney's chair, her thighs overflowing the seat, gazing unseeing down the prickly pathway to the beach. Could she still hear the distant crash of waves in the rising tide? She slept peacefully most of the time. What was she thinking?

Emily and Caroline strode along the beach, greeting the residents, avoiding the dogs which chased each other in mad circles, kicking up the sand. Behind the palms and casuarinas stood substantial homes, fortresses behind solid bars. Emily paused as the sun rose over the coral islands of the bay and touched the boats gently swaying in the golden water, their sails furled. A grey heron stood motionless on a sandbar, then struck with lightning speed, dashed its catch against a rock and gulped it down with one swallow.

A wild-looking fisherman, dreadlocks tossing around his head, cycled towards them with his *kikapu*. He unloaded the contents of the basket onto the sand for them to inspect and choose and weigh carefully on ancient kitchen scales, ready for the ritual of bargaining.

Ethel used to be an expert at beating him down to a fair price, but Caroline was nearly as good, and Emily marvelled at her patient insistence. Parrot fish was their favourite, but this had become a rare delicacy now that the hotels had the monopoly.

When they got back to the house, Ethel wanted to know why they were here.

"I've come to see how you are, Ethel – the doctor called me, and I've brought Emily with me."

Ethel peered at Caroline with eyes glazed, and Emily came to kneel at her chair. She felt fingers lightly touch her head and looked up. Recognition dawned in her grandmother's eyes.

"My Emily," she whispered. "How are you? You have grown so big. Tell me about yourself."

"I'm very well, *kukhu*."

Ethel nodded. She closed her eyes and looked as if she were going back to sleep. Suddenly, she lifted her head, her eyes bright and searching. "Tell me about yourself," she said, her voice clear and demanding.

Emily glanced at Caroline for encouragement. "I'm very well, *kukhu*," she repeated. "I'm working in Kakamega now."

"Remember I told you about Amayoni last time I came to see you, Ethel?" said Caroline. "Emily and Paul are helping the village people."

"Emily and Paul?" The old lady turned to Emily. "You're together?"

Emily shook her head. "We're working together, *kukhu*." She looked at Caroline apologetically. "But I have some more news. I haven't even told Caroline yet – I may be getting married soon."

Caroline gripped her shoulders. "Sam?" she said.

Emily nodded.

"I'm so glad! I thought you two looked different when you came back from Lamu, but with all the other things to think about," she included Ethel in a wide gesture, "I never got round to asking…"

"…And the time didn't seem to be right to tell you."

"It's absolutely the right time now!"

They both looked at Ethel.

"Sam – our Sam?"

"Yes. Isn't it wonderful!"

They waited, wondering why Ethel remained silent. Her eyes stared into the distance, then her lids closed. Emily looked at Caroline in alarm.

"She's gone back to sleep."

Ethel slept for several hours, but her breathing was steady so they left her and went to prepare dinner. Together they helped her to bed.

In the morning Emily wore a white bikini and Caroline a black swimsuit and they hired a glass-bottomed boat. They gazed at remote fish weaving through the murky green waters beneath their feet, then Caroline put on flippers and slipped into the sea, adjusting her goggles.

"Come and join me," she called. "The fish look much brighter out here, than looking through that opaque glass."

But Emily wasn't tempted. The thought of brushing against one of those slimy monsters in the water made her shudder with revulsion. The gently rocking boat brought on a wave of nausea. She looked with longing towards the distant shore where a camel plodded after its keeper, inviting tourists for a ride. She endured the discomfort of the hot sun and the sickening heaves of the sea until Caroline climbed over the side, dripping water and shaking droplets from her hair.

Ethel was awake when they got back. Emily waved as she

slipped off her sandals at the steps, relieved to see her grandmother's eyes once again bright and alive. They ate breakfast, Ethel sipping at some fresh orange juice and taking a spoonful of *posho* porridge.

"My time is near," she said. "I want to be buried at my home in Kakamega."

Emily nodded. It was a reasonable request, although Caroline looked surprised.

"It's our custom to go home to die," said Ethel.

"But your home has been here for years."

"She means the custom of our people, Caroline," said Emily. "Although I don't know any relatives in Kakamega, she probably does. Everybody needs to return to their ancestors when they die."

Caroline was silent.

It would mean a great deal of organising and discomfort for Ethel, but she was adamant. The expense was no problem, as Boney had provided well for her, but they had to act quickly. The doctor had not given her long to live. Emily sent a text message to Paul for help, and he used his contacts to hire a van and driver for the journey upcountry. Not another word was spoken about Emily's engagement, and she tried to swallow her disappointment at her grandmother's lack of interest. Death was, of course, a more serious matter than marriage, she told herself, as she climbed into the back of the vehicle and sat beside Ethel who lay strapped onto a stretcher. The doctor had given her a sedative, and a nurse was in attendance, but Emily wanted to be with her on this final journey.

As Caroline closed the rear door, Ethel raised her head.

"Charles!" she called out. "Tell him I want to see him!"

Chapter 34

He is getting old. Charles gazes out of the window at the cabbage patch which Sister Brigid has kept going all these years. He watches her bend over a row, then massage her back as she eases herself upright. She must be feeling her age, too. She waves towards his window and he drops his pen. It is time for the morning tea ritual. Only a few lines of scribble give evidence of the passing hours.

He is tired. His brain is not working as it used to, and the burning issues of the moment no longer fire his imagination.

Charles shakes himself mentally. There is nothing wrong with him. He still has much to offer his vibrant country. They need his wisdom and experience, his ability to think laterally and capture the overall picture, so easily lost in the urgency of day to day reporting. The trouble is, not many of his articles are published these days. He has been side-lined in favour of sensationalism, politics and greed. Is it worth carrying on?

Perhaps it is time to get back to grass roots. He hasn't been to Kakamega since Jackson died, and it will be good to see how the Amayoni project is progressing. The concept of empowering communities to take responsibility for their own progress, rather than relying on political aid, is one he has supported in his articles. But he is tired, and he thinks of Ruth.

Charles grabs his crutches. He can't remember the last time he used his prosthesis. He glances round the bare room. Nothing has changed since he came here with Ken and the boys. His possessions are few, his needs minimal. It will be no big upheaval to leave, and nobody will miss him.

"Of course we'll miss you, Charles," says Sister Brigid.

"But none of us is getting any younger, and you're lucky to have a home to go to."

"A home?"

"I know you've been estranged all these years, but your family is there."

Home. He hasn't lived anywhere he could call a home since his brief years with Ruth in Nairobi. A spirit moves within him, and with lightened steps he swings his crutches aboard a *matatu* to take him up-country. He settles into the back corner of the vehicle, makes room for a large *bibi* who presses up comfortably against him, and closes his eyes.

Chapter 35

It was a long and tedious journey. The sedatives kept the old lady asleep for the duration, and Emily wondered why she'd insisted on going with her; except it gave her the opportunity to reflect. She loved her grandmother. So stoic, peaceful and down-to-earth; accepting of whatever life threw at her without complaint. Her loyalty and devotion to Boney had reaped the benefits of requited love, and when he retired to the coast, she'd deserved her time of fulfilment and luxury with him.

But she'd also suffered the stigma of a mixed relationship. The old settlers at the coast wouldn't have anything to do with Boney because of her. And her family in Kakamega had cut her off as one who had betrayed her race. Did she have a family? Emily hadn't thought about it much. Certainly nobody near Amayoni had come forward since she'd worked there. Yet her grandmother wanted to go back there to die. The ancestral pull was strong.

Ethel's luck had reflected on Emily, for Caroline had taken her home to Likoni and treated her as Paul's little sister while she trained to become a secretary. Dear Paul; his obsession with birds, and his affectionate concern for her well-being, his friendship.

Through him, she'd found Sam. It was strange that he, too, was an integral part of Caroline's unusual family, and yet they had never met before.

Ethel stirred and moaned. Emily leant over her, and the nurse lifted her head to offer some water.

"We need to stop soon," she said. "We're nearly at Nairobi."

Emily reached for her mobile phone and sent a text to Sam

at his office. Perhaps he could meet them for lunch at the Fairview Hotel? They had said a hurried goodbye on their return from Lamu before she went to Watamu with Caroline. She missed him. A peaceful feeling of pure love thrilled through her. They'd waited too long. Marvelling that her fears of sex had dissipated, she hoped they would marry soon.

He was waiting for them in the hotel car park. They opened the rear doors of the vehicle to let in the fresh air under cover of a flame tree and made Ethel comfortable, then they retired to a table in the garden.

Sam held her hand and Emily gazed into his eyes. There was no need for words. A meeting of minds, an absorbing intimacy and affection stirred between them. What heights of ecstasy awaited them?

Sam's lips widened and his eyes creased into a smile. He gave her a faint nod. "We'll wait until the knot is tied," he whispered uncannily, brushing her brow with a gentle kiss as he rose to return to the office.

***

Sam wondered what Emily would do when they were married. He knew she would miss her work at Amayoni, but his career at the museum came first, and he had to live in Nairobi. It was one of many problems to be solved.

He must talk to Paul. Perhaps Emily could work with him in Nairobi on the expansion of the charity's ideals to other villages in the country. Sam had been reading Charles's newspaper articles on a loan system enabling people to take ownership of their lives by starting up businesses. He must find out more about it.

It was many months since they'd met up. Sam reached for his mobile phone.

His childhood friend never changed, although he noticed a greater thinning of hair round Paul's temples as they sat opposite each other at the Five Bells. The years fell away, and it was as if they were boys again.

"I hear Amayoni is going from strength to strength, Paul. Emily is full of news about the villagers growing their businesses, and she says that by the end of the year, the loan scheme will be self-sustaining. Is that true?"

"It is indeed. They have embraced the concept which works a treat, and over the past three years, there's only been one defaulter. The ladies take their businesses seriously, but it needs supervision and training. Has Emily explained it to you?"

"Vaguely, I suppose, but you know women…!"

"Have you heard of the Grameen system?"

Sam pondered while he cleaned his plate and emptied his glass. Alex Gomez came to the table for his usual greeting and enquiry that everything was to their satisfaction. By the time he left, Sam remembered where he'd heard the name.

"Did I read about somebody winning the Nobel Peace Prize a few years ago – for setting it up?"

"That's right, Professor Muhammad Yunis from Bangladesh. The concept is simple, and the Grass Shoots Charity has modified it. They injected the initial capital and showed the villagers how to organise themselves into groups and decide who among them deserved to receive a loan. The ladies are given support and training, and repayments with interest start immediately. As soon as the money comes in, it is given out to someone else as a new loan."

"A veritable money-go-round!"

"Something like that."

"Sounds as if it could work in other places around the country."

"Possibly." Paul paused. "We haven't thought that far ahead. Our efforts are concentrated on Amayoni. There's still so much to do."

"There's a hidden agenda to my idea, Paul. You know Emily and I will be getting married soon, so she'll come to live here in Nairobi with me. It will be a wrench for her to leave Amayoni. I haven't discussed it with her yet, but I was wondering…"

Sam stopped. Paul's mouth opened and his eyes went

blank. He put down his fork and lowered his head into his hands, elbows resting on the table. In the silence which followed, Sam watched his friend trying to overcome his shock. In the flush of their love, he'd not realised how close Paul had been to Emily.

Paul looked up, visibly trying compose himself.

"You've been courting for so long, we all thought it would never happen – I'm glad for you both."

Somehow, the words didn't ring true. Paul's reaction was a mere semblance of politeness and congratulation.

"It's been a long time, I know. But something happened in Lamu, and now—"

Sam stopped, watching Paul's face. Their eyes met.

"Forgive me, Sam. I've always had a soft spot for Emily. Of course I'm delighted for you. Don't mind me. I'll get over it." Paul pushed his chair back, slamming it against the wall, and got up to stride out of the restaurant, ignoring Alex's polite farewell.

Sam called for the bill, then walked back to Museum Hill deep in thought. Why should one man's joy have to be another's distress? But at least he'd sown the seed, and Paul would get used to the change. It couldn't have come as that much of a shock, surely?

***

For Caroline, the shock was a joyous one. She couldn't wait for the wedding, and allowed her mind to go off in flights of fantasy. Just think – two of the people she loved most in the world, getting together. Skin colour was no barrier to love, and her beloved country had yet another example of how to conquer its ethnic differences. Of course the ceremony would be at the coast, her home.

But first things first. Could they manage to hold the wedding while Ethel was alive? That would be wonderful. Under the circumstances, maybe a wedding in Amayoni would be better.

She telephoned Paul. He'd only just heard the news, and

sounded distraught. Wedding talk was clearly too soon for his comfort.

"Come now, Paul. You've had several years to get used to the idea; surely you don't begrudge your best friends their happiness? Although I must admit they've made quite a meal out of their courtship."

Chapter 36

It is just as if he's never been away. Ruth greets Charles like a long-lost friend. Maybe she will come to look on him in a more intimate manner in time, and in keeping with their advanced years.

Maria has developed into a self-assured leader, commanding respect for the work she does in the community, and she is full of enthusiasm.

"I can't wait to show you round, *baba*. You'll be amazed. Our crops are producing bumper harvests thanks to the improved quality of seed. We have a mill now, and people all over the district send their maize to us for packaging. And most of the homes in Amayoni are now made of brick."

"So, Ken's business is flourishing?"

"Ken is a wealthy man, with many branches all over the district. Joshua runs the original brick works, helped by the twins. They even own two lorries. You must go and see them. I'll send word."

Ken is there to greet him, a stocky man of note, oozing self-assurance, and Charles discerns the faint signs of a paunch showing at his waistline. Ken tweaks his tie before shaking Charles's hand.

"Good to see you again, *Bwana* Charles," he says. "Joshua will show you round. You'll see many changes. And now I'm sorry I must rush away; I have a meeting in Kisumu. You're here for a while?"

Charles nods. "I hope so."

"We'll catch up later."

He watches Ken walk towards a sleek black Mercedes. The driver holds open the door for him, and he pulls out onto the newly-graded road, speckles of dust already masking the car's gleaming polish.

Charles adjusts the jaded tweed jacket he has carefully preserved over the years, and fastens a single button across his lean frame. With a secret smile he speaks appropriate words of approval as he swings his crutches along the paved pathways in Joshua's wake, while the twins chatter beside him, pointing out new developments. The place has certainly changed.

"Louise is here," says Joshua. "Have you seen her?"

"No."

"She's brought some new tourists. They're staying at the lodge. We're building two cottages in the grounds, and you must go and see the first one we made last year."

"Tourists? That's a new development."

"We call our sponsors tourists now. They come to see the progress in Amayoni, and then go off on safari, using the lodge as a base. We're building the cottages at a discount, and the Manager gives us a commission on every booking. The people have stopped cutting down the forest and the birds have returned, so we get many bird-watchers from all over the world."

"That's sound business policy, and good for Kenya too. Don't tell me – Ken had a hand in all this?"

"He certainly did. It was his idea from the beginning."

Charles remembers his original dreams when Louise broached the idea of sponsoring children through school, and Ken was one of her first beneficiaries. The charity has made a difference to the people of Amayoni in so many aspects of life, and again he wonders what motivates these do-gooders. They are energised and full of the joy of giving, and seem to receive little but grateful thanks in return.

A kind of reverse mission idea develops in his mind. The Europeans have lost touch with down-to-earth reality in their sophisticated world, which he remembers only too well from his Oxford days, and perhaps Africa has the answer to their need. Amayoni offers an opportunity for them to experience the grass roots of life – the bare bones of existence. We've been giving them this education without realising it, he thinks.

Now is the time to exploit that need, develop the potential it offers, and stop his people from grovelling in grateful thanks for every handout. All this time we've been giving the donors value for their largesse. We can hold our heads up high, knowing that for every giver there is a receiver, who gives back or passes on, to make the world go round.

Thoughts chase themselves around in his head as the words come to mind. He must re-educate his people: not the power-hungry politicians, but the ordinary *wananchi*, and by what better means than the one he does best – through the newspapers.

We are a proud nation, he thinks, but not so proud that we don't appreciate the value of giving and receiving. We need not grovel before the world, because we possess the key to the purpose of life. The people must no longer bow their heads. We must train the western world to learn valuable lessons from us: patience, resilience, joy at the smallest of blessings, and above all gratitude. Not self-effacing, demeaning, grovelling gratitude, but thanks for what we in turn have received for what we give.

Words tumble through his mind as he takes up his pen, pulls out a notebook and sits on a log outside Ruth's home. The pages fill, and he reaches for another notebook.

The afternoon fades into night, and Maria stands before him.

"Emily has been in contact, *baba*. She's arriving soon, and Sam and Paul will be here for the weekend with Caroline. Emily's grandmother is coming home to die and she wants to see you."

"Emily's grandmother?" That is a surprise. Emily was an orphan, and nobody has mentioned a family before.

"I didn't know she had relatives here, either, *baba*."

"That explains it," Charles muses. "I've always thought Emily looked familiar. Which village does she come from?"

"I don't know. And I don't think Emily knows, either."

Chapter 37

The final part of the journey was on familiar roads and tracks. Ethel had given the driver instructions to her sister Hannah's home. Sitting in the passenger seat, Emily could not believe her eyes when the car turned towards Amayoni. They passed through the main village street and headed northwards.

They stopped on a deserted stretch of track. Rough scrub and long grass crowded the sides. An overgrown path led over a low bank and away to the right.

"It's down there," said the driver. "You'd better go and see."

Emily stepped out into the lowering glow of the evening sun. Treading cautiously in her flip-flops, she tried to part the grass stalks obscuring the path. She had never come this way before, and yet it was so close to Amayoni. Prickles brushed against her legs as she took tentative steps forward. As the path broadened, she moved more confidently and approached a patch of dappled shade.

It moved.

Her breath caught in her throat and a silent scream wrenched through her body. She was going too fast. She could not stop. With a gigantic leap she launched herself upwards. A flip-flop fell onto the large yellow and black patterned coils beneath her, as she frantically stretched her legs to the uttermost and landed beyond the snake. A puff adder.

The momentum rushed her forwards off the path, which veered to her left. She stopped, heart pounding, and cautiously followed her tracks back. The thick sluggish coils of the venomous snake were disappearing into the grass.

It must have been just as frightened as she was, she told herself, especially when hit by the flip-flop. But the thought didn't calm her. How was she going to find the nerve to pass this place on the way back to the car?

Shedding the remaining shoe, Emily turned and ran, making her bare feet pound as heavily as she could on the earth. At every step, she emitted piercing shrieks of fear, making enough noise to frighten other reptiles which might be lurking in her way.

Long minutes later, she stopped in a small clearing, panting for breath. A bedraggled hut faced her, its walls showing bare sticks and untidy patches of mud plastered with cow dung. Strands of thatching straggled from the roof. The warped planks of a makeshift door creaked open, and a tiny wizened woman emerged, clad in tattered rags.

"What do you want? Who are you?"

Emily stepped forward. "Excuse me, please. There's a *nyoka* on the path. I was so frightened."

"Did it bite you?"

Emily shook her head.

"That's lucky."

The woman waited, and Emily wondered what to say next. "Are you Hannah?"

The sharp button eyes widened, studying her closely. "*Ndio* – I am."

Emily took a deep breath. "I have brought your sister, Ethel. She's in the car." Emily jutted her chin over her shoulder. "She's my grandmother."

Hannah's eyes narrowed. In the silence which followed, Emily endured her hostile scrutiny and took a step back.

"I know of no sister."

The words hung between them.

"Ethel – your sister Ethel, who worked for the *Bwana* Boney, and when his farm was taken over, she went with him to the coast. She is my grandmother. My mother died when I was born. I'm sorry I never heard of you before now. I thought we had no other relatives."

Hannah spat on the ground with venom. "I do not have a

sister. I have not had a sister since that *mzungu* took her." She turned away.

Emily stood there. "She's dying, Hannah. Ethel is dying. She's been alone for many years. She's come all the way from Mombasa to see you. She's waiting in the car."

Hannah paused at the door of her hut.

"I remember you, and your mother," she said. "And you look as if you have succeeded in life."

Emily nodded, taking a step forward. "I work in Amayoni village on the project there. You've heard of it?"

Hannah leaned an arm against the side of her hut, and Emily went to her.

"You're all right, Hannah?"

"I am very poor. My family has left me and gone to Nairobi. How can I take care of somebody else now?"

Emily looked into the hut, allowing her eyes to become accustomed to the dark. A pile of rags lay in one corner, and a heap of ashes were piled beside a sooty pot in the middle of the dirt floor. Looking up, she saw the evening sky through the shreds of thatch.

"Ethel has money."

"I'll have nothing to do with her tainted money," snarled Hannah. "She has shamed her people. But you…"

"Come with me and see her, Hannah. She has come here to die, and she really wants to see you. That snake – I'm frightened to go back on the path on my own, and it's nearly dark."

The old lady reached for a long stick propped against the wall of the hut and trotted up the path, swishing the stick from side to side at the encroaching grass. Emily followed, chatting loudly to warn away reptiles.

The driver was tapping impatiently on the steering wheel. "It's late and we have to find somewhere to stay."

Emily opened the back of the van and stood aside for Hannah, the frail bird-like frame in stark contrast to the enormous hulk of her sister lying under a blanket and overflowing the narrow stretcher. Ethel stirred and grunted, lifting her head. She held out her hand. Hannah stared at her, ignoring the invitation.

"There is no place for this woman in my house," she said.

Emily felt inclined to agree. It would be a logistic nightmare, as how were they going to get Ethel down that path and settled comfortably in such a derelict place?

"We'll have to go to the lodge," she told the driver.

Hannah stood by as Emily closed the door. "You'll come and see me again, Emily?"

That was a surprise. Perhaps there was hope for a reconciliation after all.

"I'll come back," she said. "I'm sure we can help you in some way."

She watched the frail figure of her great-aunt disappear into the gloom. Somehow, it was comforting to know that she had a family, after all.

Ethel's health deteriorated quickly in the days that followed, despite the care and attention lavished on her at the lodge. She had given up the fight, but she told Emily there was still one thing on her mind.

"I must speak to Charles before I die."

The people she loved most in the world were gathered in this wonderful place against the backdrop of thick forest. Emily could hardly believe it. Everyone was connected in one way or another, united in their involvement with Amayoni. The great blue turacos were back, flopping clumsily around the trees, punctuating the conversation with ugly raucous calls quite out of keeping with their exotic appearance.

Louise was here with her family, and Caroline had arrived from the coast. Emily caught Paul's eye and he paused his hand on his binoculars, looking at her with such feeling, his eyes brimming with emotion. Her heart lurched. She'd never wanted to hurt him.

Even Charles had said he would come. She looked for him in vain across the lawn. Perhaps he had gone in to see Ethel. Her grandmother's looming demise was the only dark cloud hovering over the day. Since coming to the lodge, she had refused all visitors except Emily, but she appeared not to hear any mention of Sam. It was as if Ethel were in the final stages of preparation for her departing.

Emily flitted between the groups on the lawn amid the buzzing murmur of vibrant conversation. They were all here.

She joined Sam at the top of the steps as champagne was poured and distributed among the guests. He pulled her to him, and there in front of everybody, he lifted her chin and kissed her. Conversation died around them. Sam pulled away, but kept her hand gripped in his.

"I expect you guessed when you saw the champagne," he announced. "Emily and I love each other, and it is time to commit. I know you've all been wondering when this would happen."

A murmur of mirth rippled through the gathering and they started to clap, but Sam stayed them with his hand. "Emily's grandmother, Ethel, is here in the lodge as you know, preparing to depart this world." He paused as everyone bowed their heads in respect. "Caroline;" he started down the steps towards her. "May I ask you, as the head of our unusual but wonderful family, to give us permission to marry?"

Caroline came forwards, then she looked beyond Emily and put her hand to her mouth. A strangled bellow came from the depths of the lodge behind them.

"No…!"

Emily turned, and the masterful figure of Charles in a smart pin-striped suit towered over her. Sam jumped back up the steps to stand beside Emily, taking her hand, but Charles strode purposefully past them. He helped Caroline up the steps.

"Caroline – there is much to explain. Please forgive me…"

He turned to Emily and Sam, and parted their hands with a flourish, standing between them.

Sam recoiled, his eyes smouldering. He snatched his arm away from his father.

"How dare you!"

The pain and anguish in his voice cut through Emily's heart, and she also pulled away from Charles's grip. But he grabbed her again, keeping her away from Sam. He shut his eyes and screwed his face into creases of misery.

"It is my fault – I will explain." He paused, looking first at Emily and then at Sam, holding them apart with arms outstretched on either side of him. "You cannot marry each other."

Sam violently wrenched his arm so that Charles lost his balance. Instinctively, Emily jerked on his other side to steady him.

"Thank you, dear," said Charles.

Sam's face hardened. "You have no right to stop us marrying!"

Charles lowered his voice. "I've been talking to Ethel. She has revealed, and I have accepted, that I am in fact your father, Emily. There is no question. I had no idea; it was a random act with your mother in my dissolute days. I am sorry…" He turned to face the crowd on the lawn below them. "I am proud that this wonderful woman at my side, whom we all love, is in fact my daughter."

The people gasped and broke into a cacophony of questions. Emily was unable to absorb what he had said.

"You are my father?"

Charles drew her towards him. Thoughts raced around in her head, conflicting emotions tearing her apart. That meant Sam was her brother. She pulled away, looking for him. She couldn't see him anywhere.

Caroline looked distraught, and Louise came up the steps to talk to Charles.

Where was Sam? Emily pushed through the disintegrating crowd, ignoring their shocked glances, and found him hidden behind a bush near the river, throwing pebbles into the water. She stood beside him and picked up a twig, tossing it at a churning rapid. He looked for a stone and dashed it into the ripples, and another, and another with increasing force, his face twisting with rage and agony. She touched his hand.

"It's not you, Emily."

"I know."

He picked up a large boulder, heaving it off its anchoring

earth and shouldered it with a great splash into the water, disturbing the flow as a chattering of birds fluttered in the forest opposite. They watched as the current found new ways round the obstacle.

"I'll never forgive him."

He turned away, his shoulders heaved and his deep rooted sobs tore at her heart. She could say nothing. She prayed that one day, he and Charles might once again reconcile.

Then the enormity of what had been revealed dawned on her. She had found her father.

She put her arm round Sam and they held each other, undergoing new feelings, now understanding the reason for their special, intense love, and thankful they had held back from consummation. She sobbed again. She didn't love him any less, but now it was a different kind of love.

Tears fell and she croaked, "We'll still be friends?"

"Of course – we're brother and sister!"

"Come." She beckoned him back to the lodge.

But he stayed by the river. "I want to be alone."

The lawn was deserted. Emily walked towards the lodge, diverting along the flowerbeds, glancing absentmindedly at the plethora of colours. A sunbird hovered among the red flowers of a bottle-brush tree, its translucent feathers shining a metallic bronze against the foliage.

In a corner of the lounge, Charles and Caroline were in earnest conversation. Emily went towards the fireplace in the centre of the room where the families were sharing a pot of tea. Paul rose to offer her his chair. His soft grey eyes communed with hers, brim-full with understanding and love. She lowered her gaze, not yet ready for new emotions.

"Would you like a cup of tea?"

She nodded.

The waiter came to her. "The nurse has sent a message. Your grandmother wants to see you."

Emily got up. Of course, how could they have neglected Ethel, alone in that bedroom? She must be wondering what's happened. As Emily arrived at the door, the nurse rose, finger to her lips.

"She is sleeping, but it won't be long," she whispered. "The doctor came, and the priest was here just now. Call me if you want me."

Emily went to the bed. Her grandmother's large frame lay in a motionless heap under the blankets. Her ashen face was peaceful against the pillows, surrounded by a halo of tight white curls. Her breath, faint and irregular, whispered across Emily's face as she bent to kiss her cheek. She took hold of a hand and the fingers moved in a tiny twinge of response. She squeezed harder, and stroked Ethel's arm. The eyes were closed, but her lips widened into the faintest of smiles.

"Hannah – you will look after her?" Her voice was a barely discernible croak, and Emily had to listen closely.

"Of course, *kukhu*. It's all right. I love you." There was nothing else to say.

She stayed there as the light faded in the window. The nurse came in to close the curtains and switch on the bedside lamp.

"She is not in pain," she whispered.

Emily nodded. "I know."

Far into the night Emily kept vigil, communicating with gentle touches, remembering happy scenes of her childhood; sometimes drifting into a doze, then awakening with a start to feel again the faint thrill of life through the wrinkled fingers. Often, her eyes pricked with unshed tears; but she didn't want to upset her grandmother with selfish misery, and forced happier thoughts into her mind. This was a sublime moment. Peaceful, sad, but inevitable. Emily bowed her head and opened her mind to the presence of her God.

A murmur of exhalation, and then silence. The hand beneath her fingers went limp. She let go and rose, not looking at the body on the bed. It was not her *kukhu* anymore. Emily felt the spirit rise and fill the air around her, saying goodbye as she finally let the tears fall.

Suddenly, she felt tired. So tired. She called the nurse and stumbled down the corridor to her room, to fall into a long, deep sleep.

EPILOGUE

TWO YEARS LATER

"Look."

Paul stopped the car and pointed out of the window. Emily watched a large majestic bird tread through the long grass thirty yards away, the grey head and thick crested neck moving backwards and forwards in time with its strides. Focussing on its purpose, it ignored them utterly.

"It's a kori bustard. Almost extinct in Kenya forty years ago, they were sold to the Arabs as a status symbol. Now, dozens of these birds enjoy freedom from fear in our little haven."

"One of the good things that have come out of Independence!" joked Emily.

She traced its camouflaged progress as it passed through the scrub parallel to the track. The car crept forwards, and the stately bird disappeared behind some bushes.

They were on the way to his plot near Lukenya, twenty miles south of Nairobi. Paul stopped again. Another large bird with black quills protruding from the back of its head was pecking at something on the ground.

"A Secretary Bird!" cried Emily, before Paul could speak. "At least I can identify with that one."

"He's probably got a snake," he said. "Did you know when they catch one, they fly up and drop it from high in the sky to kill it? I saw that happen once."

"Clever. Cruel, but clever."

He turned the car off the track and tooted the horn for the Masai guard to open the padlocked gate.

"Why do you bother with a gate and a lock, when there's

not even a fence on either side to stop people from coming in?"

"I suppose you've noticed that there's a ditch alongside the road, so not even the best of four-wheel drive cars can get through? At least it's a deterrent against thieves who can't clear out our possessions in one fell swoop if they haven't got getaway transport nearby."

"I never thought of that." But his mention of thieves caused her some concern. How safe were they going to be on their honeymoon in this place in the middle of nowhere?

Paul drove through the rickety gate with a wave at the guard, who handed him a bunch of keys. The winding track through long grass hadn't changed. Was it really two years since Paul had brought her here on the way to see Caroline at the coast? So much had happened since then.

He stopped at the clearing, and nestling in the dip below them was a pretty stone cottage comprised of two adjoining rondavels, their slate grey conical roofs blending perfectly into the surroundings.

"Wow – I never imagined… This is beautiful. You have been busy."

She jumped out of the car and went round to the front of the building. Steps led up to an open veranda overlooking the dam. It was not as full as when she'd last seen it, and the water no longer surrounding the island. A couple of impala were drinking on the far side.

"I thought we were going to camp in tents on our honeymoon. Paul, this is amazing!"

"Wait until I show you inside," he said, fumbling with the lock. The heavy iron door scraped along the concrete floor as he pushed it open. He levered it upwards for an easier swing, but kept her at bay. "Don't go in yet."

Before she could protest, he swept her off her feet and carried her over the threshold. Continuing into one of the rooms, he deposited her with a flourish onto a high double bed. She sank into the soft folds of a duvet as he joined her.

Slowly, savouring delicious sensations as his hands brushed over her, she allowed him to undress her. Then all else was forgotten as with infinite care, patience and love he drew her close. He throbbed gently into her, penetrating parts of her she never knew existed, until she opened to him and enveloped him with love and ecstasy.

When night fell, Paul got up, wound a *kikoi* round his midriff, and scraped the front door closed, shooting in the heavy bolts.

"It's the only access," he said. "We're perfectly safe here. And we're quite alone."

She studied the windows, strongly barred.

"Feel hungry? I've arranged some provisions."

She nodded, opening her arms as he came close, and pulled at his *kikoi*. "Hungry for more of you... The food can come later."

Emily woke before dawn and gazed in wonder at Paul asleep beside her. Her heart lifted at the memory of last night, a night that had been everything she could have dreamed, and more. The bed was the same height as the window, and leaning on her pillow she watched fingers of sunlight dapple the bush. On the far side of the clearing, two figures clad in blankets and wielding spears loped purposefully across her field of vision. She nudged Paul awake.

"Who are they?"

He stirred and yawned, then rose on his elbows to look through the window.

"They're our extra guards," he explained casually. "We're having problems with sand thieves trespassing at night. They come in lorries with floodlights and dig it out to take away and sell to Nairobi building contractors."

"That's awful."

"Yes – we've tried deterring them and telling them to go away, but they take no notice. The police do nothing, but the residents have employed the Masai to keep an eye on them and report developments. They also report on any poaching in the area."

He pulled her towards him, nuzzling at her neck. "You don't want to be worrying about things like that now. There are far more urgent matters to attend to…"

She sat on a camp chair, her feet resting on the low wall of the veranda. Before her, a herd of Thomson's gazelle trooped towards the water hole, the leader taking tentative steps, looking from side to side, ready for immediate flight. Paul came up behind her and placed a hand on her shoulder.

"Here's my wedding present for you, Mrs Clayton," he whispered in her ear.

He laid an oblong package on her lap, brightly wrapped and adorned with a red rose.

"Wasn't it a wonderful day? Did you enjoy it as much as I did?"

Paul's mouth twisted down and he gave her a rueful smile. "In retrospect, yes," he said. "I must admit I didn't relax until after the formal part was over. That speech of mine kept me awake at nights for weeks."

"Oh Paul, it was a perfect speech – what I can remember of it! And weren't Maria and Laura wonderful as my bridesmaids?"

Emily fell silent, remembering the joy that had surrounded them all. Even Sam, as Paul's Best Man, did his duty by Laura with such aplomb that she wondered if something more permanent might come from it. She did hope so, especially later in the evening watching them gyrate in perfect synchronisation on the dance floor. He was quite a bit older than Laura, but what did that matter?

"And it looks as if Sam and your father might be making amends again," said Paul. "I glimpsed them toasting each other in a corner of the room at the reception."

"Caroline's was the only sad face on the day – but we can excuse her tears, can't we, my love? Isn't she a wonderful mother to us all? And we've had such a happy-ever-after day."

They kissed, and sat together watching Africa awaken under the rising sun.

"We'll have to make it so, won't we," he said. "But you haven't opened my present – you'll need it here."

Carefully, so as not to disturb the antelopes, Emily picked at the sellotape, prised the paper away and opened the box. In it lay a small pair of binoculars. She looked at him, her eyes dancing with mirth. He picked them up by the strap and gently placed them round her neck.

"Try them. They're lightweight, and now you won't have to share mine."

She raised them and focussed. The gazelles leapt closely before her eyes, their tiny tails flicking constantly back and forth over the white patches of their backsides. The delicate black nostrils flared as they tested the mud and tiptoed towards the water on dainty legs.

The animals passed through and she lowered the glasses. Paul touched her arm and raised a finger to his lips, pointing towards their left. A large shape emerged from the bushes, enormous shoulders tapering down into haunches which almost touched the ground. It lumbered with awkward gait towards the mud on the near side of the island, then stopped, turning its ugly head from side to side, looking along the way it had come. She could hardly see its mottled brown form camouflaged against the background.

Paul raised his binoculars and Emily remembered hers. She held her breath. Three smaller furry forms followed their mother and with a final furtive pause, the family disappeared into the reeds.

"I'm so glad my hyenas are still here," said Paul. "I've watched them many times, and the little ones are growing fast. Their den is on the island. They leave at dusk every day to go hunting and return early in the mornings." He turned to her and grinned. "Want a cup of tea?"

He brought Emily a mug and they sat in silence, watching and waiting as a herd of impala trooped by. A giraffe peered at them over the dam wall before gracefully venturing to the water's edge and splaying its front legs in ungainly fashion to take a drink. Warthogs snuffled in the mud below; the sun warmed the land, and the animals disappeared. They would come through again in the evening, Paul told her, on the way back to their night pastures.

A heron stood motionless over the water, and weaver birds chattered in their nests in a nearby thorn tree. Paul pointed out other little brown birds, her new binoculars revealing distinctive flashes of colour. He showed her how to distinguish the markings, study the beaks and name the birds with the help of his bird-book. He produced a notebook and pen. It would be fun to make a list.

"I'll turn you into a birdwatcher, yet!" he said, rejoicing in her enthusiasm.

Then they pottered around the house, Emily opening cupboards and inspecting the provisions he had bought.

"You've thought of everything," she said.

"Of course. I'm an old hand. And now I'll cook you a full English breakfast on the gas stove."

Afterwards, he brought out an intriguing collection of lights to charge their batteries on the window sill in the blazing sun. There was even a solar battery connection and lead for Emily to charge her mobile phone.

"We have no electricity?" she asked.

Paul smiled. "Perhaps one day," he said. "But these little lights are just as good, and I prefer the subdued glow of hurricane lamps at night, they're much more romantic." He indicated light fittings on the walls. "You can see I have planned for electricity when it comes to the area. My most valuable possession is the generator, but it's hidden underneath the window seat. I only bring it out to pump water from the dam up to the top tank."

Later, he led her on a walk round the property, showing her the survey beacons buried in the undergrowth. No other sign of demarcation disturbed the vista, broken only by discreet clumps of bush harbouring the houses of other owners, each with their own special outlook.

"We'll meet the neighbours next weekend for our regular exchange of news," he said. "And we're having our Annual General Meeting, which you'll find interesting."

Every afternoon they went out in the car, exploring different parts of the estate and visiting several water holes and dams. Emily added to her list of birds. The rivers were dry and the grass parched, but animals were in abundance, and game paths meandered between the symmetric network of dirt roads which separated the five acre plots.

Leaving Paul to check over the generator one morning, Emily went out by herself to savour the magic of their special place. She'd followed Paul often enough along the game path from the dry river bed bordering their plot. Reaching a bend, she looked to her left.

There was a loud snort of concern. A wildebeest stood poised for flight. They eyed each other, frozen with tension. He was big; he tossed his horns and stamped a foot, then snorted again. Emily stood her ground and so did he. Only a few yards separated them, and a feeling of unease spread through her. Paul was out of reach in the house on the other side of the dam. If she retreated, the animal would chase her down. She held her breath, and eyed the surrounding long grass, looking for an escape route – and the wildebeest lowered its head. To her great relief, it continued sedately on its way across her path. She had broken the confrontation, and it no longer saw her as a threat.

For one long moment she had been a mere creature out there facing danger, tasting the fear experienced by wild animals every moment of their vulnerable lives. It was a humbling experience.

During the regular radio call-up that evening, they were told that a guard had been attacked by a hyena the night before. The Kenya Wildlife Service had been called, but were slow to act and the *watu* had hunted down the animal and killed it. The guard was taken to hospital.

"I hope it wasn't our hyena," said Emily. "We didn't see it come in earlier, did we?"

"We weren't looking," said Paul, signalling her to hush, while he listened to the rest of the report. It was a large old female with infected rotten teeth. They also heard news of an eland which had been killed by poachers and the carcass chopped up for meat.

The next day, on their excursion in the car, a lone figure walked along the road towards them, a bright new bandage on his arm. Paul stopped to talk and the man saluted him smartly.

"You're the person who was hurt by the hyena?"

"Yes, *bwana*."

"What happened?"

"I was off duty, sitting outside my hut, when it suddenly came and attacked me. I fought and fought it off." He demonstrated in dramatic fashion. "It ran away."

"You're all right now?"

He grinned broadly. "Yes, *bwana*. I've been looked after very well."

The sand thieves were active again. They were becoming bolder as the weeks went by, and hardly a day passed without fresh signs of activity. An ambush was planned for the night before the residents' AGM, but Paul received a message in the morning saying it had failed, as the thieves didn't turn up.

"We think the police must have warned them," he told Emily on the way to the meeting, which was convened at the site of the illegal sand mine. "Their low wages are no competition against the bribes offered by the contractors. It's happened before, and we'll have to decide what to do."

The road wound in a large arc to the left away from their plot, and then Paul pointed the car at some tracks veering off to the right, following several 4WDs through the thick scrub. When they found a patch of shade to park under, it seemed to Emily that they'd travelled a semi-circle round their own plot. She saw the rim of the dam wall less than a mile away and nudged Paul's arm.

"I know," he said. "It's quite close to us. That is why the extra guards live at our place."

"You didn't tell me."

"I didn't want to frighten you. The thieves are only interested in the sand. They're not dangerous, so long as we don't harass them."

The residents congregated, placing their camp chairs to face a table under the shade of a stunted thorn tree. Then they went to examine the area, stepping over large thorny branches which the *askaris* had scattered in the grass as a deterrent to the intruding lorries.

A scene of sheer devastation faced them. Great gashes had been made in an area of previously pristine bush. Deep holes were gouged out of a hillock, creating tunnels under the bush. Heavy lorry tracks criss-crossed the area. Trees had been carelessly undermined, and stood high above the clearing, clinging precariously with their roots atop pillars of sand.

The residents returned to their chairs reeling with shock. They had to do something, but what?

The meeting came alive, and everyone started talking at once. Emily listened as ideas were bandied to and fro. The need for immediate increase of *askaris* was acknowledged, but something more had to be done.

"What's happened about the fencing project?"

"Fencing is a waste of time," said someone. "We've tried before, and within a week all the wire disappeared. We've planted a hedge on the Lukenya boundary, which will eventually grow into a thick barrier. But what are we going to do in the meantime?"

"We can't rely on the authorities. The police are hand in glove with the thieves, and the local council is in disarray, with constant changes of leadership."

"Now is the time to use crampons," said one die-hard resident. "I've always said the only effective remedy is to use fixed nails hidden in sacks beneath the sand to puncture the lorry tyres."

But Paul, together with prominent African businessmen who valued their weekend retreats, vehemently opposed the idea. "There'll be reprisals if we do that," he said. "People have already suffered break-ins, especially those who live nearest to the site."

Emily shuddered, wondering if she would ever sleep easily here again. Paul leaned towards her, whispering in her ear. "I haven't had any break-ins," he said, patting her shoulder. "I've made sure those iron doors are impregnable, so don't you worry."

"Why don't we dig deep ditches?" somebody said. "We

could make them so that vehicles can't cross, but animals can."

But it would take too much time and man-hours, and there were no resources.

"We need more money."

"We also need a plan, and a budget. Perhaps we should call in a consultant…"

Hands were raised in horror. It could cost millions of shillings per month. They couldn't afford it.

"We must clamp down on security at the main gate on the Mombasa Road, and have a system of passes. We need more up-to-date information from our members, on when plots change hands, and on legitimate construction projects, so the *askaris* know which are the bona fide lorries."

There was so much to discuss and decide, and faced with the horrific evidence, the will to act was strong. A new committee was formed, and Paul voted on as Treasurer. Membership subscriptions, hitherto ignored by most of the owners, suddenly became the focus of attention. There was a hush in the proceedings, and Emily stirred, finding herself becoming more and more concerned by what she'd been hearing. This was their little piece of paradise, and they must defend it with all their might. She'd gained in self-confidence since her visit to the UK, and she knew exactly what she had to do here. She rose to her feet and turned to the new Chairman.

"I am your new Treasurer's wife," she said, ignoring the startled look on Paul's face. "And I believe we have a wonderful opportunity here to make things work. If you'll allow me, I'd like to help in true African fashion. We can't just talk; we must do something. Come on folks – let's see how much we can raise for our Association. *Harambee* everyone!"

Emily gestured extravagantly with her arms, and called out to the prosperous members with their gleaming 4WDs parked around the place, cajoling them into pulling together. One member sidled forward to place his overdue subscription on the table in front of the new Chairman, and then another, and another. The trickle turned into a queue, and Paul turned up his hat to hold the offerings. But more was needed.

Emily had another idea. "*Mpesa, mpesa* – if you haven't got cash or cheques with you, use your mobile phones! Paul – what's the Mpesa name for the association?"

Paul did not know if the association even had an on-line Mpesa account, which was the country's new way to transfer money. The previous Treasurer was not present.

"No matter – we can use Paul's account until he gets it sorted."

The meeting agreed the procedure, and building on peer pressure, Emily shamed the members into coming forward. She named each person and announced the amount as they added tens of thousands of shillings to the coffers. This was amazing; she had never felt so impassioned before.

She wilted into the camp chair beside Paul.

"A new Emily has sprung before my eyes. You look as if you're in your element – I'd never have thought it of you!" He squeezed her hand. "I'm so proud of you, Emily."

"I don't know how I did it," she said, taking a deep breath. "It was hard work, but it's worth it. Look at the result! And I have a feeling that before long we'll have an army of *watu* working on the boundaries, digging deep ditches alongside the hedge to deter thieves, and at the same time ensure the wild animals can get across."

"We have a special place here. A multi-cultural society in a peaceful environment, with a chance to prove that taking ownership can work from the grass shoots up."

"We're fulfilling my childhood dream, Paul. Of course there'll be problems, but with a will, there's always a way."

THE END

Glossary

All translations or explanations of words from Kiswahili, unless otherwise indicated.

Al Shabaab – jihadist terrorist group based in East Africa
Amayoni (Kiluhya) – birds
Anglo Leasing Scandal – corruption scandal involving high-ranking Kenyan government officials that came to light in 2004
asante sana – thank you very much
askari – uniformed guard, soldier
baba (Kiluhya) (*pronounced 'baa-baa'*) – form of endearment from a child to his or her father
bhajia – fried Indian snack recipe, made of batter with varied flavourings
bhang – cannabis
bibi (*pronounced 'bee-bee'*) – wife
boda boda – motorised bicycles originally used for transporting customers from 'border to border' between Kenya and Uganda; evolved into motorised taxis throughout Kenya. From 2008, small Chinese 250cc motorbikes were imported into Kenya free of customs duty.
bundu – wilderness, bush
bwana – of Arabic origin, used as a respectful form of address for a man
Dambisa Moyo – Zambian-born international economist and author of *Dead Aid: Why Aid Makes Things Worse and How There Is Another Way for Africa*
Dawa cocktail – medicine. A concoction made from vodka, ice, lime and honey.
donga – steep-sided gully created by soil erosion
dudu – insect
duka – shop
Egerton University – originally Egerton Agricultural College, founded in Njoro in 1956. It became a university in 1987.
FMG (Female Genital Mutilation) – ritual removal of

external female genitalia, prevalent in Africa

Grameen system – an internationally recognised banking system (pioneered by Nobel Laureate, Bangladeshi Professor Muhammad Yunus) which provides credit without collateral to micro-businesses

hapana – no

harambee – 'Let us pull together.' Although popularised as a national rallying cry by Kenya's first president, Jomo Kenyatta, the word hails from an injunction to a Hindu deity, first associated with the indentured labourers who built the Kenya-Uganda railway.

intercropping – growing multiple crops (such as maize, beans, squash) simultaneously, which provides mutual benefit to the plants

jambo – hello

jembe – a large and heavy hoe

Jumba la Mtwana – the 'large house of slaves', a ruined village and former slave port north of Mombasa

kelele (*pronounced 'keh-leh-leh'*) – noise

kali (*pronounced 'kah-lee'*) – fierce, sharp

Kamba – ethnic group of Bantu origin, concentrated in Kenya's eastern province; closely related in language and culture to the Kikuyu

karibuni – welcome (plural). The singular form is *karibu*.

khanzu – long white cotton or linen robe worn by East African men

Kibera – a huge slum in Nairobi

kikapu (*pronounced 'kee-kaa-poo'*) – a commonly used soft basket made of woven straw

kikoi – a colourful length of cotton, fringed at each end, often worn round the waist

Kikuyu – a large ethnic group in Kenya of Bantu origin from the central parts of the country around Mount Kenya. There has been a longstanding rivalry between Kikuyu and Luo politicians since Kenya's independence.

kiondo – handwoven handbag made from sisal with leather trimmings

kitenge – length of colourful multipurpose cotton

kofia – round cap with a flat crown worn by Swahili men in East Africa

kuka (Kiluhya) (*pronounced 'koo-kah'*) – grandfather

kukhu (Kiluhya) (*pronounced 'koo-hoo'*) – grandmother

Lamu – Lamu Island is a popular tourist resort off the east coast of Kenya. The Old Town, a world heritage site, is the oldest and best preserved Swahili settlement in East Africa.

Lamu Fort – served as a prison from 1910 to 1984 to both the British colonial regime and the Kenya government, before it was handed over to the National Museums of Kenya in 1984. Efforts to turn the Fort into a museum were started with technical and financial assistance from the Swedish International Development Agency (SIDA). With its inception as a museum with environmental conservation as its general theme, Lamu Fort is basically a community centre for the people of Lamu Old Town.

Luhya – a large ethnic group in Kenya, of Bantu origin, from the north western parts of the country

Lukenya – hills at Athi River, south of Nairobi, used as a training place for rock climbing

Luo – a large ethnic group in Kenya of Nilotic origin from the south western parts of the country. There has been a longstanding rivalry between Luo and Kikuyu politicians since Kenya's independence.

Machakos Stage – Machakos Country Bus Stage, which people called 'Machakos' although it was miles away from the town of the same name. It is a bus terminal in Landhies Road, Nairobi, near the large Muthurwa market.

madaka – large niches in the walls of Lamu houses, serving as local patios, from where people sit and watch the world go by

mkora – ruffian

makuti – roof thatching built with dry vegetation such as straw, reeds, grass or leaves

mama (Kiluhya) (*pronounced 'maa-ma'*) – mother, mum

mandazi – Swahili doughnuts

Masai (*pronounced 'maa-sigh'*) – an ethnic group in Kenya, mythologised for its people's fearlessness and attachment to

their pastoralist traditions
Masai manyatta – a masai settlement, or compound
matatu (*pronounced 'maa-taa-too'*) – often colourfully-painted minibus which is the predominant form of public transport, associated with congestion and road accidents
memsahib – originating from India, where it was a title of respect for colonial wives. It has become a term of respect for any female employer by servants in a household.
mia moja (*pronounced 'mee-yah mohjah'*) – one hundred
mihrab – a niche in the wall of a mosque at the point nearest to Mecca, towards which the congregation faces to pray
Mpesa – M is for 'mobile' and 'pesa' is Kiswahili for 'money'. The name given to a money transfer tool using mobile phones, which originated in Kenya and has been imitated elsewhere.
muezzin – crier, who calls Muslims to prayer
mwivi (also *mwizi*) – thief
mzee (*pronounced 'mzeh'*) – old man. Used as a term of deference by those who consider themselves much younger.
mzungu (plural: wazungu) – a person of Caucasian origin, hence 'white man'
mzuri sana – very good
NGO – non-governmental organisation. A channel for independent funding.
nusu-nusu – literally half-half; used to describe a person of mixed race
Ol Donyo L'Engai – a volcano in Tanzania which erupted in 1966 and 2007. Its lava uniquely consists of carbonatite, which is of a lower temperature than molten lava and is often less viscous than water. It quickly turns from black to grey.
panga – machete, used as a tool or weapon
pole (*pronounced 'poh-leh'*) – sorry or apologies, according to the context
porites coral – bilaterally symmetrical finger-like stony coral
posho – ground maize meal
puff adder – a sluggish, venomous viper species, which

basks on warm pathways; prevalent in savannah and grasslands throughout Kenya

quelea – a small brown bird hated by farmers in Africa. It is voracious and occurs in large numbers, destroying crops.

Rais (Arabic) – president, great leader. A respectful form of address.

Rene Haller – Swiss naturalist, known for his commitment to environmental restoration of a quarry wasteland in Mombasa. The Bamburi nature park and sanctuary are named after him.

rungu – a knobbed stick, weighted at the end

safari – journey

salaams – greetings

shamba – farmland, smallholding

Shanga ruins – an archaeological site in Pate Island, part of the Lamu Archipelago in the Indian Ocean

Shauri ya mungu – literally 'Affair for God', meaning 'It's up to God'

shenzi – mongrel

Somali pirates – piracy off the coast of Somalia was a threat to international shipping from the second phase of the Somali Civil War in the early 21st century, reaching a peak in 2008

syce – Arabic origin, common word for a groom

totos – children

Undugu Society – literally 'brotherhood'. A non-profit organisation founded in 1973 by Father Arnold Grol, a Dutch Catholic priest, to assist and rehabilitate street children in Nairobi.

wabenzi – literally 'those with (Mercedes) Benzes', 'fat cats', well-to-do, 'the haves'

wageni – guests

Wangari Maathai – Kenyan environment and political activist, founder of the Green Belt Movement and 2004 Nobel Peace Prize Laureate. Author of four books, including an autobiography, *Unbowed*.

watu – people

Bibliography

Dambisa Moya: *Dead Aid: Why Aid is Not Working and How There is a Better way for Africa.* Penguin, London. 2010

Wangari Maathai: *The Challenge for Africa.* William Heinemann, London. 2009

Fantastic Books
Great Authors

CROOKED CAT

Meet our authors and discover
our exciting range:

- Gripping Thrillers
- Cosy Mysteries
- Romantic Chick-Lit
- Fascinating Historicals
- Exciting Fantasy
- Young Adult and Children's Adventures

Visit us at:
www.crookedcatbooks.com

Join us on facebook:
www.facebook.com/crookedcatbooks

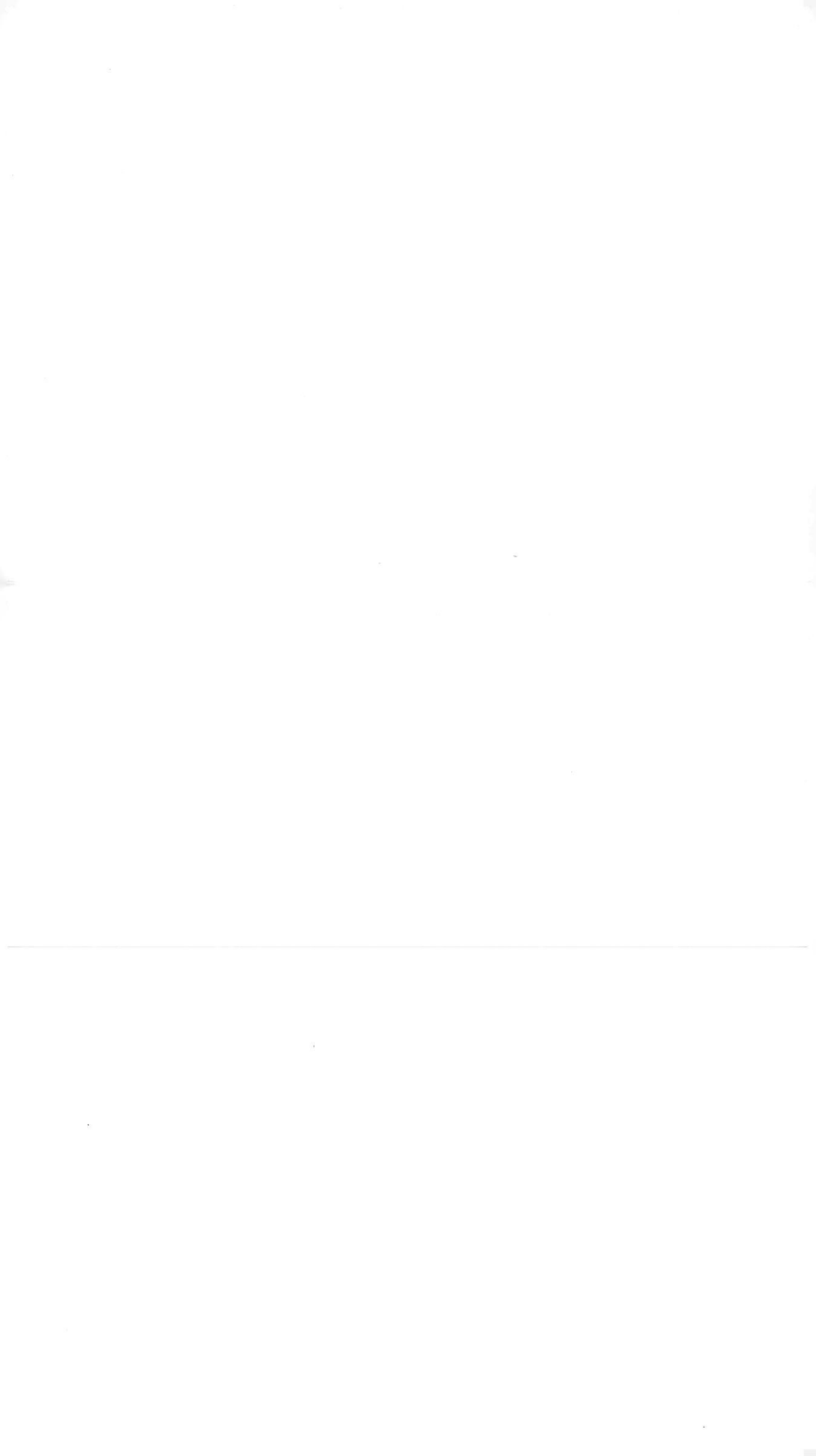

Printed in Poland
by Amazon Fulfillment
Poland Sp. z o.o., Wrocław